PRAISE FOR THIS BOOK

A fantastic tale, full of pace and steeped in the sense of the place. Hilton really knows Havana—and there is no substitute for that."

Matthew Parris, author
*Inca Kola: A Traveller's Tale of Peru* and *A Castle in Spain*

Almost everyone falls in love with Cuba, intoxicated by its climate, its scenery, its buildings, its music and its people. Some, like Chris Hilton, are lucky enough to fall in love with a specific Cuban. Not so difficult of course, but much harder to write truthfully both about Cuba and about a relationship. In this, Hilton's book is a triumph. He is a delightful guide to the very special atmosphere of Cuba in the last years of the Castro family, and his book should find many readers.

Richard Gott, author
*Cuba: A New History*

ABOUT THE AUTHOR

Chris Hilton has been a factory worker, a dealer in
modern first editions, a landscape gardener and a part-
time university lecturer (among other occupations).

He has visited Cuba over thirty times and has lived
there twice. The events described in this book took place
in the early 2000s, during the final years of Fidel Castro
and the coming of the internet, and proved to be life-
changing for those involved: the author, his friends and
his enemies.

Names have been changed for the protection of all.

# The Attraction of Cuba

A NOVEL

## Chris Hilton

ENVELOPE BOOKS

*The Attraction of Cuba* is a revision by Stephen Games of Chris Hilton's 2012 novel *Caliente*, an extract from which appeared in *Booklaunch*, Issue 3, Spring 2019.

Published in the UK and the USA in 2023 by EnvelopeBooks
www.envelopebooks.co.uk

EnvelopeBooks, 12 Wellfield Avenue, London N10 2EA, England
editor@envelopebooks.co.uk

Cover design by Stephen Games | Booklaunch

Main text set in Quadraat 10.3/13.6

A CIP catalogue record for this title is available from the British Library

ISBN 9781915023124

# Havanasis

by Richard Blanco

In the beginning, before God created Cuba, the earth was chaos, empty of form and without music. The spirit of God stirred over the dark tropical waters and God said, 'Let there be music.' And a soft conga began a one-two beat in the background of the chaos.

Then God called up Yemayá and said, 'Let the waters under heaven amass together and let dry land appear.' It was done. God called the fertile red earth Cuba and the massed waters the Caribbean. And God saw this was good, tapping his foot to the conga beat.

Then God said, 'Let the earth sprout papaya and coco and white coco flesh; malanga roots and mangos in all shades of gold and amber; let there be tabaco and café and sugar for the café; let there be rum; let there be waving plantains and guyabas and everything tropical-like.' God saw this was good, then fashioned palm trees—His pièce de résistance.

Then God said, 'Let there be a moon and stars to light the nights over the Club Tropicana, and a sun for the 365 days of the year.' God saw that this was good; He called the night nightlife, the day He called paradise.

Then God said, 'Let there be fish and fowl of every kind.' And there was spicy shrimp enchilado, chicken fracasé, codfish bacalao, and fritters. But He wanted something more exciting and said, 'Enough. Let there be pork.' And there was pork—deep fried, whole roasted, pork rinds, and sausage. He fashioned goats, used their skins for bongos and batús: he made claves and maracas and every kind of percussion instrument known to man.

Then out of a red lump of clay, God made a Taino and set him in a city He called Habana. Then He said, 'It is not good that Taino be alone. Let me make him some helpmates.' And so God created the mulata to dance guaguancó and son with Taino; the guajiro to cultivate his land and his folklore, Cachita the sorceress to strike the rhythm of his music, and a poet to work the verses of their paradise.

God gave them dominion over all the creatures and musical instruments and said unto them, 'Be fruitful and multiply, eat pork, drink rum, make music, and dance.' On the seventh day, God rested from the labours of His creation. He smiled upon the celebration and listened to their music.

*'Havanasis'* from *City of a Hundred Fires* by Richard Blanco © 1998.
Reprinted by permission of the University of Pittsburgh Press.

*No one is ever old enough to know better.*
Holbrook Jackson

# I

# Anything is possible in Cuba

I got to know Cuba through José. And I got to know José through two rather unremarkable Brits who were staying in the same hotel as me in Havana on a Christmas break in 1998.

One of them turned out to be a late-night drinker and we often sat drinking mojitos into the early hours, but both became holiday friends and the other seemed glad of some company during the day. Both were teachers, a little unadventurous, but they'd been to Havana before and they knew their way around. They showed me the sites and we had some fun moments.

One morning at breakfast they said that a Cuban friend, a young man, a physical education teacher, was going to take them to a local junior school. Did I want to come along? Oddly, I did.

The friend turned up after breakfast. He was black and in his mid-twenties, very well-dressed, very handsome, shortish but powerfully built, cool and polite but with what I sensed to be a dark humour in his eyes.

'This is José.'

They seemed proud of him and treated him like an acquisition—a trophy friend.

We walked up Obispo, the long narrow street beside our

hotel in Old Havana, then turned into a pretty, tree-lined square and from there into a meandering house that turned out to be the school. It was full of happy, noisy children in maroon uniforms that indicated their age group.

José had a quick chat with a teacher, went off and reappeared a few minutes later with a class of twenty or so children whom he led, crocodile fashion, out of the school and up to the park opposite the Inglaterra Hotel. We followed, sat on a bench and watched José coach the children through a strange set of exercises, which they appeared to enjoy. They ran a few small races, all cooperating willingly with whatever games he devised, and the Brits cooed and commented on how happy they all seemed.

After about thirty minutes José called time and we all walked back to the school, where we decided it was time for lunch. José had another brief exchange with the teacher and then we went off to a restaurant on O'Reilly, where the food was cheap and we could drink mojitos on the balcony.

The meal was José's reward for the tour. Conversation with him was easy and I asked him about a situation I'd found myself in a few nights before. A German woman who lived in Cuba had invited me to a poetry reading. After a meandering taxi ride, we'd ended up at a large villa with a lively party in progress and not a poet in sight. The patio held three large metal baths filled with cans of beer submerged in cold water. Bottles of rum lined the perimeter. A band played salsa and everybody seemed to be doing just as they pleased, which was everything. Expensive cars lined the street; occasionally one would move off to take a group of prosperous drunks off for more alcohol elsewhere.

The German woman, who was enormous, got red faced and bad tempered whenever I danced with any of the women, and by 3:00 a.m. I'd decided that I'd had enough. I suggested we leave but it was impossible to find a cab. She proceeded to have a panic attack, convinced she was going to be raped and murdered, which I thought unlikely, but I flagged down a passing car and paid the driver to take us back to Old Havana.

'How could this be?' I said to José.

After all, Cuba was a socialist country, the last bastion of equality and justice. Who owned the villa? Who owned all those cars? Who were all those people?

He'd been smiling and laughing throughout my story, trying only slightly to hide his amusement. His eyes showed more than just humour when he replied, 'This is Cuba. Anything is possible.'

The teachers retired for a siesta and I was glad to have some time apart from them for a while. Coming to Cuba had given me a feeling of excitement I hadn't known for many years and I wanted to explore it. I asked José if he'd like to go for a drink that night and we arranged to meet at the Sevilla Hotel but we didn't stay there. José took me to a peso restaurant where we ate and drank at Cuban prices and where he asked me a lot of questions about my life.

'What about you?' I said.

'What about me?'

I took a sip of my rum; José had introduced me to Silver Dry, pure and white. He said the sugar in mojitos gave bad hangovers; Silver Dry was different: it was organic Cuban rum. Accompany it with occasional bites, drink water with it, don't overdo it: no hangover. It was clean.

'Well,' I said, 'you're not a teacher for a start.'

He spluttered on his drink.

'No?' he said. 'So what am I?'

'You're a hustler,' I said. 'You just borrowed those kids. And what were those games you were putting them through?'

He could barely speak for laughing but he didn't admit anything. I liked that.

'So you had taste of Cuba,' he said, referring to the party. 'You like?'

'Apart from the German, yes.'
'Did you find woman? I can find you one.'
'That's OK.'
'Why no?'
'I don't know. I'm fine.'

I got back to the hotel at about 2:00 a.m. With no sign of my British drinking companion to share a nightcap, I ordered my own large Silver Dry. After a day in company, I now became melancholy alone. The barman was reserved rather than talkative so I sat on my own with my thoughts. I'd enjoyed seeing the Hotel Ambos Mundos a few days earlier: the twenty-four-hour bar, the airy high-ceilinged lobby, the monochrome photographs of Hemingway, Fidel, Ché and assorted gangsters. Hemingway had stayed there while writing *For Whom The Bell Tolls* and my travel agent had recommended it. It oozed character—romantic, corrupt and promising.

I nodded to Jorgé, who was on security. I'd come in the previous night to find him minding the hotel alone. He'd come behind the bar to serve me and, between each drink he poured me, he'd stood erect and disapproving, like a soldier. I'd tried to engage him in conversation and had only broken through by buying him drinks. He was a true believer in Fidel and the revolution and by seven the next morning he'd drunk at least eight Cuba libres—rum and Coke. Between us we had solved most of the world's troubles. When the day staff arrived he'd been stumbling around talking happy nonsense. They'd given him a few funny looks but said nothing. I thought I may have got him sacked so I was pleased to see him still here this evening.

I'd hardly got started on my drink when something bright and shiny came up in my peripheral vision. In the bar mirror I saw that a Cuban girl had seated herself next to me; she was smiling determinedly at my right profile. She wore a bright red T-shirt; enormous gold earrings swayed and sparkled. I turned to her; she'd gone for the red-hot poker look: red jeans to match. I wasn't in the mood, said 'No gracias' and turned back to the mirror. My reflection didn't improve my mood. She wasn't in the least discouraged and asked in precise, beautifully spoken English, if she could have a beer. I bought her a beer.

I continued to ignore her while the barman ignored both of us. She smiled unconcernedly. Jorgé chatted to his security colleague by the door. I couldn't figure out how she had got into the bar. During my stay I'd seen a few men, not the best advertisements for the Caucasian male, attempt to take Cuban girls to their rooms. They were politely but firmly stopped at the lift by hotel security and told that it was against the law. Single Cuban girls were generally not allowed into hotels at all without good reason.

Officially, prostitution is illegal in Cuba and foreign visitors can be locked up for making use of it but the law was far more honoured in the breach than the observance. I'd seen Cuban girls with tourists and I'd had any number of approaches. Prostitution struck me as not just rife but normal, and I'd turned down offers not because of any moral distaste or lack of desire but because I couldn't see how it all worked and didn't feel comfortable with it. I'd also not been impressed by many of the men I'd seen parading with stunningly beautiful Cuban escorts on their arm. I didn't want to look like them.

But here she was and nobody seemed to notice. Jorgé and his friend had found something fascinating to watch through the window, the barman was being inscrutable and the hotel's more respectable residents were tucked up nicely in bed. I wondered if I'd overdone the rum, because if anyone else could see the lady in red, drinking beer and smiling, they didn't show any sign of it, and there was ceertainly no protest. But things change after midnight, no matter where you are in the world, and she'd been allowed in. She must know somebody. Interesting.

Fed up with my reflection I turned towards her. The smile remained in place, an impish child-like smile that seemed to say, 'OK, what shall we do next,' as though we'd been together all day. Her hair was cut short above her ears, curly, but she'd sort of straightened the top two inches and gelled it upwards. It could have looked masculine but Cuban women don't do masculine and I was suddenly aware that she was unusually beautiful. Her brown eyes flashed at me in the light. How do they do that? Mid- to late-twenties, light brown skin, high cheekbones, tapered chin, carefree smile, perfect white teeth.

If I'd wanted her, I'd have felt intimidated. I was in my late 40s then and though I thought I was in good shape, my reflection disagreed. I was pale and tired and the day's drinking had jaded my appetite for anything other than sleep. I'd buy her a beer, have one more rum and go to bed. Yes. I ordered: same again. The barman somehow managed to serve us without acknowledging our presence.

'Take the drinks here,' she said. 'Is more comfortable.'

She indicated some small tables away from the bar, next to the windows and the street. I said no, that I would drink up and go to bed.

'Me too,' she said.

'No,' I said. 'I go here ...' and I pointed above me, as if to my room on the fifth floor, '... and you go there,' and I indicated the door. She smiled as though I was being very silly, picked up the drinks and took them to a table. I followed.

Her name was Irene. She asked me where I was from, what I did, whether I had any family, whether I was alone. Her English was good, though she said she spoke only 'a little'. Where did she learn? At school. Did she live in Havana? No, she was from Santiago. Did she have family? Yes, some in Havana, and a young daughter back in Santiago. That took me by surprise; I hadn't expected it, nor the frankness of it. I'd expected her to be guarded. Instead she was completely natural, which made her bright and easy to talk to.

I'd finished my drink and I wanted another. She changed to rum and ordered some snack biscuits.

'Are you hungry?'

She nodded. I gave her five dollars.

There are 24-hour bars along the length of Obispo. She took the money and rose to go.

'You stay here,' she said.

'OK. After this,' I raised my drink, 'I sleep.'

'Me too'.

Ten minutes later she was back. She had some chicken and what appeared to be hot crisps. She offered me some. No thanks. She offered the change. I shook my head.

'When you finish I go up, you go out,' I said.

'No. I stay with you.'

'It's not possible.'

'Is possible. Give the man ten dollars, no problem.'

So that's how it worked. I looked over at Jorgé. He and his friend had been watching us, now they looked away quickly. Jorgé was talking very loudly, indicating how dark it was tonight, or how large the moon, or something equally important.

I thought about it. I wanted to want to, but I really didn't want to—not at 4:00 a.m. And yet she had no intention of going anywhere. Every time I said I was going upstairs she replied, 'Me too,' and shrugged, as though it was inevitable. I wondered if she just needed a room for the night, what was left of it, but she didn't seem concerned. She didn't seem concerned about anything. Perhaps it was the rum making her so; or maybe this was what her job entailed; or maybe she was genuinely enjoying herself.

I tried another approach, took twenty dollars from my pocket and put the note on the table. She stared at it evenly.

'Take this,' I said. 'Now I go this way, you go that way. Do you understand?'

'Yes, I understand. Is a present for me.'

'Yes, a present. Now you have to go.'

'No. I stay with you.'

She sipped her drink, shrugged and smiled. I gave in. Apart from anything else I really needed to sleep.

'You go to your room,' she said. 'Five minutes.' I walked to the lift. Jorgé dragged himself away from his conversation and followed me. He opened the concertina doors. I handed him ten dollars.

'Do you know her?' I said.

'Irene. Yes. I know her family. A good family.'

He was soldierly again. His moustache was intimidating. Had he set this up? Enjoyed our conversation from the night before? Or just noticed the cash? He may have been a true Communist but everyone needed an angle to stay above the peso economy.

'I've not seen her since I've been staying here.'

'She likes you.'

'She doesn't know me.'

'She likes you.'

In my room I cleared stuff off the other single bed. I didn't feel any different about wanting to sleep but was curious about what she had in mind. A knock at the door. Jorgé had brought Irene. She walked past me into the room and looked around. I was about to speak when she came towards me with a look, half predatory, half amused, and kissed me full on the lips for a very long time. Her kiss woke me like an electric shock and, suddenly, I was wide-awake, tingling, alive and ready for more. She broke off, studied my face and smiled.

'Wait here,' she said, and disappeared into the shower.

I waited.


I flew home two days later. José came with me to José Martí airport. We sat at a bar waiting.

'You come back?

'Definitely.' I surprised myself by how sure I was. 'But it

won't be until this time next year—Christmas. I hate Christmas in England. And I have to make some money. I'll try and stay for a few weeks next time.'

We exchanged addresses and numbers. I hated goodbyes and I didn't want to go home. I never do.

'You leave Cuba and you no have a Cuban woman.'

'You think?'

He gave me his full attention.

'When?'

'She's been staying in my hotel room for the last three nights.'

'And you like her?'

'Yes. She was fun.'

'Fun?'

I explained. He shook his head and laughed.

'How much you pay her?'

'I didn't pay her. We went out and I paid. I gave her a present on our last night.'

'That means she like you. She was beautiful?'

'Yes.'

'Was she good?'

'None of your business.'

'So, she was good!' he said. 'All Cuban women are good. That's why men come here, fall in love. The women—not inhibited, not like in Europe. Men come, women come, then they come back. Everybody love Havana.'

'I'm not in love,' I said.

'Sure?'

'I'm sure.'

'When you come back, you be in love.'

'I don't think so.'

'We will see,' he said.

*When you go in search of honey you must expect to be stung by bees.*
Joséph Joubert


# 2

# Yamilia, Havana, Christmas 1999


I got to my room at the Ambos Mundos at 10:00 p.m. Cuban time—3:00 a.m. my time. Due to meet José the next day, tonight I wanted to prowl alone. Two large white rums revived me and I wandered up Obispo, which was then still sparsely lit: quiet, dark stretches interspersed with bursts of brightness, music and laughter from the bars, shadowy figures moving in and out of side streets and doorways.

Obispo was changing. Building materials littered parts of the narrow street, now being ugraded for tourists. The crumbling, tall, colonial buildings were being slowly, very slowly, restored. Bulbous, long necked bottles containing a rainbow of coloured perfumes lined the top shelves of a pharmacy that had been rubble a year before. Behind a long hardwood counter were rows of herbal medicines, hand-labelled with their names and medicinal properties. The previous year I had watched workmen, in a mess of dust and debris, apparently doing little or nothing other than occasionally hand sawing a plank of wood. Yet they had purpose and worked at their own pace. There would be no real profit in what they were doing—the bottom line wouldn't make sense—but this was craftsmanship for its own sake: beautiful, unique and idiosyncratic. Cuban.

An echoing clatter of heels on concrete interrupted my thoughts. A long shimmering white dress emerged from the gloom, and moved, not at all gracefully, towards, through and past the pool of light where I stood. I lit a cigarette and watched as it went. The dress flowed loosely around a pair of strutting legs but clung tightly to a prominent Latin bottom, defying gravity as it swayed hypnotically between me and a patch of gloom. The low cut of the dress revealed a glint of gold against light-brown skin. Intrigued, I threw my cigarette into the street and followed.

Ahead of me, I saw long black hair swept back, something red holding it in place, and an expression of severe indifference—even anger. She appeared to be having trouble with her heels, looking down and, I thought, cursing them as she walked.

Near the end of Obispo she stopped in response to a shout from some boys on a street corner. As I got closer I heard her no longer cursing but laughing and joking with them. Looking up for a moment she gave me the briefest of glances.

As I approached she set off again. I closed the distance and walked beside her; even in heels she was small. She stared straight ahead, ignoring me. Only when I spoke did she acknowledge my presence.

'Buenas noches.'

She looked up at me but didn't stop or speak.

'Do you speak English?' I said.

'You are English?'

'Sí.'

'¿Hablar Espanol?' she said.

'Muy poco.' Very little.

'I no speak English.'

'You just did.' She laughed and the harshness left her face, utterly changing her. As we walked, she stared at me, a direct, challenging and confident stare that demanded to know what was coming next. I was having the same thoughts.

'Would you like to have a drink with me?' I said.

'Like? What is like?'

'Happy. *Feliz*.'

'Happy,' she repeated the word, was silent for a few long seconds as she clacked and tottered on her heels, 'OK, me happy.'

'You said you couldn't speak English.'

'*No hablo inglés*.' I don't speak English.

We reached the end of Obispo, emerged into the weak light of the Plaza de Armas, silent apart from the chatter of tourists at a pavement restaurant. Much of the square was bathed in shadow. Replica gas street lamps gave a pleasant, low, seductive glow; opposite us the Santa Isabel, rumoured to be the height of luxury and the haunt of Hollywood actors in its heyday, bathed in their yellow light—three storeys and twenty-seven rooms of expensive exclusivity. Bats darted from the darkened museum to the castle and the tall ceiba trees lining the square. It could have been a quiet provincial scene, but if you listened carefully you could hear music, just a few minutes' walk away.

'Where shall we go?' I said.

'Where you want?'

'I don't know. Do you live in Havana?'

'*Sí*.'

'So take me somewhere.'

We walked to a very public tourist bar by the seafront. Crowded tables spread outside and over a wide pavement. It appeared to be full and we joined the queue waiting to be placed. She shouted at a waiter, who smiled and greeted her; they embraced and kissed cheeks. He found us a table close to the usual smiling, energetic musicians. The female singer waved to her as we sat down. I ordered rum and she had a beer. Suddenly feeling very tired, I explained that I'd been travelling for sixteen hours.

'Where you from?'

'London.'

'What you work?'

'Computers.'

She lowered her head and smiled. When she raised it again she checked out my jacket, hung on the chair. Her eyes moved over my shirt, watch, shoes and lastly my face. She spent a long time there. Some women can check you out and appraise your worth in a millisecond. This woman was as subtle as a sledgehammer. I held her gaze, wondered if she was mulata: half Spanish, half African. Her skin was a light, tawny brown but appeared to change with the light, her large, almond-shaped eyes dark, almost black as she weighed me up. Although she seemed to be in her early twenties, her eyes and manner spoke of experience way beyond her years. I couldn't place her: Latin, African—Indian? Was there still Indian blood in Cuba? I thought the Spanish had wiped the Indians out, but wasn't sure.

'How old you are?' she said.

'Forty-eight.'

She thought about it. Her thought processes showed on her face like subtitles

'How old me?'

I thought: twenty-three.

'Twenty,' I said.

Her face lit up with pleasure.

'*Veinticinco*,' she said. Twenty-five.

I didn't know about dollar shops then. How some lived above, or way above, the peso economy. I just thought that this was a poor country trying its best in the face of spiteful sanctions. I looked over her clothes. Cuban people of all ages manage to look good, no matter what they wear; they put something together but do it with style. This woman had style but it hadn't come cheap: gold around her neck and wrist, a nice watch, the new-looking silk dress—I wondered where it had come from.

'Where did you get such nice clothes?'

It was a clumsy question.

'You think we no have good clothes in Cuba?' she reacted. 'You think you come from rich country and we have nothing? I buy from Hemingway Marina, from Habana Libre. You come here and you think we are shit.'

'No. I don't think you are shit. *Lo siento*. I'm sorry. I don't know Cuba. Your clothes are very stylish. I didn't know you could buy them here.'

Her face darkened, her lips compressed and white with anger. She wouldn't look at me. She stubbed out her cigarette, almost destroying the ashtray. Her eyelids flickered. She sat back in her chair and looked around for a distraction, found it in one of the waiters and shouted out a greeting, smiling as the storm clouds disappeared. She turned back to me, all as before.

'What is your name?'

'Chris. *¿Como te llamas?*'

'Yamilia.'

'What is your work?'

'*Enfermera.*'

A nurse. Had she always been a nurse? No. Before that she had been a gymnast; she had represented Cuba at the Atlanta Olympics.

'You've been to America?'

'To America? This is America. To *Estados Unidos*. Sí. And I live in France two years.'

'Where in France?'

'Monte Carlo. And Genoa in Italia. I see the cars in Monaco and the *pelicula* in Cannes.'

'*¿Pelicula?*'

'Sí. Movies.'

'The Cannes Film Festival?'

'Sí.'

'Why were you in France?'

'Un *medico*.' A doctor. 'He come to Cuba and take me to France.'

'And you came back.'

'Sí. *Estupído*, much money, very stupid.'

'So you came home.'

'Sí.'

If he'd sent her home or she'd come by choice, I didn't ask.

At around 2:00, the bar began closing. Yamilia now looked happy and relaxed, and hadn't made any suggestions. I was very tired and didn't *need* a woman but I wanted her. I wanted to ask her to my room but didn't want the invitation to feel like a transaction: what if I wanted to see her again? I looked up. She was watching me with an age-old stare, wise and knowing.

'Me no *prostituta*,' she said.

I met her eyes. Sometimes they would slide away as she talked. Not now. She held my stare and smiled. I decided to resolve any conflict in the morning, or afternoon, or whenever I woke up. If I woke up.

'Come to my hotel for a drink.'

'A drink?'

'Sí.'

She pondered what a drink might mean.

'OK.'

At the hotel it took five minutes for the bar staff to appear and serve us. It was a twenty-four hour bar, but there were no customers.

'They sleep,' she said. 'They no like. They no happy.'

Happy. She repeated the word, shook her head and laughed. Then she shouted an order at the barman who jumped and served us two large rums. After the first beer, she'd matched me, rum for rum, all night. She held her drink well; apart from talking more freely than at the start, I saw no signs that she'd been drinking at all. We sat away from the bar by a large open window looking out onto Obispo. She shivered.

'*Tengo fría*.'

'You are cold?'

It was late December, nearly Christmas. The temperature was around seventy degrees Fahrenheit. 'Take my jacket.'

I stood up, took off my jacket—charcoal with pin stripes—and spread it over her shoulders like a cape. She put it on, released her hair and fluffed it around her ears and shoulders. It spread behind her, thick, shiny and slightly curled. She shook it and pushed it back from her face, pulled the jacket round herself and hugged herself. I couldn't take my eyes off her. Was she disconcerted by my stare, as I had been of hers? Did she have any idea of the effect she was having? My uncertainty made her even more attractive.

She picked up her glass and clinked it against mine.

'*Salut!*' she said.

She laughed and pointed to the window.

'That man. *Mira*. Look.'

I turned and looked out at the street. A man stood there, his arms held out, palms up in supplication. He was around thirty, with long gelled hair. I couldn't tell if he was a tourist or a local. When Yamilia didn't respond, he shook a fist, pointed to his wristwatch, then walked off. She laughed again.

'He's *cómico!*'

Maybe that's who she'd been rushing to meet in her high heels: a date.

'*Sí, cómico,*' I said.

As she relaxed, her voice took on a seductive deep tone: personal, attentive and interested. Her laugh was sexy and musical; whenever she smiled or laughed I wanted to make her do it again because it made me feel good. I asked her to come to my room.

'*No es posible.*'

'It's possible.'

In the room she walked straight to the balcony and watched the street below.

'Hemingway write famous book here,' she said.

'Here?' I said, joking, meaning this room.

She stared at me as though I was insane.

'No. Not here, upstairs. In room for tourists.'

She had a toned gymnast's body, not the slight East European version but one with all the Latin curves in miniature. She was almost entirely physically passive at first but I sensed her gauging my desire. She was alert, interested and calculating. When I climaxed, loudly, she propped herself on her elbows and watched. Rather than sleepy, I felt energised. As she dressed I put on a pair of baggy shorts, picked up my wallet and flicked through it.

'You want give me money?'

'You want me to?'

'I have money,' she said, as if the subject of money was so vulgar she wouldn't lower herself to discuss it. She finished dressing and sat on the other bed. I told her I'd been learning Spanish and quoted silly phrases at her.

'We put on the TV after dinner. They go to school by bus. I washed my hair today.'

She sat, chin on hands and watched me. I was high now. I launched into a monologue, part English and part awful Spanish, about Fidel and Cuba and the United States. She sat and looked and listened.

'What you say?' she said.

Then she undressed again, pulled my shorts off and made love to me. She smiled the whole time. Warmer, perhaps more herself now, but still holding something back. Somehow I doubted she was a nurse. I was left in no doubt at all that she'd been a gymnast.


She dressed quickly. It was 5:00 am.

'When you out of bed, you call me.'

She wrote down her number and left.

I got up six hours later and ate a late breakfast on the roof of the hotel. It was a gorgeous day, like a late, warm, English summer. The quality of the light alone revived me. Later in the lobby, in the afterthoon, I listened to an enormous Cuban, whose backside spilled over the piano stool, play lovely music on a Steinway. He said Hello. He remembered me from the year before. Everybody at the hotel remembered me from the year before.

José turned up at 5:00 pm. I told him I'd met someone the night before and had spent the night with her. He smiled approvingly. Then I said I was going hire a car and see the country with her. He looked disappointed for a moment but then said, 'It will be good for you to see Cuba: see how *las cubanas* live.'

I told him I'd call him when I got back and that cheered him up, and we settled in for an evening of rum and conversation, in which the allure of Cuban women figured highly on our list of talking points. At some point in the evening I said I had to phone Yamilia and arrange to meet her the next day.

'Yamilia?' said José. 'Your girl?'

'She's not *my girl*,' I laughed. '*My escort*, perhaps!'

'Yamilia? Not Yamila?'

'I'm pretty sure.'

'Yamila is popular name; Yamilia? Not so common.'

He asked me to describe her and as I did so, his eyebrows furrowed. I asked him what was up. Did he know her? Maybe, he said, and we left it at that.

The following morning I went for a walk after breakfast and hired a high-range Audi, realising uncomfortably that I wanted to impress her. I browsed the book stalls in the Plaza de Armas as I waited for the allotted time. Returning to the hotel I scanned the lobby. She wasn't there, so I sat at the bar to wait. The barman mixed my mojito and studied me curiously,

'Your woman is here,' he said. 'She wait twenty minutes.'

I turned and checked the lobby again. It was almost empty.

In the far corner a young girl sat alone on a white sofa, a soft drink on the low table in front of her. She wore a brightly coloured striped T-shirt with old jeans and sneakers.

I watched the barman as he mixed lime, sugar and mint leaves into the white rum and soda. I paid and raised my eyebrows in query. He nodded at the girl. I looked again. She sat primly with her hands in her lap, unsmiling, staring straight at me. Yamilia? I felt confused and embarrassed. Finally she smiled and I went to her table.

'You don't know me,' she said.

That was true. She looked eighteen—or maybe less. She was different, Asian today, perhaps Balinese, a tiny, golden Asian; hair bunched behind her head, pulled tight to her scalp. She smiled prettily; I found it hard to speak. Only her eyes and the sensuous turn of her mouth told me who she was. She wore no make-up and, with her hair back, her face looked thinner, smaller—still supremely confident though, enjoying my confusion.

'You look different. I didn't recognise you.'

'You like?' She said, with a coyness that didn't suit her.

I shrugged.

'You're OK.'

She kicked me.

'I hired a car.'

'Sí?'

'I want to see the country. Do you want to come with me?'

'Where you go?'

'I don't know.'

'Can we go see my mama?'

'Where is your mama?'

'La provincia de Camagüey. One day drive.'

'OK.'

The drive was my first real experience of Cuba outside Havana. The three-lane freeway was mostly deserted and the kilometres sped by comfortably, without the driving needing too much concentration. I was free to take in the mainly flat farming land, the fields of tobacco, sugar and coffee, the various exotic fruit and vegetables, and the occasional green rolling hills. Towering royal palms swayed, fragile-looking but indestructible, above thatched farmers' cottages. The sky appeared vast, an endless horizon, like the Big Sky in America's Midwest but incongruous for a small island.

We settled into an easy companionship of conversation, music on the car radio and silence. I watched Yamilia occasionally, still fascinated by her changeability. She was lithe and tomboyish, often clambering over the seats to retrieve something from our luggage or to sleep for a while. She seemed able to sleep at will and then be wide awake again. We spoke English and she asked me to explain words she didn't understand. I'd put a word into context for her, give the Spanish equivalent if I could, and it quickly became part of her vocabulary. She sometimes mixed Spanish, French and English and had a gift for languages that I lacked completely.

When we stopped for petrol, we'd eat and drink at the roadside cafés and restaurants. They were depressingly similar in appearance to cafés and restaurants all over the world but most definitely Cuban in terms of service and atmosphere: unhurried, casual, mostly friendly, sometimes indifferent. Yamilia seemed happy and I wondered what she was enjoying: me, the prospect of seeing her mother, the change of scene, the living in the moment. Would she be like this in any company?

Yamilia was curious about my life, about life in England, about everything.

During a conversation about money she said, 'You come from good country. I come from shit country.'

Then I remembered her indignation from two nights before when I'd implied that good clothes couldn't be found in Cuba. This was something I would often encounter with

Cubans: a mocking criticism of their country contradicted by a fierce pride in being Cuban and an extreme sensitivity to criticism of it.

Havana to Camagüey took ten hours, with a few rest stops. Long stretches of almost-deserted motorway were punctuated with men, women and children selling bunches of bananas, onions and other assorted farm produce. They walked to the middle of the road waving their stuff. The *campesinos*, farmers, I'd met, mostly in small towns and villages seemed happy enough—poor but not really lacking anything. But to stand in the hot sun all day on the slim chance of making a few pesos spoke of hardship I hadn't encountered. And in the country hardship was everywhere.

In the nineteenth century it was possible to ride the length of Cuba without leaving the shade of trees. Sugar plantations changed that. Although there were protected forest areas, thanks to the now burgeoning eco tourism, large stretches were fairly dull and treeless. Life in the country was controlled chaos. The working day was long, with a strange selection of archaic vehicles chugging back and forth, sometimes pulling trailers full of people. Ancient lorries belched black smoke at every gear change; overtaking could result in a cloud of toxic, foul-smelling fumes wafting through the open window. An abiding memory was of long lines of Cubans everywhere, all over the country, waiting for a non-existent bus, or a lift from a friendly face, or for a price they could afford, or crammed into the back of a lorry, standing room only.

It was dark for the last two hours of the journey. In Cuba half the vehicles drive without lights and many of the drivers are drunk. There are donkeys, goats, cows, dogs, pedestrians, jay-walkers, inebriates, bicycles, motorbikes and children playing—mostly in unlit streets. I was having trouble negotiating it all in the gloom. More than once I was forced onto the verge, steering a fine line between clipping an oncoming truck or mowing down pedestrians. Yamilia showed no concern; these were just everyday hazards.

'They don't care,' she said. She meant Cuban drivers, although you could say the same of Cubans in general. Something is history and unimportant the moment it's happened. I found it a refreshing and infuriating attitude to life.

Her mother's cottage was in Lugareno, a village thirty miles beyond Camagüey. Just before arriving, we stopped at a roadside bar, where Yamilia bought masses of beer and rum. I saw why when we arrived. She had obviously phoned ahead and we were greeted by a mass of grinning, laughing, over-excited people of all ages. I was overwhelmed by them all despite Yemilia's introductions and glad to find a rocking chair on the porch where I could take refuge.

Yamilia couldn't stop hugging her mother, detaching herself to introduce me to someone else and then clinging to her again. As I sat in the chair, someone thrust a glass of rum into my hand, and I became more sociable and felt my Spanish improving. Slowly, before the night turned into a blur of fiesta, music and dancing, I managed to figure out who was who. Many were friends and neighbours who had just turned up for the occasion. Of her family, Yamilia's mother and one of her sisters, Ramira, lived in the cottage with Fifi, one of four brothers and occasional resident. Her father, whom her mother hadn't spoken to in ten years, was visiting for my benefit. Zenaida, another sister, was also visiting. Yamilia turned out to be the baby of the family, a late addition and the favourite, spoilt and watched over by everyone, particularly by her mother. They were protective of her and concerned but at the same time indulgent. Baby or not, she had left home at fifteen and survived alone in Havana for ten years. She was probably tougher than any of them.

Her mother was dark-skinned with a gentle, long-suffering expression. Ramira was also dark and Fifi, tall, beautiful and manic, was even darker. He smiled constantly and seemed to be in a permanent state of excitement.

'Fifi is crazy,' said Yamilia.

'He seems OK.'

'A little crazy is good.'

'And he's a little crazy?'

She watched Fifi for a while and shrugged.

Ramira, according to Yamilia, was 'simple', in her mid-thirties, had never left home 'and never fucks nobody'. Zenaida, who had her six-year-old son with her, was lighter-skinned than Yamilia, equally beautiful but taller, older and fuller of face. Maybe they had different skin colour because they had different fathers. That's common in Cuba. Compay Segundo, of the Buena Vista Social Club, boasted that he had sired over 20 children, though officially he had only five sons, and he smoked and drank rum till has death at 95. Castro was said to have had at least 15 children. All stories in Cuba are exaggerated and exaggerated again, endlessly. It is difficult to know what the truth is but there is a semblance of truth in all the stories. As for Luis, Yamilia's father, he was Haitian: tall, slim, handsome, dignified and pale skinned. He sat with me on the porch, avoiding his wife.

When I rented the car, I'd been expecting a driving tour of a few days. I ended up spending three weeks with Yamilia's family in Lugareno and lived more intensely than I had ever lived before. At New Year's Eve I supported Luis as we wove our way unsteadily home from a party at the village hall, where a horse had been one of the guests of honour. A week later I bought a live grain-fed pig, which was trussed up and put in the boot of my car ready for that night's fiesta. I watched as they killed and prepared it. They fried the skin first: the scratchings. A villager said that if I ate scratchings all night I could drink as much rum as I liked without getting a hangover. He was right.

Fifi liked to drive my car, and as we drove around he would pick up as many hitch-hikers as we could fit in. One day we drove back to Camagüey with eleven people in the car, music blaring.

Yamilia didn't ask for money. I once asked her if everything was OK. She studied me as though I were a child.

'When is everything OK in this life?' she said.

One night as we lay on a beach in San Pedro, I told her that some of the stars she could see were not really there, that they had died and disappeared many years ago, that they were so far away and that the light took so long to reach us that we didn't know they were gone yet. She turned to face me from where she lay, pointed at her head and said,

'You have something wrong here.'

I liked to sit in the rocking chair on the front porch and read. I'd finished all but one of the books I'd brought with me and was now down to an old English-language copy of Plutarch's *Lives* that I'd found on a bookstall in the Plaza de Armas before we'd left Havana. It was pleasantly entertaining, because the story of Anthony and Cleopatra reminded me slightly of my relationship with Yamilia. I'd been reading it one lazy afternoon when I put it down for a moment to light a cigarette.

Yamilia picked it up, flicked through it and asked me about one of the illustrations. I explained how Anthony and Cleopatra had fallen in love and how Cleopatra had decided to kill herself when she heard that Anthony had died by his own hand, thinking she was dead. She was now trying out poisons on her slaves, to see which one caused the least painful death. The illustration showed one of her slaves writhing in agony at her feet while she considered her choice; another, already dead, was being carried away. Yamilia studied the picture with some fascination, gave me a beautiful smile and walked away, singing a Cuban song that I didn't recognise.

We could get rum at any time. All over Cuba there are bars in the middle of nowhere, open twenty-four hours a day. Well-frequented, they serve the local population: farmers, drivers, lost souls—anyone who needs a drink. We were served by such a bar half-way between Lugareno and Camagüey, where Fifi would drive for supplies.

We were also arrested and fined in Santiago for riding two on a bike, something everybody did but which gave the police an opportunity to make a little pocket money.

Further along the coast we lay on black-sanded beaches beneath the Sierra Maestro, the mountain range that runs across the foot of Cuba and where Fidel, Che and eighty compañeros launched Cuba's first successful revolution.

And climbing to the highest point of the Sierra Maestro on a clear night, we watched the shimmering lights of Haiti and Jamaica across the water, a hundred miles away.

On the drive back to Havana we stopped at a roadside bar. I noticed Yamilia had taken $200 from my stash in the glove compartment. I asked her to give it back. She widened her eyes and smiled.

'Give it back or you walk home.'

We sat in the car facing each other.

'Me? Walk?'

She reached over to the backseat, picked up my jacket and got out of the car. She put it on, patted the pockets and smiled through the window. The jacket contained my wallet and passport. She walked towards the restaurant smiling over her shoulder. I waited a few minutes before following and joined her at a table.

'You see all these places, fiestas, photographs of my life, stay with my family? And you don't like I take $200?'

She had a point, but I sensed danger in giving in. I gave her $150.

Before we reached Havana I stopped on a small bridge by a lake where I wanted to take some pictures. I got out and leaned against the railings with my camera. Below was a man-made outlet with sheer concrete sides, perhaps part of a water supply. Clear shallow water flowed gently under the bridge.

Yamilia asked if she could use the camera. I said she could and lectured her about being careful and keeping the strap around her wrist so as not to drop it to the water below. She listened patiently and then ran off a few photographs.

When she returned, she handed the camera back and I rested it on the railings for support, intending to use the zoom. And I dropped it. I hadn't used the strap and the camera fell into the water twelve feet below. 'Fuck!' I said, angry at the lost camera and particularly the lost photographs, and embarrassed at my own incompetence after all my lecturing of her.

'I get it,' she said.

She walked around the side of the railings and along a grass verge above the concrete sides of the outlet, and stood above a thin metal pipe below the top of the wall. She shimmied out of my jacket, lay it on the grass and crouched at the edge before slipping over, holding the top of the wall for a few seconds and then dropping into the water below.

She walked out to where the camera had fallen, picked it out of the water and shook it.

'Is OK,' she said. 'We can dry in the sun.'

I stood above the metal pipe, wondering how she was going to get out.

'Catch,' she said, and tossed the camera up to me.

I lay it on the grass next to my jacket and turned to help her. The metal pipe was way above her reach. The wall leaned at a very slight angle, pockmarked with a few bumps and dips. She used them to gain a grip and sprung herself up to the pipe two feet below me. I moved closer to the edge to pull her up. She was swinging by one arm, smiling up at me; her arms were thin and barely muscled, but she seemed quite comfortable supporting her weight.

'Chris, you get out of the way,' she said between laughs.

'I'll help you,' I said.

'No, get out of the way.'

I stepped back. She jerked her other hand to the pipe and swung her feet up onto the grass, then pushed on the pipe to move her upper body up too. Only then did she take my hand as I pulled her to her feet.

'You must be careful with your camera, Chris,' she said, 'and keep strap around your wrist so it don't drop in the water.' She threw back her head and laughed as she walked back to the car, her soaked trainers squelching. 'Come: we dry it in the window.'

It was late when we got back to Havana and the Ambos Mundos Hotel. We ate at the rooftop restaurant, then went down to the lobby. It was my last night but we were both too tired to go out. After three weeks together, we would have to make do with a few hours before reception called and asked her to leave.

Jorgé showed Yamilia to my room. I was already on the bed. She lay down beside me. The ringing phone woke us as the first dim light of my last day crept onto the balcony. She lay with her arm draped across me; both of us still in our clothes. I watched her sleepily as she got up and gathered her things. She bent and kissed me. 'Phone me later.'

'OK.'

She stopped by the door and turned around, momentarily confused. She looked down at her clothes and at me on the bed.

'Mmm,' she said. 'Chris and Yamilia sleep.'

My flight was at midnight. I checked out of my room at midday and settled down in the bar. When José came and met me, as we'd arranged, I couldn't stop talking about the trip. I still believed that it was just Cuba that I'd fallen in love with; that Yamilia had just been the catalyst.

José listened. He was glad I'd seen life in Cuba but didn't say much.

'I think I'm going to come back here to stay,' I said.

'When?'

'Soon.'

'What you gonna do here? How you live?'

'I'll see.'

'You got money?'

I smiled enigmatically. I didn't know whether I had money. By Cuban standards, I was probably loaded. It depended how I chose to live—and what my financial situation was back home.

'You say goodbye to your Yamilia?'

'I have to phone her.'

'You know I know her,' he said.

'So?'

'*Ten cuidado*, Chris.' Take care.

'Why?'

'Just—take care.'

I thought I needed to be careful too but I wasn't sure why. I wanted to see her but some vestige of self-protection, a desire not to get involved, prevented me from picking up the phone. I thought of myself as a free man. I'd enjoyed our three weeks together. Everything was new. If we got any more involved with each other, things were bound to get mundane. I'd become the prisoner of her expectations. I didn't want to be trapped in that way: that wasn't what I'd come to Cuba for. So I didn't phone.

An hour later she turned up in the bar. Ignoring José, she glared at me.

'You no phone,' she scowled. 'You say you phone and you no phone.'

'I'm sorry,' I said helplessly. 'We got talking and … .'

She turned to José and stretched an imperious arm towards the front doors of the hotel.

'You: go!' she ordered. 'You, come,' she said, looking at me.

At eleven I was at the airport with Yamilia. In the taxi she said, 'José is your friend?'

'Yes, I think so. You know him?'

'He is *un cuchillo*, a knife man,' she said.

'He's what?'

'He's a *pandillero*, a gangster. When anyone make trouble, they send him. You need take care. People see you together, you get reputation. You no want that.'

I'd only ever enjoyed the time I'd spent with José. I'd found him charming and amusing and relaxed and, without knowing what I was talking about, I spoke up for him. Yamilia got increasingly angry and we had an argument that hadn't resolved by the time I had to go through passport control. I turned my back on her and walked away, convinced that I didn't care but also convinced that she'd follow me and say sorry and that we'd kiss and make up before I flew off. She didn't.

As the plane sped down the runway I still thought I didn't care. As soon as we settled on to the flight path I ordered a large rum, chatted to the hostess and opened up the book I'd chosen to read. But I couldn't concentrate. I had a pain in my chest that felt like a heart attack. The stewardess asked me if I was OK and whether there was anything she could do for me? No, there wasn't anything she could do for me.

I looked around the first-class cabin: a few men playing with their laptops; no women. I felt dizzy, couldn't collect my thoughts. I'd imagined that I'd made myself tough and impregnable and unreachable by anyone. So what was this? I was aware that the hostess was watching me. I didn't know what to do. I tried reading my book but couldn't even see the words. I ordered a bottle of rum and drank through the lot as I sped towards England and work and everyday life. The life I'd had under so much control.

At Gatwick I phoned Yamilia.

'I'm coming back.'

'You come back? When?'

'I don't know. I have to work things out.'

'You full of bullshit.'

'No. I'm coming back. I'll let you know.'

*Don't trust a brilliant idea unless it survives a hangover.*
Jimmy Breslin

# 3

## Escape Tunnel

I had no real idea how I would get there, I just knew that I would—that I needed to. Life in England wasn't working. I needed to find a new way of living. I was so bored that I'd been spending more than I earned just to keep myself distracted. I was borrowing heavily and had run up several credit cards to their limit. I could sell the small terraced house that I owned but otherwise I had nothing of real value.

A review of my finances told me that leaving for *anywhere* was a good idea. I had to make money—the kind of money I wasn't able to make in my tedious job. Maybe the sort of money that involved taking risks. And somewhere abroad, where regulations were looser and the rules less restrictive and the life more rewarding. Where opportunities were ripe for the plucking. Cuba. Of course.

But how?

Needing financial advice I placed an ad in *Private Eye*. It appeared in March.

ESCAPE TUNNEL COMPLETE
BAGS READY TO PACK
Discreet legal and financial advice needed to avoid mishaps.
Credentials and requirements to Box 1096.

A reply arrived a week later. It was from Paul, an inmate of an open prison serving two years for fraud. He invited me to visit him. Over the next few months I visited every weekend.

Paul was allowed out on weekend passes. I would drive him to a nearby pub and we would make our plans. Or rather, he would make our plans. I merely followed his instructions. We would put together a fund and use it to buy Cuban assets, which he would sell to investors through an office in London which he'd set up when he got out of chokey. We'd both put money in so we were equal partners and I'd fund my share by taking out a loan on my house. I'd be the link man in Cuba, scoping out options, and I'd refer them back to Paul, so he could take a view of them and add them to our portfolio. What exactly the assets might be—property, goods, exports—we wouldn't know until I was there on the ground. But what I would certainly need was a large float, so the contacts I met would take me seriously as a business partner. In short, I'd need to spend freely in order to attract the right attention. I thought I could probably manage that.

Paul's first instruction was: don't arouse suspicion—so I waited. During the summer I went back to Cuba briefly, to prove to Yamilia that she could rely on me and to prove to myself that I really was crazy about her, and then I let the autumn slide, until one Friday evening in November, I simply shut down my computer at work, tidied my desk and switched off the desk light. I had told people in the office that I'd booked a two-week holiday and they wished me the best as they left.

Jo watched me as she put on her coat. We'd been close over the last six years and she'd helped me through some tough times. She seemed to sense that something was up and was probably offended that I hadn't confided in her.

'See you,' I said, simply.

She smiled, a not-altogether-friendly expression.

'See you Chris. I'm sure you'll have fun.'

Out in the damp, cold evening, car doors slammed and

engines revved. I watched her as she pulled out of her parking space. I waved. She waved back and drove off—shaking her head, I thought.

Left alone, I sat in the empty car park and smoked a cigarette. Then I drove through the grey, bad-tempered Friday-night crawl to Gatwick Airport. I left my car in the Pink Elephant long-stay car park, booked into the Hilton and spent the next three hours roaming the airport, drawing dollars and sterling from various ATMs and exchanges. The next morning I did the same again and posted my Pink Elephant ticket to Paul. The car belonged to him now.

At 4:00 that afternoon I boarded a Cubana flight direct to Havana. Paul, now free and tagged, called as I sat on the runway.

'All set, pal?'

'All set.'

I had $100,000 in an attaché case and considerably more than that in a Channel Islands bank account, accessible in Cuba.

I didn't set foot in England again for another two years.

*Many people die at 25 and aren't buried until they're 75.*
Max Fritsch

# 4

# Arrival, November 25, 2000

The lights of Havana below stirred an excitement in me bordering on euphoria, a childish feeling, but still level-headed, tinged with the knowledge that I'd done this myself. I'd had a dream, made a plan and here I was. The city appeared warm and welcoming to me then. This wasn't just another holiday. This was my home. Home free.

Yamilia was waiting for me. Over the course of the previous months, she was the one person I'd stayed in contact with. My flight to Cuba needed a soft landing and she was going to be my runway. I'd told her vaguely about my wanting to make a new life for myself in Cuba and I'd asked her to fix things up for my return. As far as I was knew, she'd done everything I'd told her. She seemed cautiously excited. So was I.

A taxi took us to a flat in Villa Panamericana, a neighbourhood on the north-east edge of Havana, just near the coast. I was in a daze, exhausted, but also wide awake and buzzing. Yamilia was strange too, maybe not quite believing that I was actually here, after months of worried phone calls, doubting not so much my ability to return to Cuba but my desire to return to her. The owner of the flat was Rosa, whom I paid up-front for three months. I wanted to show that I meant this.

We went to the only club in the district at the Villa Pan-americana Hotel. I floated in and out of alertness, cashing dregs of spare adrenalin. Yamilia didn't suggest a quiet night or sleep. She'd got to know me pretty well the year before, knew that I'd have bursts of energy, that I'd be tired and then wake up suddenly, so she let the evening go at my pace. The pace would change when we fell into bed.

She laughed as I danced my strange salsa, mixed up with every other dance I'd ever danced and every emotion I was feeling. I danced with the energy of the damned, thinking that such nights were precious, that any could be my last. And on that night—and many to come—as the rum did its best to soothe my jangled nerves, I felt truly, miraculously alive. Night seemed to welcome me. The early hours in particular are the time for hedonism. If you get the balance right, it makes up for everything else. Get it wrong, and you become sad and irredeemable, prey to violence and corruption. My plan for a new life was working out and I dared God to stop me. I threw back my head and laughed.

As I danced and drank, I looked into Yamilia's black eyes, searching for kindness, not sure if it was there. At some point later, I stared into her eyes again and felt that she was trying to swallow me up. In bed she held onto me as if to save herself from drowning and I, in turn, tried to disappear into her.

And then I remember waking to a smile and coffee. I'd slept for fifteen hours.

The next day we took a taxi to the Cubacel phone company in Miramar, among the rich and the foreign embassies. At that time only Cubacel's cellular phones worked in Cuba; you had to buy and rent from them. I called Paul in London as we took the return journey.

'Where are you?' he said.

'I'm in a taxi on the Malecón with Yamilia.'

'The Malecón?'

'The sea front in Havana.'

'So you're mobile. How does it work?'

'I bought a couple of phones. I have to pay for the phone time. It means going to the phone company for top-ups. It's slow.'

'Phones?'

'I bought one for Yamilia too.'

'Is that wise?'

'Local calls only on hers.'

'OK. Is the phone time expensive?'

'I don't know.'

'The seafront in Havana. Beautiful woman by your side. You bastard.'

'I know.'

*I prefer young girls. Their stories are shorter.*
Thomas Mcguane

# 5

# Villa Panamericana

Villa Panamericana lacked the noise and chaos of downtown Havana, which was fine. Modern flats, some nice houses, a few rows of shops and the hotel built for the Pan American games in 1991. A one-street township with a couple of small supermarkets, some bars and restaurants, dollar clothes shops and the hotel. Havana was a twenty-minute taxi ride; the hotel had a good pool and a decent club and the Playas del Este, the Easterly Beaches, were just a few miles away.

I became comfortable shopping and in the bars; knew people to say hello to and practise my Spanish with. We even had a tame policeman for a while. I liked him. He came to the flat with his girlfriend and always brought a couple of beers. After a few weeks he stopped coming. I asked Yamilia why.

'They move him another place,' she said, 'Fidel no like them get comfortable.'

Yamilia could cook, and occasionally did, but mostly we ate out. At other times, especially when we wanted to have people round, we asked Rosa to come and cook for us. Rosa was trim, fortyish and white, with the usual long black hair and tolerant of, rather than friendly towards, Yamilia.

Two weeks in I met Raúl, a local doctor, and Lucia, his nurse. When I went down with a fever, it was Raúl that Yamilia called. Raúl said my fever was brought on by exhaustion and my change in lifestyle—a cleansing process.

The first few weeks went better than I'd dared hope for. Yamilia accepted my permanence and saw that I wanted to stay. The tension of our previous times together, her doubts that I would ever return for good, and the rage of our goodbye at the airport were gone. My body adjusted to the fact that I didn't have any work to get up for, didn't have a mortgage to pay and could do anything I wanted in a sunny, exciting country with pleasure-loving people. My health and my temper improved. Sleeping with a beautiful woman every night, a woman whose sexual appetite seemed greater than mine, brought an almost Zen-like calm. I felt lighter, younger and full of spare energy. I began to like people again. I realised I'd been carrying a burden of stress on my shoulders for years: everyday stress that many people feel, struggling through the same stultifying routine of too much work, too little money, too little living, day after day, trying to erase the boredom, and not sleeping enough. Despite what happened later I will always remember those first few months. I think of it now and my heart lifts, the back of my neck bristles. It is unrepeatable.

I recalled a conversation with Paul while he was still in the open prison. By then we'd been planning for a few weeks and I thought it was time I should mention Yamilia, surprised that he'd never asked if I had any ties. Perhaps, in his late-thirties, he thought that a near fifty-year-old like me wouldn't be bothered with women or perhaps that I was gay. I don't know.

'There's a woman,' I said.

'Oh. Not good.'

'Why?'

He studied me sagely.

'You have a path you want to take. They have a different path. Always. And it's only their path that matters.'

'I see.'

'And they panic. In this business that's not good.'

'This one doesn't panic.'

The very idea seemed alien to him.

We spent many of our days at one of the Playas del Este, the white sandy beaches just east of Havana, facing the southern tip of the Florida Keys, less than 100 miles to the north. They were popular with tourists but still felt comparatively deserted, so long and wide and plentiful that there was more than enough beach for everyone. I soon took for granted the warm turquoise sea, fine sand and swaying palms—postcard views—but I didn't lose the cool excitement I felt but never showed, an excitement about the future, about the fact that I was beginning to think that this might actually work out.

Yamilia didn't demand anything; she wasn't greedy. We already had a TV, so we bought a music system and she got hold of some bootleg CDs. The furnished flat didn't need anything else. When I gave her money for clothes, she always bought me something in return. For a while we both lost a part of us that was manic and self-destructive. We didn't drink so much: there seemed no need, and although we still went into Havana regularly, often until the early hours, mostly our weekdays were spent in idleness—in the house, at the beach, at the pool—and our evenings with friends or just with each other. I read a great deal and she didn't disturb me, listening to music through headphones or doing something else. She even read herself sometimes, but that was more to impress me; she didn't see the point of books, and was bored by most films too. She appeared rooted in real life, feet on the ground, at least during those first weeks.

She seemed anxious that I was happy. Cubans are demonstrative, open people. They show their emotions. Although I was very, very happy, unless I was laughing, dancing or in mid-orgasm, Yamilia doubted my contentment. I am by nature thoughtful, was happy simply to be, and didn't feel the need to grin all the time to prove it but Yamilia was confused by my occasional silences, mistaking them for unhappiness. She thought sex would cure any moodiness on my part, which was true but could be exhausting.

What she got up to when we weren't together, I didn't know. As for me, I'd meet José. We had to meet in bars; Yamilia wouldn't allow him in the house. She wouldn't tell me why and nor would he. He had warned me about her often; what I couldn't tell was whether they had been lovers and had fallen out or whether there was something else. Whatever it was, Yamilia wouldn't let him near me, which meant I had to lie to her about meeting him—the first lie of our relationship.

Meeting José was important to me. For one thing, in spite of our age difference—him mid-twenties, me late-forties—I counted him as a friend and a welcome male counter-balance to Yamilia. And then he knew people, had contacts—was involved in stuff. I never knew exactly how he made his money but he obviously sailed close to the wind and I found it amusing that he had no moral qualms about it—found it amusing, too, to be associated with his little hustles, if only at arm's length, by virtue of our friendship. It was all so much more alive than my friendships in England, especially when José started calling on our friendship to help fund him, which I was delighted to do, because it pleased him. If what he was involved with was illegal or dishonest, there was also something wonderfully innocent about it.

I was even amused that he cheated on me—and that he didn't realise that I was knew he did. If we were out and it was my turn to pay a bill, he'd add a bit on top and then pocket the difference. Or get the bar staff to accept Cuban prices and pocket the difference between that and the tourist rate that I forked out for. I didn't mind in the slightest; it was part of the entertainment. This was Cuba: it was what I had come for.

When we met for drinks without Yamilia's knowledge, he'd often fish for information about my life and plans but he stopped telling me to watch out for her, knowing that I was beyond his influence. Besides which, his association with me was financially life-enhancing, and he didn't want to kill the golden goose.

What I'd come to understand was that Yamilia's history was history. Nothing in the past mattered. Even if I'd found out something very bad, it would have made no difference. This was my Year Zero. What mattered was what happened now and from now on; I would succeed or fail on that. Knowing how wild and reckless Yamilia could be, and how unstable I was, I didn't hold out much hope that we would last long. I thought from the first meeting that my time with her would end in tears but so far I hadn't regretted a minute; I was as happy as I'd ever been: what was there to regret? Let life do its worst, let fate take its course, let it all end in tears. 'Thou blind fool love, what doest thou to mine eyes?' I knew perfectly well what it was doing. I didn't care.

Many evenings with Yamilia began at Cathedral Square in Old Havana, slowly drinking rum and watching the world go by. It was important to drink slowly, eat occasional snacks and sip water. That way one became slowly mellow as the sun set and day turned into night. The air itself seemed to take on new life as it grew cooler; the darkness beckoned eager voices, music and expectation. We drew attention from European tourists, often middle-aged women. They gave me darting glances of disapproval, quickly turning away if their stare was returned. It didn't help that Yamilia could look eighteen. We drew looks from the men too, not of moral outrage but envy. If they watched for long enough, they would see us talking, joking, laughing and touching. We were usually like this when life was just life, when history and plans and business didn't intrude. The stares then became wistful; some would even smile. I enjoyed feeling that I had what they wanted.

It's a common notion that all relationships fail first in the bedroom. Not in my experience. Relationships fail when people stop communicating. I know people who have been together for years who have no idea what their lover has been doing, thinking or dreaming. *Hable con ella.* Talk to her. Despite not having much skill with the other's language, Yamilia and I always talked. Rum improved our conversation, breaking down barriers and providing inspiration.

I didn't always sleep well. It wasn't worry; I felt pretty good. It was more the heat and, when I did fall into a light sleep, the noise. Cuba was rarely silent and I'd come from a quiet country cottage. I read if I wasn't too drunk. Yamilia slept the sleep of the innocent, at any place and at any time.

Well, not quite always. I woke one night to find her fighting somebody or something in her sleep, sometimes clawing, sometimes punching at the air. I rolled her gently onto her side and stroked her hair until she began to snore. I wondered who she was fighting and hoped it wasn't me.

On another night, we ate in one of Havana's *paladares*, the entrepreneurial private houses with a licence to serve food, where you sit at small tables in what was, in effect, their front room. I said something that amused her and she couldn't stop laughing. She laughed so much she fell off her chair and lay on the floor of the restaurant, clutching her stomach as gasping uncontrollably. We drew stares from the tables around us; she was barely aware.

We set off for a club in Miramar. As I drove along the Malecón, she unzipped me and sucked as I drove. It was exciting and wouldn't have taken long but you can't drive far along the Malecón without having to stop—for junctions, lights and traffic. I still regret that I didn't just ignore the lights and risk a massive pile up. But I moved her and the moment was lost. As I parked by the club, Yamilia studied me and said, quite seriously, 'Did you find that erotic?'

'Just a little, Yamilia. But inconvenient.'

I liked to dance and liked to think that I was a competent

dancer. On occasions, maybe I was. Yamilia stopped once as we were dancing and said with astonishment, 'Your dancing is correct!'

But mostly I just jigged about, an approximation of salsa. It didn't matter. I knew that nobody can move like the Cubans and I didn't try to compete. I merely let myself go and concentrated on not bumping into anyone else. Yamiliia didn't seem to mind. At one point on this evening, I looked up and there she was, moving towards me, drinks in hand, hair braided with red ribbon, a mischievous look in her eyes that drew me in. And I was happy with that. Then she smiled, smiled at me, for me and with me. And I was happier still.

Before it got light we left the car and took a taxi home. During a night we usually drank a couple of bottles between us. There was no staggering, no slurring of speech and no tantrums. I never saw her appear drunk or anything like it but as soon as we got in a taxi she would fall asleep, head lolling from side to side, mouth agape. I would carry her into the house, sometimes in my arms, sometimes over my shoulder. I would meet neighbours on their way to work and we would wish each other a pleasant morning. The next day I would sleep until midday at least. Yamilia would wake up early, in a foul mood, and get it out of her system by cleaning the house and singing along to the music on her headphones. Later she would take a siesta.

I enjoyed the evenings when people came round. Rosa, if she cooked, brought her son and maybe a friend. Raúl sometimes appeared and Lucia came with her husband, son and daughter and dominated the whole evening, talking mostly about *sexo*, her favourite subject. Lucia's fourteen-year-old daughter, seemingly unembarrassed by this, was a promising swimmer and we often went to watch her in competition. The events, which felt like school sports days to me, were shown on the national news programmes.

Lucia developed a bond with Yamilia and became a regular visitor to the flat. She found Yamilia entirely natural and liked her saying and doing what felt right and being exactly what she was. They talked for hours and I knew they talked about me. Lucia began to take an interest in our health, our love life and our plans. Yamilia, after a few drinks, would talk about beautiful mulatto children with green eyes. Lucia would look on approvingly. I was being groomed for fatherhood. I didn't find this anything like as disturbing as I'd expected.

While Lucia took an interest in our relationship and coached me on my sex life, Raúl would give me advice on the perils of smoking and rum, and I would come to rely on him many times over the next eighteen months.

Raúl checked up on me once a week. A serious man of around thirty, he took my blood pressure, listened to my chest and nagged me about smoking and drinking. He was waiting for documents that would allow him to travel to the USA and had no patience with Fidel's socialism, earning perhaps fifty dollars a month for his skills, the top wage for skilled professionals. While Lucia had quite a large apartment above her surgery in Villa Panamericana, Raúl lived alone in a modest flat like ours. One morning after a check-up we chatted over coffee. He asked how we spent our time, where we went. I told him I'd given some money to a music school and to some young dancers for equipment.

'Why? Do you like ballet?'

'Not really.'

I told him about a programme I'd seen in England about young Cuban musicians, talented but lacking good instruments, and dancers who made their own costumes.

'Would you like to go to the theatre or the cinema? Cuba is good for the arts.'

'Yes.'

'Would Yamilia be interested?'

'No.'

'I think you should do these things. It would be good for you.'

As we talked, there was a loud banging at the door. It was Luis, one of Yamilia's uncles. I had met him briefly. He was a gardener for Havana's parks, a small wiry, light-skinned, muscular man. As I brought him into the room he followed me closely, pleading with me in agitated Spanish, clearly under the impression that I had a clue what he was saying. I looked to Raúl for help.

'He says Yamilia is a thief. He says Yamilia bought him a TV and now has taken it away. It was his TV and she has taken it.'

'Why did she take it?' I said.

Luis waved his arms frantically as he shouted, veins pumping on his neck and forehead. He must have come from Havana to see me and the sweaty, tiring journey hadn't lessened his anger. We had met when Yamilia had taken me to his flat. He was in his forties with a young wife and baby. The flat was bare and depressing; life was evidently a struggle. Although she made me feel welcome, his wife didn't disguise her low opinion of Yamilia. I wondered if she was the catalyst for his coming to meet me. Raúl continued to translate.

'She took it and gave it to the family, he says.'

'Her family?'

'No. The family here in Havana.'

'What family here in Havana?'

'The family of Lazaro. They are not good people. They ... .'

Luis interrupted us with something Raúl couldn't translate. Se aprovechan de la gente. We searched for a dictionary. He found what he was looking for and jabbed a finger at the word

'He says they "prey" on people. He says Yamilia must be a weak woman for them to prey on her. Not proud enough to resist. A shameless woman.'

He was too angry to make much sense, shouting, his face too close to mine. I found his accusations crude and wild and any sympathy I might have had for his lost television had now evaporated and I asked him to leave. He was shocked and deflated, unable to fathom why this clear injustice had failed to move me.

'Tell him I'm sorry about his TV,' I said to Raúl, 'and maybe I can do something for him later.'

Luis nodded, unconvinced, his pride hurt at being dismissed.

'And tell him I like shameless women.'

'What was all that about?' I asked, after Luis had left.

Raúl spread his arms wide.

'It's hard to say. People get a reputation. There's gossip. It's hard to rebuild your name once people have labelled you.'

'Yamilia, you mean?'

'Chris, it's hard but a lot of people don't like her.'

'Because of them or because of her?'

'It's hard to say. She's strong-willed; sometimes insensitive. It causes friction. For a man, this can be hard enough; for a single woman, far from home, it can make her ... unwelcome. '

It was hard to hear this but I was aware that it was true. Yamilia was a force of nature. A lot of people would have wanted to shut her down. What I liked about her was precisely that she was so extreme.

Raúl asked what I knew about Luis. I told him about my visit.

'The television would have been be a big thing for him,' he told me, 'a source of entertainment and a distraction, as for anybody. You have introduced money into Yamilia's life. That has changed her. Because of you, she can help some of her family but not everyone and not automatically. Why she gave Luis and his wife the TV and then took it away, I don't know, but you can understand their pain. As for you, people know that you're the source of her money and assume that you now control her. Es complicado. The longer you are here, the more people will come to know about you. Some will take you as you are; some will think only about what they can get from you.

Money makes a difference. There are bad people everywhere. You will be bored with me telling you but you must take care, not just of your health but of the people around you and the assumptions they make about you.'

Then he surprised me by asking for a beer. I joined him, out of respect.

'I can understand why you have come here. Cuba is hard for Cubans, but not for you. If you are clever, you can do what you like. Women are more available here. I think you should slow down, learn to speak Spanish, find out more about this place and see what is possible for you. What you do—the clubs, the dancing, the drinking—I can see why in the beginning, but now, why? You are an intelligent man; there is more than that for you here.'

'And Yamilia?'

'I like Yamilia. I like both of you. But you need people around you who will help you. You are vulnerable until your Spanish improves, until you understand more about life here.' He flashed a rare smile, 'Take it easy, slow down and enjoy your life. Thanks for the beer.'

*If you don't make mistakes, you aren't really trying.*
Coleman Hawkins

# 6

# Magic Night

A few days later Yamilia took me back into Havana to meet some 'good friends'. She said I would have a good time, that they were nice people. The taxi dropped us by the Ambos Mundos.

'We will take a bicycle taxi from here,' she said.

A fat taxi cyclist waited by the hotel. We often used his taxi. Bicycle taxis are a quicker way of negotiating Old Havana's narrow back streets. A CD player was attached to the handle bars and he'd listen to its music constantly. Enormous, black, very smiley and friendly, he'd been pedalling tourists around Havana for years, which was desperately hard work. I wondered why he hadn't either lost weight or had a heart attack.

The journey lasted a few minutes. We stopped at a semi-decrepit, tall grey building and paid our panting, sweating driver his fare. Yamilia phoned ahead. In spite of her earlier enthusiasm, she seemed small and nervous in the dark deserted street.

We climbed the steps to a third-floor flat and were welcomed by a tall, grey-haired man in his fifties. Yamilia introduced him as Lazaro. Lazaro—the family she had given Luis's television to. This was going to be an interesting evening.

He took both my hands in his, pressed them together as though we were both at prayer, nodded and bowed obsequiously. He held my hands for far too long, muttering greetings in Spanish as though I was a visiting dignitary. He led us along a landing to an open door and into a room with a sofa and a few chairs. We were directed to sit. Yamilia looked around anxiously. Only Lazaro was smiling. He introduced his family: his wife, blonde and glaring; and Amado, his son, fidgeting restlessly in an armchair, sighing loudly, running his fingers through his long gelled hair, impatiently and pointedly not acknowledging me; and a boy of about eight or nine, who I saw had Down syndrome, asleep in a playpen in the corner of the room. I was sure that I'd seen Amado before. Where? Yes, the night I'd met Yamilia. The angry person who'd shaken his fist at her and pointed to the time on his watch.

I wondered what Yamilia's relationship with them all was.

The usual artificial flowers and some travel posters added a little colour to the flat. Why, with the abundance of real and beautiful plants everywhere, did they love the synthetic? Perhaps it was the struggle to keep real flowers alive against the constant rationing of water. Lazaro placed a bottle of Silver Dry on the table next to me. He opened it, tipped some into the corner of the room for their household saints and poured me a glass. I gestured for him to take some and he thanked me at length, as though I were the host offering my own drinks. Amado declined, his skin jumping with energy and impatience. He ran out of places to look to avoid looking at me, sighed heavily, pushed himself out of the chair and stomped to the back of the house.

Lazaro offered us slices of cold pork from a large flower-patterned plate. When we had taken a slice each, he put the plate next to the rum, indicating that it was only for us. I was ill at ease and the general atmosphere was tense. His wife clearly thought that wasting food that cost a week's wages on me was not a good idea and, although Lazaro might be welcoming me to their home, she wasn't going to. If these were the good friends I was supposed to meet, it wasn't going smoothly. I couldn't believe that Yamilia thought I'd be so naïve not to see through this, but she was a different person here, edgy and reticent. She touched my arm.

'The magic show will be here soon.'

A skinny young man arrived with a holdall. He had a boyish, pale face that emphasised red lips. His hands were delicate and feminine, with long thin fingers. He wore a red jacket, black trousers with thick shiny seams and a white shirt with a black bow tie: the Magic Man. Over the next hour he performed tricks and illusions that were the equal of anything I'd seen from celebrity magicians on TV. He made things appear and disappear. He did unfathomable card tricks, he even produced a white dove—I can't explain how. Yamilia clapped and squealed. Lazaro nodded and smiled, adding the odd 'bravo'. The wife stood and glowered from the kitchen doorway. Amado didn't appear. I clapped along too and tried to show some appreciation. Where did he come from? Was he a friend? Had they hired him? I admired the show but did not enjoy one second of it.

I didn't want to offer him money but thought it was required of me. I took out my wallet and fiddled with it. Lazaro leapt up and pushed my hand back to my pocket, backed away in his prayer mode again, bowing and scraping.

'No, Chris,' said Yamilia, 'is not necessary.'

I asked for the bathroom. As is often the case in Cuban homes, the bathroom was reached through a bedroom. Lazaro pointed the way. I walked through a darkened room. Returning, I passed Amado, asleep, sprawled across a bed, fully dressed. He snorted an abrupt piggy snore, one of his legs twitched and he farted. I'd had enough.

'Yamilia, I have to leave,' I said.

'But Chris, we have more food for you.'

I didn't like the 'we'.

I stood up. Lazaro's wife snorted from the doorway and headed for the kitchen. Lazaro stood, his grey eyes showing an anger that didn't spread to his face. He spoke softly to Yamilia in Spanish. I understood him to say that it was alright, that she had done well in introducing us, and that he would speak to her in a few days.

He led us back along the landing. At the top of the stairs I shook his hand, said my thanks and apologised for leaving early. He grasped my hand again in both his and spoke; he was taller than me, a big man, so he stood on a lower step, enabling him to look at me face-to-face. I met his eyes and didn't like what I saw or what I smelt: a sweet, sickly cologne scent. I had no idea what he was saying. Yamilia stood a few steps down, watching from the shadows.

I released my hand from his grip and joined her but he followed me down, this time taking my hands more firmly. He turned and again moved to a lower step so that again he looked at me face-to-face, speaking softly, hypnotically, almost in a whisper, his tone polite, his demeanour respectful and the danger unmistakeable.

Without looking for a taxi we walked back to Old Havana in silence, keeping to the middle of the street, as most Cubans did, for fear of being killed, as sometimes happened, when pieces of masonry fell away from the crumbling buildings. After a few paces Yamilia stopped. I turned to look at her, a solitary figure in the deserted, unlit street, the glow of her white satin dress giving her a ghostly appearance.

'Chris, I no understand you. You have twenty year more than me, you have much experience. What you want? I take you to friends. You walk out. They want meet you, talk with you.'

She stamped a foot on the cobbled street, nearly toppling off her high-heels. The bad feeling in my gut melted away and I felt only the need to protect her, alone in the dark of a Havana backstreet. A tiny, beautiful woman who had come to the big city when she was fifteen years old. And she had out-toughed everybody. It had taken its toll on her but her spirit was not broken. She stood here, abandoned and exasperated.

But I was alone too. And exasperated too. What had all that been about? Was it a social visit or something else? Did Yamilia know? If she did, she wasn't saying. I would have to figure this out for myself. I walked back and put my arms round her, pulling her to me. I waited as she relaxed into me.

'I don't want to go home yet. Let's go and get a drink somewhere.'

Outside the Ambos Mundos the fat tax cyclist waited for more passengers. He called us over, invited us to listen to some music. It was reggae; he was a connoisseur and had cassettes from all over the world given to him by his passengers. We listened, allowing the music to change our mood. I asked him if he would like to join us for a drink.

'Where?

'In here,' I said, pointing to the hotel.

'Is not possible for me.'

'It's possible,' I said.

Once we were seated, the fat man told stories of his passengers. Yamilia, happy again, laughed easily at his dry delivery. He told us about the 'lord' who came to Cuba every year and always used his bicycle taxi.

'A lord?' I said.

'Yes, English lord. From London.'

'And his name?'

'Lord Chelsea,' he said.

I explained to Yamilia what a lord was.

'And he comes every year?'

'At least. Sometime more often. He come for more than ten year. Always use my taxi.'

'Where does he stay?'

'The Inglaterra, always.'

'You sure he's a lord?'

He stiffened a little at my doubt, fiddled among some

crumpled cards in his wallet and handed me a plain white card with black type: Lord Chelsea, Financial Services and Expertise, followed by an address in the Fulham Road, which I thought was probably a poste restante. Con man, I thought, and nodded thoughtfully and respectfully as I handed it back.

'How old is he?'

'Seventies. Is a lord. Very respectful man. Beautiful clothes. He pay me very good.'

'And,' I said, 'when he comes now, does he like the Cuban women?'

'Yes, I take him in my taxi.'

'And do you take him many times?'

'Every day,' he said proudly. 'Every day.'

The next morning Yamilia said she needed to go to Havana for a manicure. While I was certain that she would return with pristine painted nails, her momentary look away didn't ease the bad feeling I'd woken with. Something was up. I felt Lazaro's grey eyes still boring into me, his sickly scent lingering in my nostrils. I dropped her in Old Havana and had coffee in the Ambos Mundos. Lazaro was on my mind but not in any way I could deal with or shake off. How could I deal with it? I didn't know what had happened.

I walked to the Malecón and climbed onto the thick seawall. The sun, not yet strong, was hidden intermittently behind wispy, white clouds darting east to west. My head spun, doubts stabbed at my gut. I walked along the wall for a mile or so with the wind at my back, then turned and walked back into it. My head slowly cleared, the worry vanished. I let the wind blow it all away.

I sat on the wall watching lithe, shouting, children, all shades of skin colour, playing baseball on the wide pavement with a broom handle and a ball made of tape. Behind them on the balconies across the street, drying clothes fluttered like flags of all nations. An ancient red-and-white Chevrolet pulled over to the kerb. Its engine roared, groaning under the strain of a thousand loving retunes, services and home-made parts, but its paintwork gleamed proudly and its chrome sparkled in the sun. They don't make them like me anymore, I felt it boast. The young driver leaned out of the window.

'¿Taxi, senor?'

I smiled and shook my head. He smiled back, waved and gunned the maquina, Yank Tank, into action and merged slowly, noisily, back into the traffic with a clunking of gears as the engine, over seventy years old, dutifully groaned into another day's service. This strange, beautiful city was my home and that was enough. Whatever happened, I would deal with it.

I walked up to central Havana and the park, but it was hot and sweaty away from the sea, and so time for a cool drink. Several large tourist hotels surrounded the park. From the Plaza Hotel on the corner of Neptuno and Zueleta came the thin murmur and tinkle of an indoor fountain. Inside I was hit by a natural, airy, high-ceilinged coolness and sat down to the sound of laughter and the ring of glasses on tables. The reassuring chatter of female voices in the background greeted me when I phoned Yamilia what I supposed was the manicure salon. Her nails were done.

'Meet me at the Plaza.'

I sat transfixed as an English football match played on a large screen and stared like a man deprived. It felt good to sit in cool surroundings and watch football, taking an interest in the game and caring about the result. Two plump Irishmen sat at the table next to me, shouting at the TV. The match ended and another was scheduled to begin later.

In their mid-thirties with round, sunburnt faces, Tom and Liam had just returned from Santiago de Cuba.

'Some of the poverty there was disgusting,' said Tom, 'Seemed like time for another revolution.'

'Maybe,' I said, 'but I love it here.'

'Oh, right, don't get me wrong mate. Cracking country, cracking people. But this Marxist shit, what's in it for the people? You've got doctors and scientists driving taxis and waiting tables to make ends meet. Good idea in the first place, don't get me wrong mate, kicking out the fucking Americans, or the fucking mafia. Viva Che and all that. But it's all gone to shit. It's bollocks. Patria o muerte, for fuck's sake. Country or death. How about a decent standard of living before we start talking about dying for the fucking country?'

I told them I was getting out of Havana for a while.

'Vinales, Pinar del Rio, mate,' said Liam. 'That's the place. Not too far, lovely mountains, beautiful rivers and lakes. Beaches too, if you're not sick of them. Fucking gorgeous.'

I heard a soft rustle of silk behind me. Yamilia had a bought a new dress. She loved white silk and satin and linen. She gave a twirl.

'You like?'

'That's great, love,' said Tom, 'that's just the thing.'

She stared at them with open curiosity. I gave her money for some more drinks. Tom and Liam were silent for a couple of minutes while they reappraised the situation, watching me. Was I now one of the reasons there should be another revolution?

'Jesus, it's fucking Arsenal now,' said Liam, snapping back to life.

'So what do you do in England, mate?' said Tom.

'I live here.'

'Fucking hell, which version of the lottery did you win? Divorced?'

I nodded. Yamilia returned with the drinks.

'That's a fucking racket too, eh, mate? Divorce? You get their knickers and they get your house and car. Fucking racket is what it is. Why do we do it, mate, eh? Why do we do it?'

I laughed. Tom glanced at Yamilia and she smiled at him, answering his question simply and naïvely about why some people get divorced. She had forgotten her nails and her new dress, had missed the sentiment in Tom's voice but had recognised some of the words and had noticed the accent.

'Where these men from?'

'Ireland, darling,' said Liam.

'¿Donde Ireland?' Is where?'

I drew a crude Britain shape in the spilt water on the table top with another smaller splodge off to the left. She nodded.

'And is English too?'

'It's complicated love,' said Tom.

'You speak different,' she said.

'That we do.'

We left them and went to eat.

'We're going to Pinar del Rio tomorrow,' I said.

'¿Porque?' Why?

'Aburrido.' Bored.

'OK.'

As we walked through the lobby of the Plaza, I thought I saw someone duck behind one of the giant columns that supported the double spiral in the ceiling. He seemed to have long gelled hair. I stopped for a moment. Yamilia had seen nothing. We walked on.

The province of Pinar del Rio is west of Havana, a few hours' drive. We had intended to visit the capital of the same name but stopped in the town of Vinales because I liked its wooden colonnades and red-tiled roofs. We ate overlooking the main square with its unused-looking church as night drew in.

'Where we stay? Here?'

It was illegal for Cubans to stay in tourist hotels, which was one of the many reasons why Tom and Liam had had a point. I checked our guide and found that a few miles from town was a ranch complex with twenty cabins where we could stay.

'But we can't stay there, is illegal,' Yamilia said.

'We'll stay there,' I said. 'Don't worry.'

We got back into the car and I drove to the cabins, parking near to the reception to investigate.

It was a modern tourist complex. The cabins had showers, satellite TV, air-conditioning, balconies with spectacular views and hot tubs. There were restaurants and bars, a swimming pool, a health spa, warm sulphurous baths, mud baths, massage, physiotherapy, acupuncture, and digitopuncture, whatever that may have been. They also offerred medical checkups and more. The price included three meals a day and as many drinks as one wanted. I didn't care what Yamilia thought or what the law of the land was. We were staying here. I left Yamilia in the car and established that rooms were available. The young woman tending the reception desk was Monika, according to her name tag.

'How long would you like to stay?'

Four nights, I thought; maybe more. I glanced at the price list and studied my wad of cash as I appeared to think about it.

'Only you?' she said.

'No, I have someone with me.'

I fetched Yamilia from the car. She looked around.

'No, Chris. We can't stay here.'

'Yes, we can.'

The expression on Monika's face fell with embarrassment.

'I am very sorry, sir. But we can't allow it.'

Yamilia gave me her I told you so glare. I placed two fifty-dollar bills on the desk. Monika didn't acknowledge them, just studied us as she considered. Leaving the money, she walked over to a tall, name-tagged black man in an expensive dark suit. Slick and sleek with sunglasses, despite being indoors, he stood in the centre of the lobby looking casually authoritative, surveying his domain. They spoke for several minutes, he occasionally pointed his sunglasses at us as he listened, frequently shaking his head. But it was a long, drawn out refusal. Monika returned.

'I'm sorry. It is not possible.'

I laid three more fifties on the desk. She nodded to her manager, who walked briskly to us and shook my hand. He kissed Yamilia's cheek.

'I am Ôscar, your manager. You can park your car over there. I will send someone for your bags. Monika will take care of you now. I hope you have a wonderful stay.'

He leaned over the desk, took the top four notes and walked away. I put my passport on top of the remaining fifty. Monika picked it up.

We were in a valley of steep limestone mountains topped with pines. In the flat valleys farmers grew tobacco, fruits and vegetables. On one of our rare treks we found a high waterfall, and swam for hours without seeing another person. I settled into a routine of breakfast, swim, massage, siesta, evening meal and drinks on our balcony or in the hot tub on the back terrace. Yamilia did much the same, as well as taking every health and beauty treatment going. The place seemed to slow Yamilia's metabolism. I was happy with the impact of this on her in bed, tired of the pounding, sweaty, biting, scratching and relentlessly energetic sex that seemed to be the norm here. I think the enjoyment of slowness was a novel experience for her; she smiled at herself in the mirror, making no attempt to speed things up but allowing herself to be led to whatever happened next. In the mornings she bounced around like a child.

I decided not to mention Lazaro or what seemed to be a sighting of Amado. She had an immediate and effective defence mechanism against any enquiry anyway—anger. That didn't mean I couldn't still read the signs, which were often obvious, but this was the *big* thing, apart from money, of course. This was the invisible but malignant *thing* that threatened our relationship so far. And for the key to that, there were no signs, no slips. I wouldn't find it. I'd just win her away from it. I thought I wanted that.

She became more affectionate, softer: a touch on my arm, a

stroke of my neck, spontaneous broad smiles. You're not as hard as you think, I thought.

The last night we sat on our balcony watching the stars. We had made love and were sharing a bottle of rum. We wouldn't finish it. Healthy living made us tired earlier; we would drink two or three glasses and fall into bed.

We were sitting at a wooden table. Music floated faintly up from the club below; late night swimmers laughed in the pool. Yamilia stroked the back of my hand.

'Chris,' she said.

'¿Sí?'

'You want get married?'

*And what is bettre than wisedom? Womman.*
*And what is bettre than a good womman? Nothyng.*
Chaucer

# 7

# Perfect Women

Back home in our flat in Villa Panamericana, Yamilia said she was going out to get some shopping. While she gone, I sat listening to music, half dozing, still in sleepy mode from our break.

I woke to the sound of slamming cupboard doors in the kitchen and Yamilia talking to herself. She was stomping round the room on the tiled floor. Normally she was so light on her feet, I wouldn't hear her coming; now every step echoed. She was naked, having apparently had a shower, her black curly hair, wet, snaking around her head, face and shoulders. She moved to the coffee table, bent over in front of me, took out a cigarette and lit it. After a couple of deep drags she pointed it at me, her eyes darting and restless.

'You want perfect woman, you go to Havana,' she said.

'What's all this?' I asked. 'You were happy when we got back. Did something happen when you were out?'

'Many beautiful women in Havana,' she said, ignoring my question. She turned in the doorway and stood glaring at me. She cupped her small breasts in her hands.

'You want them big here? Go to Havana. Many women in Havana big here. You want perfect ass?'

She turned round, showing me her perfect ass. I didn't say anything. She returned to the table, stubbed out her cigarette, then immediately reached for another. She bent from the waist, legs slightly apart and made a fuss of lighting it, manically flicking the lighter and showing the diamond shape between the tops of her thighs and her bottom. I sighed and adjusted myself in my shorts. She turned and shouted at me.

'You want perfect body, you go to Havana.'

There's no such thing as a perfect woman or a perfect body. She knew I loved her just the way she was, I was sure. But suddenly this wasn't enough; something had triggered a crisis of confidence. She stood at the open window and glared out. Across the road, a parked car waited, its engine idling. The sun glinted off the windshield; I couldn't see who was inside. Yamilia could, I felt. She slapped the window frame and span round, smoking furiously and muttering to herself.

'You have the eyes of young man, big heart. You have power and money in Cuba. Age not important here. Many women in Havana want man like you.'

She turned and shouted at me again. 'You want perfect woman.' She nodded to herself in agreement. 'OK. Take perfect woman. Go to Havana.'

She set off for the kitchen again as though it was all decided; as though I'd rejected her and was about to pack my bags for Havana. She threw her cigarette in the sink and stared out of the window again. The car was still there.

'Go, go,' she said. 'Why you still here?'

Her hair had dried in the heat, wild, sticking to her back, neck and cheeks and jutting out at all angles. I moved behind her and put my arms around her waist, tried to hug her without making her aware of my erection. I stood awkwardly, slightly sideways.

'I'm not interested in the women in Havana, Yamilia.'

She let out a small sigh and seemed to shrink in front of me. She stood on tiptoe, hands gripping the edge of the sink, knuckles white. She gave me a brief sideways glance. Some of the tension slipped away. She wasn't finished though.

'I see you look at women in Havana. Woman from the ballet. She is beautiful and *muy inteligente*. She like you. She can dance, speak English, she have money. You can have woman like this.'

'You think so?'

'I think so.'

'But I haven't.'

'*¿Que?*'

'I haven't got a woman like that. I've got you, because that's what I want. That's why I came here. For you. I don't want that woman. I want you.'

She shrank further, became smaller. She'd sensed my stiffy, despite my efforts to hide it, and was backing in to me. She took a deep breath and sighed. I gathered her tangled hair, moved it from her face and spread it down her back.

'Is true?'

'Is true.'

Her face collapsed into a broad smile. She spun round and kissed me and in the same moment pulled down my shorts and started to get down on her knees. I pulled her up.

'No. Not now. We're going out. Get ready, you look a mess.'

'Mess?'

'Sí. *Fayo. Muy, muy fayo.*' Very, very ugly.

She relaxed, went to the window and shut it. A moment later, the car pulled away.


We went to the Nacional. I didn't like it much but this was a treat and I could hardly take her to one of the *paladares* or peso bars that I preferred. She had spent two hours getting ready, her hair tied back tight and close to her scalp like a flamenco dancer, set off with a mariposa and dark-red lipstick. She wore a long silk dress; almost see-through. And high-heels. She could barely walk in them, she never could, always breaking or falling off them. She drew looks from everyone, which I suppose was the general idea. I liked being with her like that, of course. I liked the envious looks from the men but it wasn't the way I liked Yamilia. She had turned herself into a doll: artificial, unreal. I preferred her in jeans and a T-shirt. I didn't tell her that. You don't tell a woman who's spent two hours getting ready that you prefer the casual look.

It wasn't as stuffily formal in the hotel dining-room as similar places in Europe or the USA would have been, but it was stuffy for Cuba. The air-conditioning hid some of the smell of cigar smoke but the band, the music, never quite allowed stuffiness: there was always the feeling that a fiesta might break out at any moment, despite the exalted company, the white table cloths, the paintings and the large ornate mirrors. Yamilia couldn't make up her mind what to eat, ordered everything she liked and couldn't eat a quarter of it. She didn't become stiffer in the stiff atmosphere; she didn't change her behaviour for anybody. The waiters were Cuban, like her, and she spoke to them the way she spoke to everybody. She was direct, rude even: I could see why she put people off. As we ate she scanned the room, criticised the diners and pointed out faces that she recognised: minor politicians, drug dealers, Hollywood satyrs and the usual pimps and whores.

'You want buy house?' she said

Eventually I wanted a house, yes, perhaps, but not yet. I hadn't figured out who everyone was yet, who I could trust, who I couldn't. My Spanish wasn't good enough either. I smiled. Today had been a good day and I didn't want to spoil it.

'You've seen a house?'

As she put down her knife and fork to concentrate her power towards me, the pupils of her eyes widened and flashed like a cat on the prowl. She had seen her chance.

'In Guanabacoa. Good house, old, colonial, high roof,

beautiful floors, big patio. Is good house on the street but have bars on windows, long way back in garden—*tranquila*, cool inside. *Mucho calor* outside, is cool in house. Big wood doors, two doors together. All blue, like the sea. Is beautiful house. You like this house.'

I was in a good mood, soft and happy. She must have known she would wear me down.

'*Casa azul?*' I said.

'Sí, a blue house,' she said, then added, '*una buena inversión. Es recomendado.*'

A good investment? Recommended? What was she really talking about? Our life together or my financial prospects?

'Recommended? Who recommended it?'

'In the newspaper, Chris!' she said, unconvincingly. 'What you think? *Un anuncio de propiedad.*' A property ad.

'OK,' I said, hesitantly. Show me the house.'

She beamed a huge and happy smile at me, as if she'd carried off a mission. and could now unwind. As we left she asked for a bag for the uneaten food. The people at the nearby tables looked at us scornfully. On the drive home, I became aroused at the prospect of the night ahead. She gazed through her window at a full moon, a perfect grey flecked disc floating above an inky sea, a silver light shimmering across the calm surface towards us, trailing us. Without turning her head she reached over and laid her hand in my lap.

'Much work for him tonight,' she said.

The next day we took a taxi to Guanabacoa, a rough colonial township a few miles to the east of Havana on a busy, noisy street. The house had big, blue, arched double-doors and barred windows. It was empty so we peered though the bars at a large, high-ceilinged reception room and a doorway through to the rest of the house. Way back I could see a kitchen and a patio. Back there the noise from the street would be dulled. The floors were a patchwork of coloured tiles. I liked it immediately.

'Who owns it,' I said.

'People who move to Spain.'

'How much?'

'Nueve-mil. Nine-thousand dollars.'

I liked it but I was content with life as it was. A house would need to be furnished and it was illegal for me to own property in Cuba; my name could never be on the papers. That would mean entrusting the property to her and I didn't want to make that commitment yet. I loved Yamilia but wasn't sure of her. There was no advantage for me. Maybe after a year or so. But Yamilia said she was concerned that my money (and she didn't know how much) would only last so long and that we needed to earn an income from a business of some kind. I did have plans with Paul, and José had come up with an idea, but I hadn't told her. There seemed to be lots of opportunities.

Back at the flat Yamilia cooked. When she wanted to be, she could be a good cook but it was a talent she rarely practised —perhaps wisely, lest I got too used to it.

'You like house?' she said as we ate.

'Sí, but not now.'

'¿Por qué no?'

'It will take time to get the money. And it's too fast for me. I want to think about it.'

She thought about this for a moment, then decided to leave it for now.

'OK. You the boss!'

*Work like you don't need the money.*
*Love like you've never been hurt. Dance like nobody's watching.*
Satchel Paige

# 8

# Tony

'With business you need help. Is too difficult for you alone. No Spanish, you no understand what happen here.'

Until now, Yamilia had had little interest in business beyond her own needs but saw clearly, before me, that I'd get nowhere on my own. Parties, bars and clubs had introduced me to dozens of people, she told me, some of them useful, but these weren't the kind of people I needed. If I wanted to make real money, I was looking in the wrong places.

That's what she told me and that's how she introduced me to Tony. Tony could fix everything for the house in Guanabacoa, if I decided to buy it, she said. He was a big man, yes; he had houses all over Havana. He had served in the army, had worked high up in the system, he knew how everything worked. I needed someone like him; I would get nowhere with people like José.

'How do you know this man?' I said.

Her eyes slid away.

'He is tío, uncle, of someone I know. He want help you.'

I made a show of seriously considering this.

'The tío of someone I know? Rosa? Lucia? Raúl? Who would want to help me?'

She rolled her eyes at the stupidity of such a question.

'Everyone want help you! You popular guy!'

And a wealthy one, by Cuban standards. Who wouldn't want to help me?

'OK,' I said, 'let's meet and see what he has to say.'

'And Chris,' she said, holding my eyes this time.

'¿Sí?'

'Tony no like people who drink.'


Tony came to the flat the next day. I was showered and sharp and only mildly hung over.

'So Tony never drinks?' I said.

'Maybe a beer.'

She said this in an unusually respectful tone. How well did she know him? There was no point in asking. She was nervous, watching from the window while we waited. When she saw his car, she went and watched through the spy hole until she saw him reach us and opened the door. I thought she should have let him knock. They greeted each other Cuban style, like long-lost friends, all smiles and kisses. He towered above her, out of breath from the stairs. Smiling and laughing, he came to me, a huge hand outstretched, gripping my hand and almost cutting off the circulation.

'Mucho gustar, Chrees, mucho gustar. ¿Como esta?'

'Mucho gustar, Tony, muy bien.'

'Bien, bien.'

He was laughing, a little nervously perhaps, but it was a natural sound, big and booming as if he liked to laugh and did it often.

'Tony speak no English. Chris, you want coffee?' asked Yamilia.

I looked at Tony.

'You want coffee, Tony? Beer, rum, freco?'

'Cervesa, por favor, gracias.'

I went into the kitchen. As Yamilia took beer from the

fridge, I poured a large rum for myself, to make a point of my independence. Despite his lack of English we got by. He spoke very slowly and expressively, using his arms, hands, smiles and frowns. I can understand a lot of Spanish if it's spoken slowly. Yamilia stayed close, listening and occasionally translating. Tony liked to talk, much of it conversational rather than business, revealing a Cuba the brochures don't advertise.

In his late fifties, he was a jovial, well-fed giant of a man. Despite an impressive stomach drooping over his belt he looked fit and vital, had a full head of thick, silver hair brushed back from his face and forehead, piercing green eyes above a Roman nose and almost feminine, sensuous lips. Beneath the smiles and bonhomie was a definite authority, though—I didn't want this man as an enemy. He'd fallen out of love with the revolution years before and made his way with whatever opportunities arose, which I gathered came mainly from tourism, particularly after the Russians had left in 1989. He thought things were slowly changing for the better and that this was a good time for business opportunities in Cuba. He could arrange the purchase of the house and had other ideas too: cars were mentioned, and antiques; he gave the impression of being able to help with most lines of business.

I was aware that his income probably came from fleecing, rather than actually helping, people like me. He'd add as much as he could to his prices, to see how soft I was. But there was something about him I liked: warmth, humour, a weary wisdom, just a vague connection that, however small, I might be able to work with.

He smiled. Yamilia smiled.

'OK,' I said, 'we'll talk again.'

We parted, agreeing to meet for a meal in the near future, where presumably something would be decided.

While Yamilia slept, I called Paul. The early hours, particularly 4:00 or 5:00 in the morning, were perfect for catching people in England at the start of their day. I drank rum and kept an increasingly eccentric diary as I waited.

'I've met someone who could be useful.'

'Do we need anybody? Can't we do this ourselves?'

'We need somebody.'

'Hmm.'

'How's England?'

'I'm still tagged. It's wet, it's grey and it's cold. I see Tony fucking Blair's grinning face every day. The whole country has foot-and-mouth disease. I'm pissed off. How's Cuba?'

'Yamilia wants to buy a house.'

'How much?'

'Nine thousand.'

'Do it.'

'This person I've met Tony he can sort out the purchase.'

'You know he'll rob you.'

'They all will, up to a point.'

'You can't do it without him?'

'I wouldn't know where to start. You still interested in the business here?'

'Absolutely. I've joined Cuba Solidarity and The Friends of Cuba. The gret thing about Cuba is there's no extradition. And most of their banking is still on paper. It sounds wonderful. I've been talking to friends in London. They think getting into tourism thing could work. It's all controlled by the state so it's obvious who you have to deal with. I'll get customers with money and you show them Cuba, the Cuba the tourists don't see. I just think we would be better doing it ourselves. Do we have to involve Pedro?'

'Tony.'

'Whatever.'

'Yes, we do. It's different here. Everything's different. Nothing is as it seems. And my Spanish is terrible. We need help.'

'Well, we need to belong to ABTA, the travel agents' association. I'm forging the application documents as we speak. It will cost fourteen grand to join.'

'Use my Amex card.'

'No, I'm using one of your other accounts before it dries up. Can't explain now. Got other plans for the card.'

'Meet anyone at Cuba Solidarity?'

'Lots of rose-glassed Guardian types, beards. Some nice women though. It's good fun.'

'I gave some money to a ballet company here.'

'Why?'

'Wanted to. Can't harm my image.'

'Hmm.'

'How's life as a free man? Drinking again?'

'Moderately.'

'OK. No more mistakes.'

'Absolutely.'

I knew of two of Paul's mistakes. Arrested at a petrol station where he was so drunk he pulled the wrong card from his wallet and again at a Leeds hotel where, after a week's residence, he forgot who he was and checked out under a different name. A clever man but with three years of his life spent in jail for excess inebriation. I wondered, not for the first time, if he'd lapse again and, if he did whether he'd take me with him.

*Love, as I have heard say, wears spectacles, through which copper looks*
*like gold, rags like rich apparel, and specks in the eye like pearls.*
Sancho Panza / Don Quixote

# 9

# *Camagüey*

Yamilia kept up the pressure to buy the blue house for a while, then announced that she was bored and suggested another trip to her mother's in Camagüey. I assumed that her mother had phoned. We hadn't been there since the trip over a year before.

We set off early but were still two hours short when darkness fell. On the way, revolutionary signs were everywhere, mostly colourful and vaguely inspiring. Che's face stared angelically, heroically, out of many; few showed Fidel. Secure in his stature he hadn't made an icon of himself: no statues, no boasting, no glorifying of his name. That would come after his death, he must have supposed. As he said. History will absolve me. Well, we will see.

Occasionally the signs were comically old-fashioned and Soviet in nature. A board outside an ancient, toxic cement factory proclaimed to its workers and passersby that they should 'Work Ideologically', a relic of Russian influence, Stalinist and incongruous among the palm trees. Nobody took any notice of it. Cubans work to survive, just like anybody else.

I took all this in from the comfort of the air-conditioned car, just as I had in Havana when I walked past long queues and into dollar shops, or as I entered clubs and hotels barred to Cubans—always accepted politely with no outward signs of resentment. And there were times on our journey to Camagüey when, for all my enjoyment at being in Cuba, I thought that Tom and Liam were maybe right: time for another revolution. After all, but for the police, and maybe the military, support for Fidel was strongest here in the country—eighty per cent, as José had said. Only in the cities did some Cubans express their grievance at their lack of access.

Although Fifi had no licence, I was glad to hand him the car keys when we arrived. We were given the main bedroom where Yamilia's mother and Sally usually slept, while they moved to a smaller room. They cooked over a charcoal grill, drew water from a well in the garden and showered and flushed the toilet with buckets of water. I adjusted to this, as I had on the previous visit, almost immediately. Life changed in the country. Although there is always a sense of community, even in the most deprived and run-down areas of Havana, it is much more evident here, with its base in farming, among the *campesinos*. Apart from the young and those who had got fat on Florida dollars, support for Fidel was common, though far from unanimous, the economy one of barter as much as money.

My money bought food and rum and new visitors to the house. We had brought the music system with us, which meant that Yamilia's mother had to suffer fiestas on most nights. We also brought the first signs of friction. Yamilia spoke to me in the garden. Not all the visitors attracted by our presence were friends; she didn't even know some of them. They were merely taking advantage of the hospitality my money provided. I had to tell them they were not welcome. As for me, I had no idea if they were welcome or not and didn't much care, but Yamilia's face was hard; she didn't like to see me exploited. I must do something about it. I saw her point. Life in Cuba is difficult; you helped friends if you could but you didn't throw money at strangers.

When the usual drinkers arrived, she pointed out the culprits. I met them at the gate while she watched. No party tonight, Boys, we're taking it easy; see you around. They reacted to my terrible Spanish and English diplomacy with typical Cuban equanimity. No problem, warm smiles, friendly pats on the back and they ambled away. *Hasta luego.* I walked back past Yamilia. She watched me as I passed. Settled, but not emphatic enough. No indignant offence on my part, no permanent banishment. Was this Englishman a soft touch?

As a break from the fiestas and to give Yamilia's mother a rest, we stayed at a hotel in Camagüey for three days. I realised how little we were alone and how well we got on together when we managed it. I paid an extra hundred dollars for Yamilia to stay with me.

The one ATM we found wasn't working so I got cash from a bank in the main square. During the inevitable wait I surveyed the bank, idly wondering how you would go about robbing it. An armed doorman was allowing only a few people into the bank at any time. While we waited, a van delivered or took away cash, I wasn't sure. Three khaki uniformed guards armed with pistols and shotguns oversaw the process, constantly on the lookout and suspicious. If you managed to get past them, the usual tourist police stood on every street corner. And then where? No borders to cross, nowhere to hide from prying eyes or the CDR—the Committees for the Defense of the Revolution, whose agents spied on the public for signs of counter-revolutionary activity. Any sudden riches would be noted and would need to be accounted for. Leave the country? They'd catch you at the airports if you only missed a traffic fine. The only way, if you were mad enough to attempt it, would be to kill anyone in your path and take a fast boat to Miami. Chance of success? Almost nil. Penalty for failure? Life in prison or, more likely, death. I doubted there were many bank robberies in Cuba. Security everywhere made sure it stayed that way and lurid soap operas emphasised the point, just in case you weren't convinced.

The same armed guards arrived at the busier, usually tourist-orientated, shops every day, to take away the profits. It was routine and only a lunatic would consider trying to rob them, but they remained alert, scanning the street and diverting pedestrians. Where did they take the money? The Treasury? A special government bank account? To Fidel? Did he sit at home counting the takings and planning fresh revolutions in Central and South America?

The soap operas, while clearly low on production values, had grittily realistic story lines, often of petty crime but quite graphic in their portrayal of small-time violence. Stabbings, muggings and burglaries were shown in all their nasty, explicit detail with no romanticising of the criminal. The criminals got away with nothing. Heroic, dedicated police officers delivered justice every time. The guilty were often shown sobbing at their fate (very long sentences) and the message was clear: Don't do it. If you do, we will catch you and you won't like it. You have been warned.

Yamilia was nervous during our three days away from her mother's house in Camagüey: nervous because her papers were not in order and because she was staying at a hotel. She didn't know the police or how to deal with them so she put herself on her best behaviour.

A small group of young girls, maybe fifteen or sixteen years old, followed us from shop to shop. One of the girls, stunningly beautiful, bursting at the seams, her skin jumping with sexual energy, posed and preened for my benefit. So confident was she that she ignored Yamilia's existence entirely: she was younger and knew that many men would kill for her—for now, anyway; in not so many years, she'd be big, very big. I glanced at her occasionally and she'd smile with smug coyness or strike a new pose, ignoring the glares from Yamilia but taunting her all the same. In Havana, Yamilia would have destroyed her but here, insecure about her status, she could do no more than frown and boil with anger.

'*Tranquilla, Yamilia,*' I said, '*ella es gorda, no estoy interesado.*' She's fat; I'm not interested. She didn't believe me. No woman would have, but she was grateful for the thought.

We visited Yamilia's oldest brother in Santa Cruz de Sur. Arriving again after nightfall I saw people on their verandas and patios, swishing at the air around them with voluminous white sheets. I soon found out why: millions of pinhead-sized biting black insects. I'd adapted to mosquitoes, which weren't really a problem, but these tiny horrors were too much. They drove me to distraction.

I covered up during the day, preferring sweaty heat to the constant onslaught of the insects—I can't remember what they were called. Yamilia's brother, Yordanis, who was a fisherman, said they were assaulted by them all day at sea. He shrugged a smiley you-just-get-use-to-it shrug that made me feel very soft. Yordanis and his wife, Alicia, gave us their bedroom, their bed and their mosquito net but the slightest gap or hole let the pinheads in, or maybe I imagined my skin crawling with them. Twice Alicia came to us, cleaned the bed and reset the net at Yamilia's request, due to my thrashing about. It was not my happiest day.

We set off back the next morning, Yordanis and family taking advantage of the car for a rare family reunion, eight of us squashed together; a blonde female hitch hiker making nine later. When we stopped to stretch our legs Yamilia touched my arm,

'You have disillusion?' she said.

'No, no disillusion.'

Fifi drove and, uncomfortably but uneventfully, we made it to a checkpoint close to Lugareno where a curious guard finally flagged us down. We filed into his office and stood, everyone talking at once, while he examined all our documents. Yamilia, Fifi and Yordanis talked at once, explaining the overcrowded car. We were just a family returning home for a reunion. Sorry, but how else would we get home? The guard asked Fifi for his licence. Fifi patted his pockets, shook his head in exasperation at his stupidity—well, what an idiot, he'd gone and left it at home. The guard shook his head, beckoned me to him. He handed me my passport and licence. I understood him tell me to drive the rest of the way and something more that I didn't understand. In the car I asked Yamilia what he'd said.

'He say you have very strange family,' she said; 'so many ages and different colours.'

They laughed about it the rest of the way. By the time we got home it was a completely different story, and a few days later, unrecognisable.

Yamilia's father owned a smallholding he ran with his new wife. His house was of similar size and design to Yamilia's, very basic, but he had a fair piece of land where he grew fruit and vegetables and kept a few pigs and chickens and goats. He understood Yamilia's desire to live in a city but said that, especially with money, we could be happy here. We have sun, sea, music, good land, rum, education and health, he said. Nobody needs any more. He put his fingers to his lips, kissed them, then waved his hand at his land and the country and the sun.

The Elian story was running worldwide at this time. Five-year-old Elián González Brotons had been found in an inner tube floating in the sea three miles off Florida's Fort Lauderdale coast, his mother dead from the crossing and his father, separated, still in Cuba. The Miami Cubans had adopted him as a symbol of freedom and were determined to keep him from being returned to the clutches of Castro and the evils of communism. Fidel, after originally showing no interest, suddenly realised the political potential of the story and a tug of war developed between the Land of the Free and the US's legal obligation to return the boy to his father. Castro used the story to whip the people into righteous indignation and patriotic fervour. Sally was full of the story, chanting Elian's name.

'Sally believe all shit,' said Yamilia. Miami's Cuban community was ninety-five per cent white. Elian was white. 'If Elian black, they throw him in the sea,' she said.

My health improved despite the fiestas. Fresh food, clean air, water and sunshine had given me a healthy colour. I didn't flinch from photographs. But sleep was hard. I lay awake in the heat, unable to settle. Villa Panamericana had a constant breeze; here there was none. And it was noisy. In the country, after dark, a thousand creatures begin their nightly chorus of croaking and screeching. Dogs bark; confused cockerels crow. I got up and read, drinking a half bottle of rum, maybe more. I didn't get drunk but slowly, after a few hours, my head began to nod and I finally slept at four or five in the morning, getting up way after the others around midday. Apart from some fuzziness I felt fine. Life was good and I had no problems, although this is probably where they began.

Then Rosa phoned. My visa had expired again and I needed to leave the country to renew it. We'd both forgotten all about it. We drove home the next day.

*The great question that has never been answered and which
I have not yet been able to answer, despite my thirty years of research
into the feminine soul, is 'what does a woman want?'*
Sigmund Freud

# IO

# Mexico

I spent two depressing nights in Mexico City. Disoriented and out of my element, I didn't venture far from the hotel, reading and just passing the time. At the airport I was advised to take a green taxi; any other colour and I could end up buried in the desert. The only incident of note came at breakfast on my first day when I had to convince a potential suitor that I wasn't gay. He finally left after twenty minutes, unconvinced.

I arrived back at the flat with a new visa barely forty-eight hours after leaving. Yamilia was out somewhere and I didn't have a key. I phoned her cellular phone, but it was dead—probably out of credit. I found Rosa, who let me in. I asked her if she knew where Yamilia was.

'She hasn't been here while you've been away,' she said.

'She's been away for two days? And you don't know where she is?'

'I don't know, Chris.'

Rosa cooked and stayed to eat lunch with me. Yamilia and Rosa got on well on the surface but now I sensed disapproval.

'She know what time you come?' she said.

I nodded.

'She should be here.'

I was unsure if I wanted to pursue this. Rosa was happy to have us as tenants and it was in her interest for us to be together, to keep the rent coming in; she wouldn't upset things without good reason.

'Does she have somebody in Havana?' I asked.

'I don't know.' Then, unexpectedly, she added, 'It's your life, Chris. You can do better.'

I heard this often. I could do better: someone more respectable, someone with an education, someone from a better background. Yamilia was needy. She had survival skills but she'd probably only made it this far with the help of short-term patrons, of which I was merely the latest. Had she treated my two-day absence as an opportunity to check out a replacement? If she was feeling that we wouldn't last, she'd want to check first that she had someone to move on to.

'Let's see what she says,' I said.

Yamilia arrived while we were eating.

'Lo siento, mi amor. My phone empty and I have no taxi money.'

Her face didn't betray it but I knew that this wasn't true. She had either spent the money I'd left her or had given it to someone.

She joined us at the table and soon the atmosphere changed—a happy house. Yamilia could do that. She could do the opposite too.

That night we ate out.

'Where did you stay?' I said.

'In Havana with my friend. The one you meet. My girlfriend. I no like stay at Rosa's alone.'

'You could have stayed with Rosa or Lucia.'

'I no friends with Rosa. And Lucia busy.'

'The money I left you? You spent it?'

'I go out with my girlfriend. Music, dancing.'

I looked her in the eyes but she couldn't hold my gaze. Her eyes slid off to the side.

She was drunk when we got back to the flat. She took a jar of honey from the kitchen and poured the honey over her breasts, allowing it to trickle down her body, then lay on the low table, legs wide apart.

'Chris, lick it off,' she said.

I was tired and pissed off. I hadn't enjoyed the food or her company, and could still taste the diesel fumes of Mexico City and Havana.

'No,' I said.

She shouted while she showered. She slammed the bedroom door against the back wall. She grabbed some clothes, shouted some obscenities, and left. I didn't see her again for two days.

While she was away, a cousin of hers paid us a visit with her fiancé, a Cuban who didn't drink or smoke. He asked, very politely, for payment for some bootleg CDs that Yamilia had bought on credit. I paid him and explained Yamilia's absence.

'Chris,' said her cousin, *Yamilia esta loca.*

That night I was with José. My cellular phone rang. It was Paul.

'What are you doing?'

'I'm with José in Old Havana.'

'Not Yamilia?'

'She's gone.'

'Why?'

'It's a long story.'

'Will she be back?'

'I think so.'

'Hmm. I'm coming out in two weeks.'

'Splendid.'

'Do I need a hotel?'

'No. We've got a room for you.'

'We?'

'She'll be back by then.'

> You have your way. I have my way. As for the right way,
> the correct way, and the only way, it does not exist.
> Friedrich Nietzsche

# 11

# Santeria

She returned full of smiles as though she had been away for five minutes. Yamilia and Lucia spent the morning shopping; they said they had a surprise for me. With bags of provisions, we took a taxi to a street of little houses by the sea, built as close as possible to what today was an angry sea. We climbed some wooden steps, to be greeted at the top by a small black woman dressed in white. She ignored Yamilia and Lucia, embraced me and whispered in my ear.

'You are about to have a taste of Afro-Caribbean religion.'

It must have been a practised phrase because Elisa had little English. What she did have was spoken beautifully, full of fun, music, eroticism and the tough-as-hell, mixed-up history that is Cuba. Yamilia had decided on a 'blessing', because three bank transfers for the possible purchase of the house had been confiscated by the USA and were sitting in the US Treasury. Each was for $9,000—$27,000 in all.

Elisa may have been five feet tall, but it was a close run thing. Attractive in a dizzy way, she was Yamilia's friend and a priestess of Santeria, the worship of the saints—a religion so complex, with its brew of Spanish Catholicism and the beliefs brought from the villages of Africa by countless slaves, that I doubt if anyone fully understood it. Fortunately, like most things in Cuba, it didn't really matter.

Elisa wore large, thick-lensed glasses that added to her comical appearance. I was to be blessed in tandem with a Peruvian girl, travelling alone, whose problems, according to Yamilia, were of a serious nature.

'She from Peru,' she whispered, as though this was one of her problems.

The girl certainly looked worried, and wore the brave smile of one about to be condemned. I suspected boyfriend trouble but didn't ask. Yamilia would tell me later.

Preparation for the ceremony took some time. It shouldn't have, but it did. By mid-afternoon everything was in place: live rooster, elaborate shrine, several large cigars, strategically placed candles, pieces of coconut shells, bottles of white rum and an audience, always an audience. The audience grew, soon including Elisa's three teenage daughters (though she could pass for early twenties), Yamilia, Lucia and any number of neighbours who seemed to have dropped for the want of some entertainment. They needed, also, to catch up on the gossip of the last twenty-four hours, discuss it, argue about it, forget about it and start all over again, and this was a convenient place to meet.

I'd learned to accept the slow, haphazard pace of Cuban life, so I settled back with one of the bottles and watched the sea pounding the rocks with a force that splattered my car with spray fifty yards from the beach. Havana was having a rough January and the Cubans behaved the way the English do when temperatures drop below freezing. They moaned about it endlessly.

Yamilia and Elisa decided that they were missing a mysterious but essential ingredient and set off to a neighbour's house in search of it. They returned half an hour later in high spirits, empty handed but too stoned to remember what they'd gone for in the first place. Elisa decided that the Peruvian girl, Conchita, would have to wait until tomorrow, having divined that her problem was more serious than first thought. Conchita wrung her hands and got down to some serious worrying, but didn't leave, seemingly intent on sticking around to see what happened to me.

My situation was fairly simple: I was going to fly to Panama and the US Embassy to request politely that the Treasury return my $27,000. My UK bank had sent three transfers via the USA and they had been confiscated *en route* because of a law the new Bush administration had enacted but neglected to tell anyone about, including my bank. Bluntly, they would confiscate any funds they suspected of being used for commercial purposes in Cuba, regardless of their origin. This ceremony was supposed to bring me good fortune for my trip and quest.

Elisa's house was the last of a two-storey row on a rough road leading to a rocky beach on the outskirts of Villa Panamericana. Wooden steps on the outside joined the two floors. A fair-sized living room was prepared for the ceremony. There were two small bedrooms, a poky bathroom with a shower, a small patio, a garden with a large wooden hut and a balcony overlooking the sea. Elisa's ambition was to go to the US to become a TV healer. She said she wanted a better life for her children. I had heard of tourists and writers paying $2,000 for Santeria ceremonies. What I was about to go through had cost me no more than fifty dollars—the price of the provisions plus a few extra items for Elisa.

I'd been to a few of these ceremonies before and knew they got messy, so I wore old clothes. By the time they were ready I was relaxed and mellow. They would be spitting rum at me later, a terrible waste, so drinking as much of it as possible before they got going seemed like a good idea. I kept the cockerel company while they talked. I knew what was going to happen to it, and so did he, judging by the look in his eyes. I picked him up and tried to calm him. I wasn't sure where his ear was, so I whispered where I thought it should be.

'Listen, I'm sorry about this. It wasn't my idea and I've always been kind to animals. This is just the way they do things here. You're an essential part of the ceremony and, let's face it: you were going to end up as someone's dinner pretty soon anyway.'

He wasn't impressed.

I was asked to kneel in front of the shrine. Triangular and rising about six feet to its peak, it had shelves containing African ornaments and relics: wooden faces and big-breasted women. There were dozens of fruits, a couple of scrolls containing handwritten Spanish poetry, mirrors framed in copper and brass, and some abstract and naïve Cuban paintings in blues and reds and yellows that looked decidedly sexual, although I wasn't sure why. The shrine as a whole was draped in muslin strips of blue; fresh flowers filled the spaces. Yamilia had raided my meagre possessions: a small basket contained passport-sized photos of me and a large pencil sketch drawn by a street artist in Havana. Small wooden and metal boxes lined the shelves, mostly containing dried flowers, though one had a mix of black and brown hair in it. I checked my head for missing locks, searching for connections between all this and my confiscated money.

Elisa asked me to speak to the shrine. I looked around the room, realising for the first time that I was the only man there. Women of varied age smiled back at me, nodding encouragement. I spoke to Yamilia.

'What shall I say?'

'Just speak, Chris. Speak what you want. Pray. You never pray before?'

I hadn't and I didn't intend to start now. I studied the shrine and noticed new objects. A photo of Yamilia at the beach, smiling and tempting; wooden figures, male and female, entwined; a painting of two eyes, one black, one blue, melting into each other and a new smaller eye of sea green emerging; and an enormous wooden penis with a large pink mariposa impaled on its tip. With all eyes expectantly on me, I decided just to go with the flow once again.

I wanted to know what would happen next. I spoke to the shrine—something like: Please can I have my $27,000? I promise to use it well and not incite Cuba into open warfare or threaten the security of the USA. I promise to uphold the American Way and not do anything silly again. Something like that. I spoke quietly, in a low respectful tone. They didn't understand a word and seemed happy enough.

'What you want, Chris?' said Elisa.

I mumbled something about wanting a safe trip.

She picked up four pieces of coconut shell. They were roughly the same size and, if thrown, would land with the inside or outside curve facing upwards. She tossed the shells onto the floor. Three landed with the outside facing up, the other one down. This must have been good because it drew a murmur of approval. She repeated the process: all four had the outside facing up this time. Yamilia clapped her hands and smiled at me, eyes blazing with light. That light may have been contemplating some serious shopping but I sensed something more visceral. Was this a fertility rite? Was it a blessing for a future child or for my potency? That would explain why only women were here. Another man would have changed the atmosphere, diluting it. José would have had me out of there in seconds. But providing they didn't intend to sacrifice me, it could only be fun, I thought.

Elisa threw the shells a few more times. The worst result was half and half but, mostly, three or four shells landed the right way up. She lit an enormous cigar, which suited her, took my hands in hers and puffed smoke at my chest, holding my eyes. She spoke at length in Spanish, a lovely melodic voice, so that I believed everything she said without understanding a word. Then Yamilia said,

'Now you must go down the stairs to the wood room. I don't come with you.'

I picked up the cockerel and a bottle of rum and followed the women down the stairs. The wooden hut was quite large, bigger than the room we'd just left. At the far end was a charcoal fire, with smoke rising and disappearing through a hole in the roof. Thick round candles lit the room. The walls were hung with coloured sheets, shades of red and pink and crimson, the floor laid with wooden boards that thumped as we walked. In the centre of the room was a low table with an enormous cake on it. It was tiered like a wedding cake, white and pink and studded with fruit: slices of peach, avocado, papaya, mango and melon.

Elisa put a portable CD player on the floor and music filled the room, slow and heavy, accompanied by drums and violin. Above the charcoal fire sat an enormous pebble, in reality a flat black rock, very smooth and speckled with white and sparkling silver. I let the cockerel go, took a swig of rum and put the bottle on the table. More bottles had appeared from somewhere. Lucia began to dance, lifting up her knees, one after the other, stomping on the boards, head back and eyes closed.

Elisa reached up and took my shoulders, guided me to where she wanted me to stand. I was light-headed, struggling to understand her. The hut was hot and smoky. It reminded me of the rites of the North American indigenous people, where they fasted and spent days in a sweat tent to become pure again. They hallucinated, saw guiding spirits in birds and animals, and emerged cleansed, with a clear path to their life.

Something sweet and heady was burning, other than charcoal. Elisa was still talking at me. Conchita came to us.

'She wants you to stand here,' she said. 'Do not move. She says you may be more comfortable if you strip to your shorts. It will be very hot and messy here.'

It was the first time she'd spoken.

'So you speak English,' I said, stupidly.

She laughed and walked away, swigging from one of the bottles. Elisa drew deeply on her cigar and blew more smoke at me, then took a mouthful of rum, stepped back, and with considerable skill sprayed it all over me. Lucia stopped dancing and did the same. So did Conchita. Then they all did. They circled me and sprayed me with rum until I was soaked. Stripping to my shorts was a good idea, particularly with the fire burning at the end of the room. They took great handfuls of the cake and began to cover me in it, rubbing it into my skin and hair. It was very, very hot. Conchita and a couple of others continued to rub the cake into my skin, like a lotion. Pieces of fruit stuck to me.

When they stopped spraying rum I grabbed what was left of a bottle. I felt happy and high. The air in the hut was intoxicating. The other women were dancing, not in any recognisable moves but in a strange trancelike stomping, with their arms waving and their heads back. Lucia stripped to the waist, speaking a strange language, not Spanish—something else entirely. It was baffling: here was my upright, respectable but sex-obsessed nurse expelling demons. She affected Conchita, who laughed and began to concentrate on my pelvic area with the cake. Next time I looked, Lucia was naked and staring at me with a fearful look in her eyes, a look I remember from old horror films where the camera homes in on an 'evil' woman's eyes and mouth until they take on an all-seeing expression that terrifies everybody. Conchita joined her. Lucia spoke to her, watching me the whole time. Then Conchita spoke to me.

'Elisa is going to kill the bird. The blood will drip on the stone. You must mix your seed with it.'

'My seed?'

She looked down at my shorts.

'Yes, your seed.'

They were making this up as they went along. Freud said the Irish are impervious to psychoanalysis. I assume he never visited Cuba.

'How?'

Elisa had the cockerel in her arms. She shouted something to Lucia. Lucia shouted at me.

'Chris. Sexo. Like this.'

She made what would anywhere else have been judged an insulting gesture. She would have been calling me a wanker. She took my shoulders and stood me above the stone. I could smell our sweat mixed with everything else. Conchita knelt in front of the stone. Elisa, on the other side, still held the now-struggling bird. I'd been semi-aroused for a while but now, as I looked down, I'd become quite keen. Lucia continued to gesture, slapping my backside to instil urgency. There was no way. Absolutely no way. I was not going to toss myself off in front of twelve unhinged women, no matter how good I felt.

Lucia shouted at Conchita. She still thought that I didn't understand and that all I needed was translation.

Conchita said, 'Chris, you must ... .'

'No,' I said calmly. 'You do it.'

So she did. It took about ten seconds.

They rubbed their hands all over me. The fire had been put out. Maybe the stone would have cracked had it got any hotter. I felt what Conchita was doing and watched as Elisa twisted the head off the cockerel in one swift movement. She held the dripping neck over the stone. Streaks of thin blood ran, hissing over the smooth surface. The music stopped. The white joined the red, the way blood runs through the white of an egg. The mixture rolled around the hot stone like little balls of mercury. I heard the sea crashing on the rocks and a brief hiss as the small white drops evaporated to thin lines, criss-crossed with blood.

Conchita was breathing heavily. I seemed to have stopped breathing altogether. Elisa pushed us aside and knelt in front of the stone. She stared intently at it as its heat swallowed the stains and they vanished.

She stood and spoke to one of her daughters. 'Get Yamilia,' she said.

Yamilia arrived, stared at Lucia, naked and out of breath, and burst into laughter. Conchita, also naked, and still kneeling at my side, turned crimson when Yamilia looked at her.

I pulled up my shorts and waited to see what would happen next, although there now seemed to be an air of finality to the proceedings. Elisa killed the music, Lucia and Conchita grabbed their clothes and Yamilia took the bottle from me and took a long swig from it. Then Elisa took her aside and they talked. Gesticulating and occasionally pointing or nodding at me, Elisa spoke softly so I couldn't hear. Yamilia listened intently, asked a few questions and also looked over at me, serious and thoughtful. I felt like a piece of livestock.

Yamilia joined me in the shower and slowly, carefully, washed off the rum and the contents of the cake. Smiling, she aroused me, stopping and starting, prolonging. Then, when she was ready, she took me inside her from behind, rushing to lie on the bed when I'd finished.

'Elisa say it is best for us this way,' she said.

Over the next week or she behaved as though she was pregnant. It may have been wishful thinking or a way of explaining the pot belly she was developing. She also referred obliquely to marriage and showed concern about my smoking and drinking; they might affect my potency. A visit to Raúl showed nothing, but now she brought the subject up regularly whenever we were on good terms. I was ambivalent. I liked the idea, but a conversation with Yamilia from some time before came back to me. We had been at her mother's house, surrounded by kids.

'Do you like children?' I had asked.

'Sí,' she had said, 'for five minutes.'

*If we publicly declare that Cuba is a threat to our security,
forty million Mexicans will die laughing.*
Mexican Ambassador

# 12

# Andy

I needed some cash to buy clothes and told Yamilia I was going to the bank but I'd also arranged to meet José in the early afternoon. I drove to the Habana Libre, a few miles along the Malecón. The Habana Libre, previously the Havana Hilton, was built by Meyer Lansky and the mafia before the revolution, keeping the then US-backed dictator, Fulgencio Batista, sweet with monthly payments in excess of a million dollars. An impressive, if slightly dated structure, its character was its history, still palpable everywhere. When Fidel came to power, it was taken over by the revolutionaries, who left their horses in the elevators and wandered from room to room while their masters celebrated. If you didn't notice the people, it could still feel like Vegas rather than Havana.

There was a queue for cash. A middle-aged man, not a Cuban, stood behind me in the line. He hovered closely, obviously keen to talk. I kept my back to him, although I could see his reflection in an opposite window. Despite the heat he was wearing jeans and a leather jacket, his long dark hair combed back and behind the ears. He moved past me in the queue and joined two young women, taking care to show that he wasn't pushing in, standing off to one side. He was easy with the girls, spoke good Spanish and was never lost for words or put off in any way. The women—he would have called them 'girls'—were cautiously interested, though not enough for him, so he reclaimed his place in the queue. He wore a self satisfied smile, carrying himself with confidence, completely at home. I avoided eye contact, was hung over and didn't want to talk

'So where do you take your women?' he said.

He was American. And this was a challenge, more than a question. Getting right to it without embarrassment. I played the tourist.

'I had a woman in my hotel', I said, 'but I had to pay the staff. Turned out expensive.'

'That's no good. Get your own place. Have as many as you like and don't pay them so much. How much did you pay?'

I halved the price a tourist would be expected to pay. He didn't believe me, but made a show of considering it.

'That's not bad,' he said. 'How long are you here for?'

'I'm leaving in a couple of days.'

'England?'

'Yes.'

He nodded, not believing me again.

The queue was slow and I felt obliged to say more—he was too close to ignore—so I asked him without interest if he lived in Cuba.

'I rent a place here. Two months here, a month back home: saves problems with visas. I buy stuff and ship it to the States.'

His dark brown eyes appraised me constantly. Smiling, although the smile never reached his eyes. Cool, unruffled, at home anywhere. He offered his hand.

'Andy.'

'Chris.'

I got my cash and my chance to leave.

'Nice meeting you,' I said, as he waited for his money.

'Sure,' he said, 'see you around.'

I parked in Old Havana and browsed among the book stalls in the Plaza de Armas. Nearby was a shop that sold memorabilia, old film stills—Bogart, Laurel and Hardy, WC Fields—rare books, photographs, and other bits and pieces. I dithered constantly over whether to buy anything. I love anything to do with old movies.

'They're second issues, buddy: don't bother.'

Same guy. He must have grabbed his money and come straight after me. He picked up a still from *The Maltese Falcon* and showed me a number on the back.

'See this: "Stroke two". It's a second issue.'

I nodded, interested despite myself.

'Even if you just want it for framing, they'll charge too much in here. This is for tourists.'

The implication was that I wasn't a tourist and that neither was he. We were in this together.

'Everything here is overpriced. Everything in this area is overpriced.'

Well—overpriced for Cuba, maybe, but still cheap. I wasn't interested in getting the best price everywhere, screwing the Cubans for every peso. I didn't say so, though. I didn't say anything. I was still a bit disturbed that he'd turned up here and didn't like him any the more for what he was telling me. I had a strong, urgent feeling that I wanted to be away from him. At the same time, I was curious.

'Let's go get a drink,' he said, 'what do you drink here?'

'Silver Dry, mojitos sometimes.'

'Let's go.'

I chose the bar on the rooftop overlooking the harbour where I was due to meet José in an hour, then immediately regretted it. He could find me there. I ordered a large rum and he had a beer. I wish I liked beer; it would have saved me a lot of trouble later.

'So you're on holiday here?' he said.

'I've been a few times.'

'Where are you staying?'

'The Sevilla,' I lied.

'That's a dump. You should rent a house. It's cheaper and you can do what you like. This whole area's a tourist trap.'

'Not all of it. You don't have to walk far to find something different. I like it here.'

'Right. You got a woman here?'

'No.'

'Wise man. Fuck them all, hey?'

I looked out over the harbour, took a sip of my rum and didn't reply.

'You find they do everything? Fucked if I can get a decent blow job. You fuck them in the ass? You find they do that here?'

'Do you?'

'Pay them enough, they'll do anything,' he said, contradicting himself.

He was baiting me, which gave me an excuse to be direct.

'I don't find this is an appropriate conversation.'

He spread his hands and smiled.

'Hey, no problem. Just curious.'

He lived out by the Habana Libre. Had a home in the USA. Travelled back and forth via Mexico. Cuba was full of valuable antiques. Even the poorest homes had something, something they'd hung on to through necessity that had become valuable —furniture, paintings, books and magazines—everything, including film stills. He bought small stuff that was easy to ship, not big time, just enough to maintain his lifestyle.

'Cubans are children,' he said. 'You have to deal with them like that. I looked over a house the other day; it was full of shit. But they had a few first editions and a signed photograph of Hemingway. They asked me a stupid fucking price for the whole houseful, shit furniture, everything. I knocked them right down. They squealed and shouted like kids so I said "Take it or leave it." They took it. I picked up the books and the photo. They shouted, "Hey, what about all this stuff?" I said, "You can fucking dump it, I don't want it" and I walked out. Animals. You have to be like that with them. The Blacks are worse. So, you want to live here?

'Maybe.'

'Fidel is a fraud,' he said. 'This whole revolution thing? It's a sham. Castro's brother, Raúl? Just a drug dealer, helping the Columbians get their drugs through the country. And now the fucking Russians.'

'You sure about that?'

'Fuck! You don't believe any of their shit, do you?'

'I try to keep an open mind.'

'Then open it a bit further, my friend.'

You are not my friend.

José arrived. He saw Andy and raised his eyebrows at me. I gave him a slight shake of the head and hoped he understood. Andy just smiled. José was curious, pleased to meet somebody new. Everybody was a potential opportunity.

'This is José,' I said, 'he's black'

Andy laughed. José didn't understand but he laughed anyway.

'José, this is Andy.'

Andy eased into fluent Spanish. I sat back and watched them talk. It gave me the chance to put back more rum. José spoke slowly enough for me to understand and Andy's Spanish was clear. They didn't talk about me and I didn't give them the opportunity by leaving the table. Andy bought us both a drink, drained his beer and said, 'OK. Business to be done. Good to meet you guys.'

He handed us both a card, shook hands and left.

The card contained his name, the Havana address and two phone numbers, one for Cuba and one for the USA. No business title.

'Nice guy,' said José.

'You think so?'

José didn't judge anybody on sight, except to weigh up their potential business value to him. I tore up the card and put the pieces in an ash tray. José shrugged and put the card in his wallet. I never saw Andy again. But José did.

'So, how is your life with Yamilia?'

'She thought she was pregnant.'

'She's pregnant?'

'No.'

He crossed himself.

'She wants to get married.'

'To you?'

'Maybe.'

'No. You cannot, Chris! You not a marrying man.'

We were silent for a while, watching the passing crowds.

'Look those men,' said José.

'What?'

He pointed at the procession of couples passing by, sometimes stopping and staring, sometimes finding a table. Middle-aged men with cameras, filming everything and seeing nothing.

'What am I looking at?' I said.

'Which of those men you think are married?'

'I don't know. Why?'

'The men who don't dare even look at the women here. Where you think they would like to be?'

I said nothing.

'Not here, not with their wives' he said, 'but they is trapped. Están derrotados. Is defeated. You want be trapped with Yamilia?'

'That wouldn't happen to me.'

He laughed.

'They thought this too.'

'Why don't you like Yamilia,' I said.

'Really?'

'Really.'

'I say you before. I think she is bad—for you.'

'You've never told me why. In what way? What do you know about her?'

'I no trust her. I think she want take your money.'

I let out a great laugh. 'That's it? I know all that.'

'You know she want take your money?'

'Everyone wants to take my money. I think *you* want to take my money but we get along OK. Of course she wants my money. It has changed her life. It can change it more. But we have fun. She knows me. She looks out for me. She worries when I'm sick. We're happy most of the time. If it were just about money, we'd be miserable. She's no worse than you. People don't like that she's a woman and sticks up for herself. She's a bit wild, sure. She's bossy.'

'*Mandona*.'

'Exactly. You macho Cubans, you don't like it. You want her to be passive. She isn't. Fine by me.'

He raised his eyebrows.

'You no look Yamilia close,' he said, holding one hand up to his face. 'You think you know her—you not see what she do. Where she go. Who she meet. You think she free agent? You trust her? You think she *leal*—loyal—to you? Who else she *leal* to? Who she *leal* to before you arrive? Who pull her string? You her boss, now, *eh*? Think, Chris: who was her boss before? How they see you? You think they happy now you her new boss?'

'I'm not her boss!'

'No? How you think they see you? You think I'm hustler? She hustler also. They think she work for you now. You win this big prize; they lose it. You come here to make money—Cuba money, Yamilia money. And one day, you go back to Inglaterra. They want this; she fear it. Then what, after you gone? She waste all this time with you. So if she gonna lose you, she gonna scam you while you still here. They want this too. And they gonna help her. *Una sociedad de negocios perfecta!* A perfect business partnership.'

I thought José was the inscrutable type, a diplomat. Most Cubans just come straight out with what they think; he was normally more guarded. I'd never heard him so unguarded, especially when it was in his interests to keep me happy.

'I just warning you, as a friend, Chris.'

'She wouldn't hurt me,' I said.

'You love her too much.'

He had a point.

'You think she love you? Or she just using you? Chris, she's a loser, like a street dog. So she do what she have to do. Before you come back to Cuba, I see her with many men.'

'How many?'

He shrugged.

'I no know. Six. Maybe.'

So, probably three or four. Yamilia could pick and choose.

'Is that so bad? In a year?'

'Is only the ones I see. You meet her on the street, right?'

I shrugged. A girl has to eat. I didn't expect her to sit at home wondering how to pay for the next meal.

'None of that bothers me, José. You sure you don't dislike her because she doesn't like you?'

'No. Is not that. Is not what I know about her. Is what I feel. I have bad feeling she lead you down a bad way. Her way. Or their way.'

That was different. A bad feeling. I'd woken up with a bad feeling too.

'OK. This is what I think,' I said. 'Yamilia came to Havana when she was fifteen. Ten years ago. Hard for a woman to survive here for that long.'

'She came the same time as me. She slept in parks to begin with, like me. After two years I had a house and brought my whole family here.'

He tilted his chin at me. How could un inglés understand?

'Not easy,' I said.

'Not easy.'

'But she was a girl,' I said. 'So she'd need help. That's only natural. Men have it easier.'

'For sure.'

'So if she doesn't have a husband, she needs a patron. Like me, I guess. You think someone was pimping her?'

'No! Maybe. She independent person but *muy vulnerable* and they protect her. They make her their property. Then, you come and you take her. Is insult to them. You in danger, Chris.'

I thought about it. Perhaps he was right.

'Do you know what part of town she considers her home?'

'No. Where you think?'

'I think I know where her base is. I think she goes there when I'm away.'

'Where?'

I told him about Magic Night.

'I think someone called Lazaro used to look after her,' I said. 'I think she found him stifling but she couldn't get his hooks out of her. It's like they've got something on her. Maybe when she went to France she escaped from that but, now she's back, she's in their clutches again. I saw how she deferred to Lazaro, how he cowed her. I also saw how she ignored Amado, his son, and how he ignored her. That was odd. You think Amado was her boyfriend?'

'Maybe. I don't know. What he like?'

'Your age. Arrogant, white, greasy, rude, probably stupid, possibly dangerous. Lazaro's not stupid but he's unpleasant.'

'I think you correct. Maybe she have some *obligación* with them. Still work with them. Maybe she want to leave them. Maybe while you here in Havana, they can't reach her so easy. Or maybe they can. Who know?'

Then José told me that one of his friends had been stabbed to death a few nights before.

'Why?'

He shrugged.

'No good reason.'

He seemed unconcerned. 'Friend' was a very loose term here.

'José,' I said, 'if tourism wasn't so important, if there weren't so many police, and if the penalties weren't so strong, would the people, you know, the people around here—would they kill me?'

'Sure,' he said, before catching himself, a little too late. Then he shrugged unconvincingly. 'Maybe. I no know, Chris.'

'Kill me for what? For my money or because I'm in the way? Do they want me around so they can exploit me or do they want me out because I upset the dynamic? '

'Either. Both. Who know?'

I tapped out a cigarette and lit it.

'I want to get away for a few days,' I said.

'With her?'

'No!'

José thought about this for a moment. Then he said, 'OK, so, come to Santiago with me. You remember I tell you about a business opportunity there—un *sociedad de negocios perfecta*? They ready to meet you.'

'Sounds good,' I said. 'When are you thinking of going?'

I wasn't up to driving home that night and, after much pleading from José, I agreed to let him borrow my car. He loved driving, despite having no licence. He loved showing off too. I took a taxi back to the apartment.

Yamilia and Lucia were drinking beer when I got back. A film was on TV, but they weren't watching it. It was late.

'Long time at bank,' Yamilia said.

I ignored her, went through to the kitchen and poured a tumbler of rum. When I sat down they were both staring at me. Lucia was nervous, not sure if she should stay.

'Many people in bank, Chris? In Cuba, bank very slow, but Chris, they stay open for you? All this time? Is dark now. You very special person.'

She turned to Lucia for appreciation of her joke. Lucia didn't understand but knew what was happening. She stood up and kissed Yamilia, came to me and we kissed cheeks.

'Ay, Chris,' she said, waving her hand at the fumes.

As Lucia reached the door, Yamilia said to her, of me, '*Borracho*. Drunk.'

'*Ciao, mañana*,' said Lucia as she closed the door.

'Where you go?' said Yamilia, once Lucia was gone.

'To the bank.'

'Is all?'

'Then I saw José.'

'Ah, José,' she said, as though this explained everything. 'Your good friend, the knife man. You have good time? Fiesta? He find you woman?'

'Just talk.'

She shook her head. José meant women and trouble.

'Where did you stay when I was in Mexico?' I asked.

'Ah, so José make trouble for me and now you come to the house drunk. I tell you, I stay with my friend.'

'You stayed with Lazaro, with Amado.'

She folded her arms and said nothing.

'You're not telling me the truth, Yamilia.'

'The truth, *verdad*?' she spat the word. 'You go drink with José and you say you just at bank. So, believe what you like.'

'Why do you go back to Lazaro? You're with me now. If you spend time with them, it makes me feel insecure. I think they're using you to get to me.'

'For what?'

'For what? For my money, of course!'

She flew at me and tried to slap my face. I caught her arm and pushed her away.

'Tell me the truth,' I said. 'Or fuck off.'

'Fuck off? You want me fuck off?'

She packed a bag in two minutes' flat.

'You fuck off,' she said as she slammed the door.

It was soon late enough to call Paul.

'We have a logo,' he said. 'We're a registered company: Eternity Travel. I'm looking at advertising and we're nearly there with ABTA.'

I told him about Andy.

'He sounds useful. Are you seeing him again?'

'I didn't like him. And Yamilia's gone.'

'Again?' He wasn't interested. 'She'll be back.'

The only reliable 24 hour bar in Villa Panamericana was in the hotel. As the sole customer on a quiet Monday night, I was keeping the sole barman from his sleep, so I tipped him well with every drink. The enormous lobby, a mass of chairs, tables, fountains and pool tables, could be lively but tonight it was funereal. I had played pool with Yamilia here.

I wasn't tired and drank one rum after another. I invited the barman to a game of pool. He told me sadly that he wasn't allowed to play on duty. I spotted a woman serving at reception, wandered over, and chatted to her. Bored and pretty in the tight blue uniform of the hotel, she wore a white shirt, knee-length skirt, high heels and a tiny jacket. She spoke good clear English, had recently trained for the tourist industry, was called Maria. I wanted to nuzzle her large breasts, eat her and lose myself in her. I was in love. I wanted to marry her.

I made repeated treks back to the bar for more rum. She was happy to talk to relieve the boredom. There were few guests and nothing for her to do, though she kept a wary eye open for the CDR. I told her I'd finished with my woman. She gauged my age and worth. I told her she was very beautiful. She smiled.

'What is your girl's name?'

'Yamilia.'

'It's a nice name,' she said.

'Yes.'

'Is she a nice girl?'

'No.'

She raised her eyebrows.

'I like bad women.'

'That is very stupid.'

I wondered if it would be possible to fuck her. Of course not; she'd lose her job. Later, perhaps. Once her shift had ended. But that would bring conditions. I didn't love her that much.

'I need a woman.'

'You want a woman, *now?*'

'Yes.'

It was 3:00. Villa Panamericana, conservative and respectable, was fast asleep.

'You will not find a woman here; it is too late. You must go to Havana, but at this time it is dangerous for you.'

'Can you call me a taxi?'

'Of course, but are you sure?'

I gave her a look intended to convey that unless *she* had an hour to spare, yes, I wanted a taxi. Whatever my look actually conveyed—drunken idiot, probably—she just smiled and lifted the phone. The taxi arrived immediately; it was just round the corner. I knew that. I could have walked. As I made my way to the door she called out, 'Where will you go?'

'Habana Vieja.'

'Be careful.'

'The Ambos Mundos.'

'It is your hotel?' said my driver.

'No, I want a woman.'

'I can find you a woman.'

'No, thanks. I'll find one.'

I woke the staff in the Ambos Mundos, had another drink and walked to Cathedral Square. It was deserted and silent, though when I stopped at its centre I could hear snoring, the whirring of fans and the fluttering of caged birds. A black jagged shadow pointed at me from the cathedral, a full moon behind it. A cat padded past indifferently. The square seemed larger with the café tables cleared away. I felt safe standing there, unsure which way to go.

I chose O'Reilly, the narrow street that ran parallel to Obispo but didn't have its bars and the light that went with them. The only light here was from the moon, made weak in the street by the tall buildings but lovely, silvery and peaceful —in tune with the silence. The lights of the Sevilla Hotel a half-mile away at the top of the street guided me as I walked past the alleys and side streets without turning my head. I had no sense of danger, just a blind faith in my safety. As I approached the Sevilla, a door opened and a girl beckoned me inside. We stood at the foot of a narrow staircase. She fired rapid Spanish at me. I didn't understand but nodded anyway. What else could she be offering? What else could I want? She wore a short skirt, light make-up, and shiny long black hair, combed straight. I followed her up four long flights. Had she known I was coming? Her balcony overlooked the street. Did she sit there all night just waiting for drunk, lost souls to drift by? Had Maria phoned her just in case I happened to pass?

On her balcony I gazed out over the rooftops. She stood beside me, spoke and beckoned me inside. This was not a social call; she was a practical woman. She said it would be fifty dollars. I looked at her long legs, her severe pretty face and her straight hair. I said that would be fine.

An hour later, to the minute, she asked for her money and invited me to leave. I hadn't finished, suggested some possible solutions and counted out another fifty. She sighed, shrugged huffily and knelt back on the bed. Later, as the night's frustration finally left me, I watched the full moon through the window, threw back my head and laughed. The laugh came from deep down; I wasn't laughing at her but at myself, the moon and the world and all its silly business. But she didn't like it. Not at all. She spewed a stream of invective at me, which I took to hint as her wish for me to be gone, and quickly.

Way down the street I realised I'd forgotten my watch. My watch: my insurance, my lifesaver. I panicked, turned round and walked back. I had no idea which house I'd been in until I heard voice overhead. She was standing on her fourth-floor balcony, watch in hand, shouting to attract my attention. She tossed the watch in my direction. I got a palm under it before it bounced out and landed on the pavement. I put it on and checked it. It was fine. As I thanked her, she yelled a parting salute. Whatever she said, it wasn't 'Take care', or 'Come back soon.' She either had no idea what the watch was or she was just honest. Probably honest. Most Cubans are, no matter what you might have read.

The barman was washing glasses when I got back to the hotel. He smiled and shook his head as I approached. I ordered my drink and carried it to reception. It was nearly seven, which was when Maria was due to finish her twelve-hour shift.

'So, did you find a woman?'

I nodded.

'Are you happy now?'

'Sí.'

She smiled. Did she know? She didn't ask where I'd been.

'Go home, Chris. Go home and sleep.'

She was right. I had nowhere else to go. I didn't look at the empty flat as I made my way to bed. A coma awaited me; I could sleep all day. An hour later somebody woke me. It was Yamilia. She lifted the sheet and climbed into bed. As she was snuggling up to me, she suddenly jumped as if an electric current had shot through her.

'You stink of fucked woman. She piss on you?'

She grabbed her clothes and stomped out. I heard the front door slam. This was becoming a ritual.

It was the smell of cooking that woke me. My stomach churned as I sat on the bed. I hadn't eaten the previous day. In the bathroom mirror, my face had lost its colour, my hair was a tangled mess. More nightmares. I waited for the shower to run cold and stood under it for a long time. Only then did I manage to get a toothbrush in my mouth without throwing up. Coffee, bread, water and fruit were on the living room table. In the kitchen Yamilia was serving ham, eggs and potatoes. She stopped and stared at me for a long moment, one hand on hip.

'Is no important,' she said. Then looking down at the plate, she told me that grease (she pronounced it 'gress') was good for the stomach when you'd drunk too much.

She nibbled bread as I ate. She wore a pair of my shorts and one of my T-shirts, her hair tied back. She looked older, concerned. When she got up to go, the phone rang. She took it.

'Is your friend, the knife man.'

It wasn't, not directly. It was the police.

'Come and collect your car. And your friend, collect him too.'

José was at a Havana police station. He'd been stopped late at night, no doubt showing off in front of his friends. Another fine. I said I'd get him in a couple of hours.

'You give your car to José?'

I nodded. She stared for several seconds, an expression of studied patience.

'You stay here?' she said.

'Sí. You coming back?' I said.

She smiled.

'Later.'


I paid our fines and brought José to the house, collecting Celia, José's new girlfriend, on the way. Rosa was cleaning the flat.

Celia was slim with a long serious face and big, mournful eyes. She solved the problem of curly, wiry hair by cropping it close to her scalp. She wore masculine, wide, round-toed black shoes with short skirts, an usual combination even for Cuba. Quiet, with a habit of listening and watching more than she spoke, her English was better than José's but she didn't make a show of it. Her voice was deep, amused, knowing and possibly naughty, as if she'd smoked since she was ten. José treated her like an accessory, rarely acknowledging or speaking to her.

I asked José about the trip to Santiago. They had booked the train for the journey in three days time.

'Will you come?'

'I don't know, maybe. Yamilia is not here.'

'Why?'

Rosa shouted something from the kitchen.

'What did she say?'

'She said you should find a new woman,' José said.

Celia was uncomfortable. After a few minutes she went to join Rosa in the kitchen. Not long afterwards she was helping with the cleaning.

'What news of the business?' I said.

'There are people. They want to rent cars to tourists. They need someone to buy the cars.'

'Is it legal?'

He grinned.

'Not so much. Legal cars, they pay *la cuota de inscripción*, the licence fee. We not register the cars, so we make *más dinero*—more money. Big money! Is normal.'

'What do I get?'

'They rent the cars. You get half the money.'

'How much?'

'I don't know. How many cars you buy? Come with us and talk with them.'

'I'll join you later. I have some things I want to do first. I'll come and get you; tell me where you'll be.'

He handed me a card with the name of a hotel on it.

'They will pay', he said and winked at me.

'Have you not remarked,' said Candide, 'that yonder
young peasant girl is a very pretty brunette?'
'She has something very taking in her countenance,' said Cacambo.
Candide

# 13
# Trinidad

I drove slowly, taking my time, thinking. I reached Trinidad as
the sun was setting. Near the south coast of central Cuba, and
a beautiful Unesco World Heritage site, Trinidad is also a
tourist trap and, not in the mood for all that, I found a *casa
particular*, a private house. The sights could wait for another
visit. They always did. I rented a tiny room with a balcony
overlooking a narrow cobblestone street.

I bought a couple of Cuban sandwiches, a bottle of rum and
sat on my balcony, my diary open, as the sun sank below the
pastel-coloured houses. My cellular was with José, blocked for
foreign calls. Yamilia would call regularly; when she heard
José's voice she would hang up.

Swept along by the flow of other people's wants and needs,
I had no time to consider anything. I wanted some quiet, some
thinking space. In a whirl of fast-spoken Spanish I often had
little idea what was going on. Yamilia still held the strongest
pull on my emotions, if not my reason. José felt like a friend—
not the most sensible of friends or anywhere near my age, like
Raúl or Tony, but still a friend. And that was it. The alternative
to them was to go it alone. I would never be short of women or

their offers of friendship but that was a dangerous path. The trouble was, there weren't any safe paths.

The balcony next to mine erupted in a mass of movement, colour and female voices. Four women were in an animated discussion about clothes, deciding what and what not to wear. A couple held masks to their faces, swapping and laughing; then one of them noticed me, jumped theatrically in surprise and beamed a smile at me.

'Ay, buenos noches, Señor.'

The others turned and four curious faces studied me like an exhibit. Beyond returning the greeting, my Spanish failed me, as it often did when meeting new people without the help of Yamilia or José. I offered the bottle. They passed it around, each taking a sip, probably out of politeness, until it was back with the woman who had noticed me. Instead of handing the bottle back, she climbed over to my balcony.

'American?'

'English.'

She nodded as though with approval.

'We can't drink now because we are performing tonight.'

'What are you performing?'

'Dancing and music. I am a dancer. Dancing, music, story and history. It's a mix.'

Her English was near perfect. In her late twenties, maybe more, with light skin, a pretty, open face, she had an easy smile that looked like it wanted to be there all the time.

'Your English is very good.'

'Thank you. How long are you in Cuba for?'

'I live here.'

This, rather than anything in particular about me, seemed to grab her interest.

'Where?'

'In Havana.'

'With a woman?'

'Before, yes. Not now.'

She responded to a shout behind her.

'*Lo siento*. I'm Noemi. I must go now.' She slapped a leaflet on the table. 'Come Tonight. It will be fun. And there is a party afterwards.'

She climbed back to her balcony and disappeared with the others. I read the leaflet: La Habanera, a woman from Havana but also, in its masculine form, the hottest of hot peppers. I could still hear the animated conversation next door. Habanera? So much for private contemplation.

The performance in a dusty, crumbling hall was chaotic, a typically Cuban mixture of high energy, colour, Santeria, love and earthy sex. I loved it. Although overtly sexual it was never crude. About twenty people made up the group. Noemi was one of the backup dancers, supporting the main theme. Sometimes two performers held the stage, at other times the whole group. At the end they spilled from the stage. Noemi poked my shoulder as the bottom-wiggling, rumba-dancing troupe danced among the audience.

I expected the party to be private but afterwards the whole group went to a nearby bar. Behind the bar were enormous grounds in what appeared to be the ruins of an old colonial property, with single detached columns, archways and dried-up fountains, mazelike in its size and strangeness. Noemi and I sat away from the others, who had shown little interest in me, assuming, perhaps, that we'd already paired off. All felt loose, free and fresh. I realised that this was the first occasion in a long time that I'd been away from what was a very small group of people, and that I rarely wandered or explored anywhere alone anymore.

Noemi and the group outdid the usual Cuban love of colour with some extravagant combinations. She herself wore baggy orange linen pants, a bright green vest and a red headscarf over her tied-back hair. Although small, she appeared strong and powerful, slim and athletic rather than worked-out, a thin silver chain around her neck, bangles and coloured beads on her left wrist and a single ankle bracelet above red leather sandals. Her slightly boyish face had hints of Chinese around the eyes, cheekbones and mouth, heightened by a thoughtful expression, although she laughed easily and often. She had bright, childlike eyes. There was nothing broken about her, no signs of disappointment with life. There was nothing broken about Yamilia but she always struck one as defiant, challenging, wary of deceit and betrayal. Noemi was easy with herself.

A full moon dominated a sky full of stars, still visible from most places in Cuba, not yet obscured by artificial light and pollution. Lizards darted around the pillars while other creatures rustled in the unkempt grounds. The night chorus found its voice. A cool breeze helped a general sense of well-being. I felt completely at ease, expecting nothing.

'Where did you learn English?'

'At university.'

'What did you study?'

'Law. I wanted to be a lawyer.'

'Like Fidel.'

She laughed.

'Yes, like Fidel, but he is also the reason I am not a lawyer. There is no reward for my skill so I prefer to dance. The money is better and this is a good life. I can be a lawyer when I'm forty.'

'Forty is too old to dance?'

'For me, I think it will be.'

She lit one of her own cigarettes and poured herself some rum.

'You live in Cuba? How long have you been here?'

'A few months.'

'And how long will you stay?'

'As long as I can.'

She nodded and smiled, to herself rather than me. I was

being sized up, accurately and quickly. I felt a little naïve in her company, as though she was holding something back. 'Why are you in Trinidad?'

'I'm on my way to Santiago. A friend has a business idea.'

'What business?'

'Are you CDR?'

'Of course! Later I will have you arrested and put in jail.'

'Cars,' I said, 'for tourists to rent.'

'Your friend can do this?'

'I'll find out.'

'Be careful with that. It can go wrong.'

'How?'

'I don't want to spoil anything for you. Just be careful who you deal with and think about everything.'

She yawned and stretched her arms behind her. She wasn't wearing a bra and smiled when she caught me looking. She took my wrist and studied my watch for a few seconds. She nodded.

'Why do you stay at a *casa particular*?'

'I don't like hotels.'

She asked about Yamilia and I gave her a brief history. She seemed to form a picture without needing to pry, satisfied that she understood or knew all she needed to know, able to draw her own conclusions without too many questions.

'I needed some time to myself,' I said.

She laughed, shaking her head.

'And here you are.'

We sat on my balcony late into the morning. Trinidad, unlike Havana, was silent at this hour. Only an urban fox, losing its brief stand-off with a screeching, arch-backed cat, disturbed us. I had drunk but felt clear-headed and pleasantly tired, as though a rare dreamless sleep might await me. Noemi stretched extravagantly and yawned.

'It's very late, I'm so tired. If you want to fuck it will have to be now.'

'I'm tired too. Let's sleep.'

I woke late the next day. The troupe was long gone. A La Habanera leaflet lay on the bedside table. On the back she'd written: 'We will be in Havana next month for one week. Find me if you want to. You snore!'

From Trinidad I drove to Camagüey and checked into the hotel where I'd stayed before with Yamilia. I ate in the hotel restaurant and returned to a new balcony above a busy street. Tonight there were no adjacent balconies or beautiful dancers to change my plans. I was happy to sip rum and people-watch. I also had good memories of times spent here with Yamilia and didn't want to tarnish them.

I set off early the next day after another dreamless sleep. On impulse I took the turning for Lugareno. An ugliness I hadn't noticed before surprised me. An enormous decrepit factory dominated the landscape with rusty overgrown rail tracks leading to the village for miles. Long redundant wagons and buildings littered the tracks which ran by the side of the road. It must have once provided a living for the inhabitants. Now it looked as though only those with funds from relatives in Miami were able to live at anythng above subsistence level. Yamilia's family didn't have any relatives in Miami.

I toyed with the idea of talking to Yamilia's mother. I'm not sure why; she spoke no English and my Spanish wouldn't stretch to what I wanted to say. I drove down the dusty uneven street of small single-storey dwellings, each with a front porch and, at the back, a large garden, usually containing a pig or two and chickens. The luckier Miami-funded houses had new coats of paint, patios and garden furniture with TVs, music systems and video players inside. Others showed their lack of investment and age. All this I'd seen before, when I'd visited Yamilia's mother's neighbours. There was no sadness to it. People here didn't waste time regretting their lot; they just got on with it. I didn't see the haves lording it over the have-nots, although it was probably there. Houses stayed full of life, children and activity, no matter what. If anything, the more prosperous became more subdued as they considered what they had, took a certain pride in it and thought about what they wanted next. And the children everywhere were just that —children. They didn't notice the disparities. All this, naïve no doubt, from a European with money in his pockets but it's what I saw and felt.

The front porch was empty as I drove slowly past Yamilia's house. I saw, down the side of the house to the back garden, Yamilia's mother hanging out washing. She was laughing at something. The wind blew a white sheet horizontal on the line to reveal Yamilia, pegs in hand, laughing at the same joke, before the sheet floated down, obscuring her again. After making me ham and eggs, Yamilia had come here, to Camagüey.

I drove on and parked fifty yards down on the other side of the street, adjusted the side mirror to the scene. Yamilia still wore my shorts, her hair a long curly tangle. She and her mother were still talking and laughing. I watched until they walked back into the kitchen, then drove away.

How many days Yamilia had been here I didn't know. Had she hitched down? That was by far the most common method of travel but not for Yamilia, if she had alternatives. Train or bus? Possibly. She could have flown to Camagüey but she'd have needed to embezzle some money from me. Had she done? It didn't matter. What was important was the thud of shock and longing that hit my chest when I saw her. The feeling that no matter what I got up to here, in business or otherwise, my life was empty without her. I really believed I'd shaken it off, that I could control it; the tension in my stomach and the way I gripped the steering wheel told me I couldn't.

But I was glad she was here, glad she was away from Havana. I wanted to drive around the block, go back and see her; stay there with her and forget Santiago. Instead I stopped at the next store and bought a bottle of rum. I nursed it in my lap, sipping regularly as I drove. By the time I'd reached Santiago and found the hotel on the card José had given me, the bottle was empty.

*There are three sexes; males, females and girls.*
Ambrose Bierce

# 14

# Santiago

The hotel was a Vegas-like structure, similar to the Habana Libre, and also built by the mafia before the Americans were thrown out. At the desk I showed my credit cards but the receptionist shook her head and said everything was taken care of. I was impressed but immediately apprehensive. José had said they would pay for everything and I'd doubted it. In Cuba you paid; they didn't. But if they did, then you were under pressure. A gift given had to be reciprocated. I began to wonder who these people were.

Santiago is hotter than Havana. Historically it was the starting place for much of Cuba's revolutionary history. Any surviving protests usually started there. It also had the top Cuban baseball team and José always supported them in favour of the Havana team, Industriales. I knew he was proud of his origins.

I took the lift to my room where the air-conditioning hit me. The room was big and luxurious: two big beds, a large bathroom and shower, a writing table, built-in wardrobe space, vanity mirror, and a wall-length window opening on to a balcony with a great view of the city. And three women. A tall blonde lay on one of the beds, reading a magazine; a black girl leaned on the balcony admiring the view. Another girl sat at a table, combing her long black hair. She had light brown skin and a studious face. Whoever had sent them had tried to cover all tastes. None of them looked more than twenty-five; the girl at the mirror could have been a teenager.

I was tired, dirty and hot. The sight of them depressed me and I felt even more tired. I thought, though, that a reaction was in order. I needed to show some authority.

'Buenos dias,' I said and threw my bag onto the bed.

I nodded to the blonde, then at the bag. She immediately began to unpack it and put things away. I took the hand of the girl at the table and led her across the room with me.

'I'm going to take a shower,' I said, as I closed the bathroom door. In the shower I asked the girl how old she was. She said nothing, just studied me with curious intensity. She washed me and let me guide her to what I wanted.

I wanted it to last about an hour. If I was cold and didn't think about or look at what I was doing, I thought I could maintain some indifference, get it over with and get some sleep. An hour later I stood behind the blonde as she knelt on the bed, thinking and watching now, just wanting it to end; bored and very tired. The black girl had returned to the balcony. Since the shower, though, the young girl had just watched, watched every move, studied our faces. She tilted her head this way and that, like a conscientious student watching an experiment. I couldn't finish. If I hadn't cared about the impression I was making, I'd have given up. The girl had other ideas. She moved behind us and, sighing with impatience, kissed the back of my scrotum. I pushed the blonde away and moved to lie on the bed but she held me upright, leaving me standing while she went to lie on the bed, her head tilted back towards me. The other two watched with amused interest. I was just tired. Then, when I was sure I was done, and that nothing was left, using her hands and mouth, she made me come again. The instant I relaxed she righted herself and, task completed, dressed in seconds.

All three stood by the door, ready to leave. I fumbled with my jeans, looking for some money. They stared, offended. The young girl tossed her hair imperiously, gave me a curt nod and, ignoring the others, left the room.

The blonde said, 'No, that was Hello to you. Welcome to Santiago.'

She gave me a look—that look, as I stood there, middle-aged and naked with my crumpled jeans in my hands. They laughed, gave me a pleasant smile, and were gone.

I slept for twelve hours before meeting José and Celia the next day. We sat outside a bar in a large plaza. I felt refreshed and drained at the same time. Ready for anything and not too concerned about what happened. Even the feelings about Yamilia were muted.

'Here they come,' said José.

Four young men stood at the table, polite, waiting for introductions. Despite the heat, they were well dressed in smart jeans or chinos, shirts, linen jackets, expensive sunglasses and mobile phones. I was wearing shorts, flip-flops and a T-shirt. Celia wore shorts too, although José had dressed for the occasion. In a reversal of their Havana roles, he was nervous, possibly in awe of the company, while Celia was relaxed and cool. I stood up to shake hands. José would have told them about me—though what he'd told them I didn't know  and yet they seemed surprised by me. Was it my presence there, or my age or appearance?

The first three gave solid handshakes and neutral expressions. The fourth turned his back on me and sat down. He spoke angrily to the others, telling them to get on with it. They sat while he stared pointedly around the square, his sunglasses still in place, looking anywhere but at me. I looked at José and Celia. José behaved as though nothing had happened. Celia giggled.

'Leris can speak English,' said José.

Leris outlined their proposal. The silent one turned his

sunglasses on me. For pride's sake I returned his stare and then blanked him completely, as though I was dealing with three people. Celia kicked me beneath the table and winked. The proposal was simple. I would buy some cars, nearly new ex-rentals, and they would hire them out to tourists. Beyond supplying the money I wouldn't have to do anything and they would give me a share of the profits. José or Celia, who travelled regularly between Havana and Santiago, would bring the money every few weeks. I wondered what could go wrong and remembered Noemi's vague warning.

'What percentage do I get?'

'Sixty-forty to us,' said Leris.

'No,' I said, 'fifty-fifty.'

Leris showed no surprise. Silent man stood up, tipping his metal chair over and clattered on the cobbled surface as he shouted obscenities at his companions. As he stomped away across the square, I looked round the table. José and the three other men shrugged without embarrassment or concern. This was apparently what Silent man did. Celia giggled and kicked me again.

Leris made a call and spoke rapidly in Spanish, followed by a Yes or a No to some questions.

'How many cars will you buy?'

'Three.'

'Will you buy more if it goes well?'

'Yes.'

'Sí,' he said into his phone, then nodded.

'OK,' he said and cut the phone.

José ordered a bottle of rum. We poured and touched glasses. I didn't want to see the cars, and I said I've leave that to José. I said I'd give José the money in a week or so. We talked for a while but the three were keen to leave.

When they were gone we sat in silence for a while, draining our glasses and then headed for another bar. As we walked Celia took my arm, linking it with hers. She looked up at me often, rubbing her shoulder against me; sometimes our thighs would touch as we walked. At first I thought she was strange, even ugly, but she wasn't, just different. Her eyes were warm, her smile open and inviting. José walked behind or in front, greeting other people and taking little notice.

As we poured from a new bottle they seemed on the verge of laughter.

'How were the women?' said Celia.

'Three women,' I said, 'very generous.'

Celia clapped her hands together, laughed and curled up in her chair, showing her pants and not caring in the least. I looked from one to the other. José drew a breath and blurted, 'They were only meant to send two.'

'What?'

'They only send two women.'

'Chris,' said Celia, 'they only sent you two women. How could there be three?' Celia drew out her vowel sounds like a Hollywood Mexican. She was a different character, as though Havana had intimidated her and frightened her into a shell. Here she was flirty, mocking and confident. She laughed her dirty laugh, enjoying my confusion.

I turned to José. 'What's going on?'

'These people, they are from the university. They have plans for the money. When I hear their idea about renting cars, I tell them about you. They ask if you would fund. They very interest, so I arrange this meeting.'

'And?'

'They want you say Yes. They ask if you like women.'

Celia burst into laughter again.

'And do you, Chris? Do you like women?'

'I say them you do like,' said José. 'The next time, they bring two women with them. They say they send them to your room.'

'And?'

'Is not only the people you see today is interest in you. Is more. Also a girl from the university. When I tell them about you, she also interest.'

'Why?'

'I tell them about the money you give to the ballet. That money. It is like million dollars here.'

He shrugged. Celia lifted her hand above her head.

'Chris is a *good* man,' said Celia.

'But this is business,' I said.

'No. Yes. Is business but they want money for other reasons.'

'So what has the girl got to do with it?'

'I tell you. She was interested. She say she go to your room with the two other women. They didn't like it, especially Arturo, but she does what she like.'

'Arturo?'

'You fuck his girlfriend, Chris,' said Celia. 'So today he come to check you out. You think you will be friends?'

'She very serious,' said José. 'She believe in Fidel. She gonna be a doctor, go to Africa, work for *nada*. When she hear about you, she asked many questions. She very interest.'

'Imagine all the people, living life in peace,' sang Celia. She stuck out her tongue when I glared at her.

'What's her name?'

'Isabel,' said Celia. 'Beautiful Isabel.'

'How old is she?'

'Eighteen,' said José.

'Jesus.'

'Chris, she is woman,' said Celia. 'She want to meet good man. She want to learn from good man. What you teach her, Chris? You teach her how to be good?'

'She is daughter of a security officer,' said José. 'Very clever girl. She very serious about education.'

'What kind of security officer? How high?'

'This high, Chris.' He measured a level above his head.

'Fuck, José. That could have been dangerous. Why didn't you tell me?'

'I not know she would come. Anyway, she not stupid.'

'He find out, he will cut off your *pinga*,' said Celia. 'What did she do, Chris? What did she teach you?'

'She competed with the two others,' I said.

'Good for you. So you have a good time!' she said. 'What did she do?'

'I'm not telling you.'

'No problem. She will tell me.'

'She didn't say anything to me,' I said.

'She no speak English,' said José.

'I can speak some Spanish.'

'Not enough for her.'

'Why won't she speak English?'

'I tell you. She is serious. Fidel not speak English for many years. Because of the Americans. She is same. She very smart. Leris speak to her before he could accept fifty-fifty. Yes, to her!'

The phone call, of course. And the women in the hotel. You just couldn't do that here without influence. I wondered what they wanted the rental car scheme to fund.

'What did you *do* to her, Chris,' said Celia.


That night, alone in my room, there was a tap on the door. It was Isabel. I wondered how she had managed to get in. Then I remembered her father. I stood stupidly as she walked past me into the room. She wore glasses, serious and studious as ever, like a schoolgirl. She picked up the book I'd been reading. At night I preferred novels, but tonight I had only an account of the clandestine war waged on Cuba by the United States. The numerous attempts on Fidel's life, the poison in his beard, the capsules in his milkshake. Ridiculous but true. The bombs in the clubs, the air raid on Havana, the Olympic athletes blown out of the sky. None of it reported in the western media.

She studied the book, glancing curiously at me. I said something to her in Spanish. She glanced at me again briefly but didn't respond. She put the book down and began an inspection of my clothes in the wardrobe. She studied the labels. She found my passport, looked through the stamps from other countries, studied the photograph, spent a long time looking at the Cuban medical stamps giving me permission to stay for treatment. She took the credit cards from my wallet and leafed through my address book. Then she found my diary. I wasn't concerned. She wasn't snooping. She was looking at another life. Taking it in. She'd chosen her path already. I envied her. I wished I could be doing what she was doing, wished I believed what she believed. She read slowly, every page, every word. She went out to the balcony. I stood next to her. We could see the lights of the city and the sea beyond it.

'*Bonito*,' I said.

No response.

'Smile,' I said.

She smiled. Then she pulled at the neck of my T-shirt, studied the scar on my shoulder, and seemed to make up her mind about something.

She stayed with me. We didn't do anything. I woke in the night with her arm draped across my chest. She looked utterly at peace. I lay awake for hours. Then, when it was light, I woke myself with my snoring. I shuddered and looked around, wiped some saliva from my chin. She sat at the table, my diary in front of her, watching me in the mirror. She came to the bedside, kissed me on the forehead and stared for what seemed like an age. Then she said,

'Smile.'

Later that day José and Celia travelled back to Havana with me. José lay asleep across the rear seats. Celia sat in the front with me, legs apart, adjusting the air-conditioning so it blew up her dress. She fiddled with a CD. She finished and sat back, passed me the bottle of rum, lit a cigarette for me. The music was some Cuban stuff about love and loss and sex and life. She sang along.

'Chris. Tell me. What did you do with Isabel?'

'Nothing,'

'OK,' she said.

Ten minutes later she leaned over and put her face in my lap. I pulled her up and turned her face towards me.

'What are you doing?' I said.

She looked, not entirely kindly, at José on the backseat.

'I know him. He won't wake up for hours.'

And she went back to what she was doing.

'Tisn't beauty, so to speak, nor good talk necessarily. It's just it. Some women'll stay in a man's memory if they once walked down the street.
Rudyard Kipling

# 15

# *Dancing*

I dropped José and Celia in Havana. Celia put an arm around a sleepy José's waist and nuzzled his neck as they walked to his flat. As I started the car they both turned. José gave a small wave, Celia winked and turned quickly away.

I heard female voices and laughing as I approached the flat. Yamilia and Rosa were sitting together, beers on the table, lifelong friends, all smiles and camaraderie.

'Ay, mi amor,' said Yamilia, 'where you go? I think you go home to England and leave us here.'

Rosa laughed as though this was the best joke she'd ever heard, told by the best friend she'd ever had. I didn't reply and walked into the kitchen to get a drink. The fridge was full. With beer and rum were fresh cuts of meat, chosen with care at a Havana market. Fruit and vegetables filled the wooden rack next to the fridge. I poured a long glass of rum and diluted it with ice, lime juice and soda water. I sat next to Rosa, opposite Yamilia and smiled.

'You look good, mi amor,' she said. 'You have health. You go to the beach?'

She looked great, carefree, the way she looked with her mother in Lugareno. An unwanted thought sprang into my mind—how it was that men, all of us as far as I can tell, are fooled by beauty. Why did I believe in this woman?—a woman I knew to be a liar and who, although she could lift my spirits, was capable of destroying me. The answer was that she radiated an energy that engulfed me, so that I just wanted to be there, in that place with her. It wasn't even anything to do with sex. I was just happy in her company. But why? Why indeed.

'I went to Santiago de Cuba with José,' I said, deciding to begin with a portion of the truth. 'And I went to Trinidad, alone.'

Her smile didn't waver, although her eyes flashed at José's name. Rosa interrupted.

'You like Santiago?'

'It's hot,' I said, 'but now I have a business, so I can start to make money.'

I explained about the cars.

'That's good, Chris,' said Yamilia, her interest piqued. 'It is important you make money here.'

I saw no sign of resentment. My making money was important to her. Whether I stayed with her, as she hoped, or left her, as she expected, my well-being was her safety net, and the prospect of it made her happy. It looked as though we were friends again, as if we were starting over. Even José wasn't off limits.

'So you go with José? And Celia? She go too?'

This with a smile.

'Yes, José's girlfriend came too.'

She nodded thoughtfully at this.

'Sí. The girlfriend of José.'

She spoke quickly in Spanish to Rosa about Celia. Rosa nodded thoughtfully before replying with something I didn't understand. They nodded sagely to each other. To change the subject I mentioned the rent; it was overdue. Rosa was cool about it but I started to count out enough for the next three months. Yamilia caught my eye and shook her head, so I paid Rosa for only a month, waiting to see what Yamilia was up to.

When Rosa left, Yamilia put on some music and took a shower. She came back with a towel round her and danced to the music. Eventually she let the towel slip to the floor, pulled me out of the chair and danced close, holding my eyes, hers full of amusement and something else. She stroked my erection as she danced, then slowly undressed me. I felt stupid dancing with my stiffy bouncing around, but when I tried to stop she said, 'No, mi amor, dance. Dance with me.'

We danced. She went to her knees and took me in her mouth for just a few seconds then moved away, dancing and laughing, completely unselfconscious of her own body movement, and then backed onto me, allowing me inside her briefly, all in time with her own musical rhythm. After an hour of this, I could hardly stand it and would have come regardless of physical contact, so pumped up was I. She knew me though, and as I was about to come she fell to her knees and took me in her mouth again until I was drained and sank to the cool tiles. A bonding session. She would stay. For now.

For the next few weeks we spent most days at the pool and the evenings at home, both happy and with no appetite for conflict. Tony phoned and invited us for a meal at his house, an invitation that could only be a prelude to business. Yamilia wanted a house, he wanted to make money and I wanted to buy Cuban assets for the London consortium. He could help, I was sure, but I didn't have to agree to anything. I could just listen and learn: it would be easier on the nerves. There was a danger that this could be taken for equivocation, especially if I did it too often, but if I got the tone right, I thought I'd be OK. So we went to Tony's.

We took a taxi. I had tried to stop using hire cars. José had written one off and nearly killed us when I allowed him to drive me to Matanzas. Rentacar were very laid back about it and just offered me another, but taxis seemed a safer option for now.

Tony's place was half-way between Villa Panamericana and the prospective house in Guanabacoa. If Yamilia knew anything about the purpose of the meal or had any ulterior motive herself, she hid it behind a flood of small talk. But what did I know? They could well have organised the meeting themseves.

Tony lived in a medium-sized one-storey house with a large dining room, a kitchen, bathroom and two bedrooms. It was fairly new, clean, breezy and affluent, but on a busy street that rarely let up on noise. Not that noise seemed to bother any Cuban I knew. It was a fact of life.

Tony greeted me with hugs, old friends already. He was cooking and damp with sweat. His wife, Adela, a plump jolly woman, was equally welcoming. She poured beers and, after showing me due respect and establishing her lack of English, chatted happily to Yamilia and took her on a tour of the house. I took my beer to the back yard where a lean, healthy Doberman patrolled. Tony served up the meal: chicken, rice, black beans and plantain. Conversation at first was limited by my Spanish, vaguely skirting my plans for the future. Yamilia told her stories, exaggerating wildly, and the meal ticked along pleasantly, the food good and the beers topped up.

After eating we sat in the late-evening sun in the front garden, talking above the noise of the traffic. Deferring to Tony, Yamilia kept an eye on me, pleased that we drank only beer. Later we moved back to the patio at the back of the house, where Yamilia translated.

Tony spoke clearly, in measured tones. Most Cubans talk to each other as if they're twenty yards apart and both deaf. He spoke softly. He said that, legally, I could not own a house because my name could not go on the paperwork. But if I was happy to live in the house, as its owner and master to all intents and purposes, then something could be arranged. Of course we would have to decide whose name would go on the paperwork.

At that point he glanced at Yamilia and then back at me. Something was implied but I wasn't sure what. Was he suggesting that the house should be put in Yamilia's name or that it should not? Although he had shown nothing but courtesy and respect to Yamilia, I sensed a different question in his eyes. Do you really trust this woman? Are you sure about this? Was I happy for Yamilia's name to go on the paperwork? He held my eyes for a few seconds longer than necessary. Yamilia watched us.

'You will arrange everything?' I said.

'Sí,' he said, still holding my eyes.

Yamilia, unable to stay quiet, added her own 'Si'.

'Sí,' I said, without looking at Yamilia, 'You take care of everything.'

We couldn't move into the new house in Guanabacoa for two months because there was paperwork to be done, and time had to be allowed for its existing occupants to move back to Spain. But Tony owned other houses, which he rented to tourists, and one of them in Bahia was empty. Yamilia suggested we leave Rosa's and move there until the Guanabacoa house was ready. She said it was a better building, the rent lower and would show goodwill to Tony.

What I couldn't tell was whether Tony could be relied on. He sounded plausible enough. If he was keeping anything back or deceiving me in some way, he was certainly a very practised performer. But did he have a prior allegiance to Yamilia that neither of them had admitted. She had told me he was an uncle of a friend. What friend? If we went into business, who was he going to be most loyal to? Did he have a separate agenda? Did Yamilia?

I called Paul.

'I'm going to buy that house.'

'Good idea. I said so before. Do it.'

'It's complicated. It may not even end up being my house.'

'Do it. It will give us a base for now.'

'I like the place. Tony seems OK. He knows people at the right level. You'll meet him.'

'Good.

'He doesn't approve of drinking. It interferes with business. He likes money.'

'Splendid.'

'What time do you arrive?'

*I bring to my life a certain amount of mess.*
Francis Ford Coppola

# 16

# Paul Visits

I waited with José at the airport for hours, long after the stragglers whose luggage had taken longest to surface. I eventually assumed that Paul had changed his mind. We were about to leave when Paul walked unsteadily into arrivals. He'd tripped over someone's luggage and been detained. Whatever security might have made of him, the decision must have been something like, 'English. Drunkard. Harmless. Will spend money.'

'So, free at last.'

'Viva Cuba Libre. Is the bar open? I need a drink.'

He had put on a bit of weight since I'd last seen him. A big man with short thinning fair hair, he'd been slim and almost athletic in prison. Now he carried a significant paunch and seemed to lean forward as he walked, dragged along by it. He was still handsome, looked confident, spoke with a booming public-school voice but seemed permanently red-faced—a professional drinker's face.

At the house Yamilia greeted him politely in English, shared a drink with us and, seeing our condition, suggested we might like to sleep it off. We didn't. As she walked to our bedroom, Paul said, '*Now* I understand why you're here.'

As for José, Yamilia simply ignored him when we arrived.

When he was still there in the morning and showed no signs of leaving, her approach changed. She seemed confused, not knowing how to behave in front of Paul and irritated by José, who clearly liked him and enjoyed his frequent, easy laughter. In front of me, Yamilia behaved as she pleased but confronted by this new, strange, male threesome, she didn't know what to do, covering her discomfort by fussing around us, offering coffee, drinks, food and tidying obsessively.

It didn't help that José was enjoying himself so much. Our conversation centred on how I'd got to Cuba, Paul's time in prison, his previous arrests, our meetings and plans, and a few close calls on the way. José understood and joined in with some stories of his own. That's all it was: boys' stuff. But Yamilia, feeling excluded and unable to keep up with our English, saw things differently. She saw conversation and laughter that she wasn't part of. She saw me and José and a new guest talking and laughing and then laughing some more. She couldn't stand it. Was he telling stories about her? She flashed glances at me, perhaps for help. I registered them but did nothing. She was boiling up to something. I wanted to see it. And I wanted Paul to see it too.

When it arrived, it was directed at José. Although José had said nothing about her to either me or Paul, she clearly imagined otherwise. She was convinced that he'd been talking about her, and not in a good way. She pointed at him, walked to his chair, wagged her finger in his face, flounced away, came back, and laughed contemptuously at a joke of her own as she listed his faults. She shook her head at the image he portrayed and at the naïvety of Paul and me for associating with such a man. Hands on hips she listed José's crimes to Paul, who, fascinated but not understanding a word, listened with polite attention. He appeared to want to nod or shake his head but was afraid to choose wrongly, so he remained still, smiling and blinking. Rosa stood in the kitchen doorway, arms folded, watching.

Receiving only rapt silence, Yamilia shook her head angrily, black hair flying, and gestured scornfully at the air for our not all understanding her. She wasn't going to lower herself to explain, if we were that stupid. The more she shouted the angrier she got. The hurricane began inside her, her hair seemed to take on an electricity, her eyes flashed, she moved in a jerkily. We stared at her, transfixed. Of course she misunderstood that too, taking it as a sign of disagreement and getting even crosser.

'Hmmm,' said Paul, 'beautiful woman. Stroppy bitch, though.'

The room was silent for a few seconds. Expressions froze as we all took in what had just happened, as if in the aftermath of an exploding TV or unexpected flatulence. Yamilia looked at Paul as if he had suddenly appeared by magic.

'What he say?'

José, cockier than usual and having clearly enjoyed her performance in a social setting, rather than its just being directed at him, or me, said, 'He says you are beautiful.'

I was grateful that he either did not understand, or had decided not to translate, the 'stroppy bitch' bit. Yamilia stared at him and then at Paul, unmoving. I had the impression that if I touched her there'd be a crackle of static and a mild shock. Paul hadn't taken his eyes off her, a look of wonderment on his face as though he expected her to burst into song or produce a dove out of a top hat. And Yamilia was suddenly aware of a roomful of people, silent and staring—at her. She muttered to herself, tossed her hair and headed for the door. Nobody jumped at the thunderous slam. We were expecting it. The hurricane had gone off to blow itself out somewhere else.

'She's left you again,' said Paul.

I knew what she would do. She would spend the day with Lucia or Lazaro or Amado or any of the other people she knew in Havana but had never introduced me to. She wouldn't go to Havana, not with new male company in the flat and José making himself at home. She would complain first and then banish whatever had caused the outburst from her mind. Then she would change the subject, talk, laugh and make herself happy. Then, probably in the early evening, because we were bound to go out, she would return, full of smiles as though nothing had happened. And, in her mind, nothing would have happened. It would not just have been buried. It would be forgotten. *Historia. No importante.*

'She will come back,' said José.

And so she did, a few hours later, armed with supplies: food, rum, cigarettes. She greeted José as though he had just arrived and she joined in, now one of the boys, drinking rum after rum much too fast, before suddenly announcing that she was taking a siesta. Her unsubtle glance in my direction showed that she expected me to join her, if only temporarily. Afterwards she swallowed a diazepam and fell into a deep sleep within a minute. Glad that she was back on a vaguely even keel, I was also glad that we were free of her company for a while; she wouldn't wake now until the next day.

Paul boasted of his prowess at chess and tried to get me to play but I didn't have the skill or the patience.

'José plays chess,' I said.

José seemed insulted by the suggestion but eventually they played. José sat, calmly sipping his rum, making his moves after brief consideration and waiting patiently while Paul, red faced and sweating, interminably pondered his replies. It was all over in twenty painful minutes. Later José said, 'This man cannot play chess.'

Paul never mentioned chess again.

We dropped José at his flat and drove along the Malecón, where I showed Paul where Fidel made his speeches in front of the US embassy. He only looked up when I pointed something out; otherwise he stared straight ahead or at passing women, who appeared not to impress him. He held a bottle of white rum between his knees, sipping regularly.

We headed for Old Havana and the cathedral.

'Can we look at Cubacel?' he said.

'Why?'

'I just want to see it.'

It was a large private house, close to where the rich lived, converted to the needs of a telecoms company. Paul stared at the building in the way foreign tourists stare at historic sites. If he'd had a camera with him, he'd have taken a picture of it.

'We need to see if we can get you free calls.'

'Not here.'

'I know how to do it.'

'Believe me, not here.'

You didn't cheat people like Cubacel. Free calls could be had, but not on their doorstep. I had already discovered people who could tap into phone lines and who offered thirty minutes of call time from their homes for ten dollars, but it was fiddly and only available at certain hours. I was usually too lazy to bother and used my cellular insead.

We drove to Cathedral Square, quiet and peaceful in the fading light. When we were settled with our drinks he began to talk about women, asking about the racial mix. He sat hunched, his head forward, obsessively, unconsciously, touching his scalp where his hair was thinning, as though encouraging it to stay, or come back.

'So what's the proportion here,' he said, 'black to white?'

'It's hard to say. I think officially it's sixty percent white Spanish descent and forty Afro-Caribbean from the slaves.'

'And is it?'

'I don't know. In Havana it seems more like fifty-fifty, perhaps whiter in the country. But it's not as simple as that. The Russians were here for thirty years; that must have had its effect. There's a Chinatown. Cuba was a playground for the Americans for fifty years. I don't know. They're a good-looking people though, whatever their lineage.'

'Hmm. I don't see much whiteness.'

He meant pale, English-winter, never-seen-the-sun, pale.

'It's a semi-tropical country. That's the sun.'

I'd seen photographs of Paul's ex-wife: pale, blonde and buxom. He also admired similar-looking singers and actors. I began to realise that there might not be much here for him.

'So what's Yamilia?'

'Her mother is black. Her father is a light-skinned Haitian.'

'So she's *mulata*?'

'No. But she's fairly light-skinned. So is one of her sisters.'

'So there's white in her. A sugar baron from the good old days?'

'I don't know. She is what she is.'

The square was dominated by the cathedral on one side with the restaurant and houses making up the other three. A Unesco site, protected for its beauty and historical significance, the houses, with balconies overlooking the square, contained ordinary Cubans. It was comparable to renting a council house in St Peter's Square or the French Quarter in New Orleans; the houses would be worth millions in almost any other country.

I was irritated that Paul hadn't noticed where we were, hadn't commented on one of my favourite places. The light hadn't quite given up for the day; the sun beyond the square was sinking fast towards the sea. A flock of small birds took off from the roof of the cathedral and flew towards their roosting place across the red-stained clouds in a fading sky. This was the quiet time, the tourists brushing up for the evening, the interval between day and night, two very different worlds, musicians taking a break, birds chattering, grackles squabbling for overnight perches in the trees.

'What do you think of it?'

He raised his head slowly, looked blearily first at me and then beyond and around. A childish smile creased his face. For a moment the square was almost silent.

'Hmm. Splendid,' he said.

'So what are you going to do with Yamilia?'

'See how it goes.'

'Do you love her?'

'Yes.'

'And ... ?'

'I won't mess things up because of her, if that's what you mean.'

'Good man.'

Paul's first thought on rising was another drink, whereas back then, mine was for food and a certain recovery time before starting again. Paul didn't like food. He drank a strange mixture of rum, wine and beer, starting very early and just sipping all day. He was happy around the flat, playing his CDs or fiddling with my laptop, but never at ease when we went out. Then he seemed overwhelmed, uncomfortable, only relaxing at the top hotels where the people were familiar to him, the same people in top hotels everywhere: functional and predictable.

Paul was thirty-eight then. He laughed often, easily and loudly; a thorough cynic, his only pleasures appeared to be defrauding financial institutions and drinking. Unfortunately the two didn't always gel and, although very smart on how to part banks from their money, he was beginning, with age, to make drunken mistakes. His last three years in prison had probably saved his life; a doctor there told him that he wouldn't last long if he continued to drink. During our prison meetings he'd been clear-headed, sober and sharp, planning my escape meticulously and efficiently. He was brilliant then and that's how I'd remembered him. Now, two stone heavier, pink-faced and hesitant, I saw the man who had managed to get himself arrested twice. On both occasions he may as well have walked into a police station and confessed. His cool confidence was gone, replaced by a jovial shiftiness. I didn't believe he'd obtained an ABTA licence, allowing us to be travel agents. I doubted he'd done much at all that was connected with business. He'd thought of a name and designed a logo—the fun parts—but as yet no sign of ABTA validation and no customers.

His days in England began in whatever hotel he happened to be in and progressed no further than the bar. Perhaps, when he was younger, he'd had spectacular successes while drinking but he couldn't do it now and he didn't know it. Anybody meeting him knew he was an alcoholic within a few minutes. It didn't matter to them. He was good company, talked easily to anybody and stayed on his feet; he didn't fall over or became stroppy and embarrassing. And being Cuban, they naturally assumed he was wealthy, like all Europeans. But could he run a business from England?

We had some fun; he enjoyed the attention he received from all who took care of him. Tony liked him too. We had a meeting at his house and although Tony disapproved of drinking, he must have assumed that whatever our condition, we were here, we were rich, so we must be able to function like this. He even took a couple of rums himself and smoked a cigarette. And Paul liked him. Tony knew things: politics, banking, tourism, crime, women and commerce. He knew what could be done and what we could get away with and Paul was impressed. But not, I thought, impressed enough to do anything about it. As I watched him, probably equally drunk, I thought he was just drifting, drifting from one situation to another, and not really conscious of a past or a future, as long as a bottle remained by his side.

His parents were rich. If all went badly for him he must have known, at least subconsciously, that he would never fall completely, never be alone, never be really and truly without money. But it could happen to me. Nobody was there to catch me if I fell. And while I decided that we would still have a go at this (what choice did I have?), I also decided there and then, as I watched Paul roar at another joke and sip his rum, that I was on my own. No back-up. It meant I would have to start thinking and behaving accordingly.

Paul's booming, confident voice and laugh attracted Yamilia's attention. I often caught her looking at him, trying to figure out what was behind the voice. He was much younger than me. Did he have more money? Who was the better bet here? But apart from wistful looks as she moved around the flat, he took little notice of her. During his second week, he spent more time with José than me, because they both liked to visit the top hotels. I understood José's attraction to them, because he couldn't get into them without an invitation from a tourist, but to me big hotels were the same the world over. Here they had a slight Cuban twist with the music but were otherwise as dull as the people who frequented them.

One night we went to the club at the Villa Panamericana Hotel. I realised that in Paul's company, it was nothing, just a large room with a bar, but that in the company of Yamilia, it was much more to me. Paul may have imagined places like the Tropicana, tourist-brochure images of long-legged beauties, smiling faces and sparkly outfits. Here was a place you could find in most towns and cities in the UK—a hall with music. Of course it was the people, the atmosphere, a unique love of life in the moment that made me love it. Paul was oblivious to the atmosphere. So far he didn't much like the people and he hated the music. We saw Cuba through different eyes.

When, a week later, I drove him to the airport, he drank so much that I feared they wouldn't let him on the plane. He wobbled, and smiled at the female official as she checked his visa. She fired some questions at him, presumably in Spanish, because he shrugged and laughed. She turned and stared hard at me, watching from a few yards away. She considered for a few seconds before noisily stamping his visa, handing him his passport and unlocking the door to departures.

'Bring me some books,' I shouted, before he disappeared.

'What sort of books?'

The security official stared fiercely between us.

'Detective fiction, anything.'

'OK. Pip, pip,' he said, waving cheerily at me and vanishing through the door.

I took José to his flat and drove home. Yamilia was watching a film when I arrived. I poured a rum and joined her.

'Paul go?' she said.

'Sí. He will come back in a few weeks to meet Rumbos.'

Yamilia shook her head.

'You will never have success with this man.'

*When I grow up I want to be a little boy.*
Joséph Heller

# 17

# The White House

The moment I paid for the blue house in Guanabacoa, Tony told me that we had to move into the empty house in Bahia that Yamilia had mentioned, while waiting for everything to be finalised with the new house. That was strange. When Yamilia had suggested this, it had merely seemed like a whim of hers; now, Tony was making it a condition of his completing the conveyancing. I could see the sense in it, from his point of view: our occupancy meant we'd be keeping the propertly let. It was also fine with Yamilia, who argued that living there would warm Tony to us and encourage him to take an interest in our welfare. It was also much cheaper than the place we were renting from Rosa. Hard to argue with the logic but I liked Rosa's place, didn't want to move out and didn't like the feeling that the two had ganged up on me.

Rosa was distraught when we told her. She appealed to me and voiced the same doubts that troubled me. Yamilia dismissed her with a contemptuous wave. 'It's not your problem, Rosa,' she said.

And we were gone.

Our short-term rental sat in a row of one-storey villas, white-painted with small, neat front lawns. Inside, it proved to be L-shaped, the long part going back deep into a luscious garden of long grass, plants and fruit trees. Three bedrooms, a kitchen, a lounge and two bathrooms jutted out from different parts of the L, the whole surrounded by a high wire fence, padlocked at the front and guarded by Dingo, another Doberman. It was fifteen dollars a day. I'd been paying Rosa twenty-five. Perhaps it was a good move after all.

Tony's ancient television set gave off sparks and minor electric shocks so I went into Havana to buy a new one, but every shop in Havana had run out. Their windows and display areas were all empty, which was odd because I knew they had been fully stocked only days before. The assistants were reluctant to explain where all the goods had gone.

Tony laughed when I told him.

'Is Fidel,' he said.

According to Tony's sources, Fidel had decided that all schools should have one TV for every six students. In a single weekend he'd cleared out all the shops and made it happen. I'd have to wait until more TVs were imported from China.

Our new area offered us local shops, a good bar where I could play pool, and new friends. Tony visited every day. First he would feed Dingo, giving him a daily portion of miserable scraps—bread, cereal and chunks of bone with slivers of meat on them—and then make us all strong, black, Cuban coffee in tiny cups. It was important to him that we got the best; it didn't matter to him that Dingo got the worst. It wasn't cruelty, exactly, but like most Cubans, Tony was indifferent to the well-being of animals. Until we arrived, he kept Dingo permanently chained, which meant the animal could never roam beyond a fifteen-foot radius. Yamilia and I let him off the chain, but only when Tony was not around. But many dogs in Cuba were kept on even tighter leashes. That was how things were. I wondered who might be keeping Yamilia on a tight leash.

Small coffee cups were also how things were in Cuba. Tony would watch in wide-eyed disbelief whenever Yamilia poured my coffee into a large white mug, English-style.

'Ay, Chris, *mucho café*,' he would say.

This was the reaction of all Cubans. They couldn't believe that someone would drink whole mugs of coffee. I was as mystified as they were.

When we sipped our coffee Tony would talk, slowly and expressively, and after a while I didn't need Yamilia's rough translations. Despite that, he decided that we needed a decent translator. José was far better than Yamilia but couldn't handle complexities and Tony wanted everything to be clear so he introduced me to Manolo, around thirty and the first unsmiling Cuban I'd met. Manolo's English was perfect. He also spoke fluent French and German, was well-educated and behaved as if he could do better than the company he was keeping, including me. He corrected my Spanish with obvious impatience and sighed at my pidgin style but understood the little nuances of our conversations, both the subtle and important things. I told him I was surprised that he'd never left the country. He told me he had a German girlfriend, whom he could go and live with any time he liked, but wouldn't, rather than couldn't, leave his wife and young son. There was a depressive air about him, as though he thought life was mostly pointless. I saw his wife rarely; she was slim, pale and pretty and didn't smile either. She never spoke to me. During our gatherings she ensconced herself with the women and that was that.

Manolo's translations changed everything. Until now I'd relied on hazy interpretations of what I'd heard; with Manolo's help I understood every word, caught every shade of meaning. Now I could have real conversations with Tony—about politics, life, women, anything—as long as Manolo was around. And he was often around. He wasn't well-off and didn't seem interested in work and yet he made himself unusually available. This was odd because he got nothing from Tony (few people did) and never asked anything from me. I'd pay for his food, his rum, his taxis, the odd book, but never gave him money. A couple of times I asked Tony about reimbursing him for his time and Tony just shrugged as if it was of no importance. I doubted this, but let it go. It turned out to be a big mistake.

Manolo did what he was told but also said what he thought, regardless of the offence he might give. He was more honest than Tony would have liked, and more candid, and consequently more powerful. He was the only one of us who understood all that was being said and this enabled him to control our conversations. It also gave me greater autonomy. We needed Manolo when negotiating the contract for the new house. We also needed him when we went to buy furniture. Yamilia loved the process of shopping and would have dragged it out for weeks. I don't like shopping and wanted to get through the process as quickly as possible. Caught between Yamilia slowing things down and me speeding them up, Manolo helped us acquire the basics—bed, fridge, cooker, bookcases, a couple of armchairs and sundries—in just a few days. It must have been a tiresome task for him.

Tony and Manolo met us every day. Tony told us that, as a fifteen-year-old during the Missile Crisis in 1962, he had served in the Cuban army, manning an anti-aircraft gun on the Malecon while they waited for the US attack that never came. Highly intelligent, he understood the politics, believed firmly in the revolution until he didn't believe in it any more, and was now a fixer, a dealer—a businessman.

Cuba was good for business, he told me. And when Fidel finally went—well, anything would be possible. And to be in at the start, like me—I could do very well. Despite his belief in Cuba, however, he had shipped increasing numbers of his family out of the country, often to Spain; my purchase of the house would help send a nephew and his wife to Las Palmas in the Canary Islands. He himself had no interest in leaving, however. He liked Cuba and was inventive in his pursuit of money and a decent living. He was always taking on challenges and enjoyed the constant battles with bureaucracy, the government and the Committees for the Defence of the Revolution. Usually he beat them, which is probably what encouraged him to keep challenging them. I found him tough-minded, ruthless and hard-working. I also found him unexpectedly admirable.

Sometimes we ate out at restaurants of Tony's choosing but often we visited his house for dinner, where the Doberman roamed free, sleek and healthy. (Why had Dingo drawn the short straw?) We also met his mother in Havana. White haired, fit and bright eyed, she had an imperious air about her. I exchanged glances with Yamilia. We were evidently up for inspection.

The mother had the top two floors of a large old building on a quiet street in Old Havana. It was well maintained, in contrast to most of the city's colonial Spanish architecture, which crumbled as fast as it could be restored. As we were shown the house I thought of Andy, the American. The house was full of the sort of antiques that he went scouting for: furniture and paintings, ceiling chandeliers—pre-revolution stuff that the family had managed to hold on to.

The first time we visited, some of Tony's large family were there as well: a sister, Elizabeth, whom I'd already met in Guanabacoa, and another sister, Loli, visiting from Gran Canaria with her husband. Tony initiated a strange conversation, for my benefit, I thought, about the film *Fresa y Chocolate*, Strawberry and Chocolate. Cuba was slowly coming to terms with homosexuality and, because I occasionally read books, he'd decided I must be an intellectual and would have elevated thoughts on the subject. Tony led the conversation and Loli condescended to join in but Tony's mother stared straight ahead as though a bad smell had invaded the apartment while Loli's husband, a veteran of the Cuban campaign in Angola, merely nodded or shook his head whenever he thought it appropriate to do so. Tony tried to include me in the conversation. '*Sí, Tony, lo entiendo,*' I said, '*Fresa y Chocolat, metro sexual y macho*,' which must have been rather less of a contribution to the discussion than Tony had been hoping for. When Yamilia chipped in, she spoke gravely of a female newsreader who was reputedly a lesbian, as though discussing someone with a terminal disease. She said later that Loli had taken her aside, lectured her about the great opportunity she had in living with me, and how she must learn to change her behaviour. That she accepted the lecture without protest, not least from someone who only knew her by reputation, was a minor miracle—but part of me wished that she hadn't.

On Sunday afternoons Tony would gather his friends round the dining table—José, Manolo and others—to take a day's break from business and catch up on gossip. He was curious about life in England, having heard mixed reports from relatives he helped to live there. They were surprised at how hard life could be, how difficult it was to get started and, most of all, how unfriendly people were, how unwelcoming and uncaring. They tended to believe the satellite images beamed to them of happy consumers in lands of plenty. Like Yamilia, they all assumed I lived a life of luxury back at home.

I gathered that the average worker in Cuba, working alternate days to maintain full employment, earned around ten dollars a month at the time; a doctor or a scientist might earn forty. So honest Cubans, outside the tourist industry—the ones who accepted their role and took the basic food allowances—how did they live? 'They eat shit,' said Yamilia.

At the same time, although many of the young, especially in the cities, were frustrated by their lack of opportunity, Castro generally seemed to have wide support. It wasn't true that the whole population was itching to escape. A few months earlier, when I'd landed at José Martí airport from Panama, where I'd gone to get my visa, the plane was full of Cubans returning home or visiting. It was late afternoon as the island came into sight: its expanses of golden sand, rolling white breakers and green palms. The passengers thrilled at what they saw, punching their fists and shouting: 'Cuba, Cuba, Cuba.' I struggled to imagine the same happening at Heathrow.

Cuba's main handicap was the American embargo on trade, first imposed in 1958 and subsequently extended. It had crippled its economy but not damaged its political system and, over the years, trade with countries not totally in thrall to the USA had grown, as had tourism.

'Where does the money go?' I asked Tony.

'Chris, Fidel is political. The people get only the minimum he think they need—for education, medicine, culture. Family businesses do better but Fidel is more interested in supplying doctors for Nicaragua, Columbia and Venezuela or supporting revolutions elsewhere.'

'In return for money, for oil?'

'Fidel only care about money,' said José.

'But not for himself,' said Tony; 'for the economy. He want political change—in Central America, South America. He have no interest in personal wealth, though not all in the government are the same. He is a Marxist; his beliefs have never changed. Of course he is also a ruthless dictator. We could not be having this conversation in a public bar.'

José was not impressed. The money was not reaching him, and that was all he cared about.

I told them I'd been reading Gioconda Belli's book *The Country Under My Skin*, in which she'd described her visit to Cuba in 1978 with fellow Nicaraguan revolutionaries. She admired Castro but resented what she saw as his desire to meddle with the Sandinista revolution. She also claimed he made a clumsy pass at her, disguising it as an invitation to discuss politics.

'The young of Havana don't give a shit about the Sandanistas,' Manolo scoffed; 'they just want what they see on television in the hotels. American culture does more damage than its bombs.'

'And trade is improved,' said Tony, ignoring him: 'rice from Vietnam, televisions from China, cars from Germany and Japan and Korea and now France. We get oil from Venezuela and now we have medical tourism. Many people come here for the clinics. Fidel spends much on medical research.' That was true. Later I'd be treated in one of those clinics as a favour from Tony. It was full of foreign visitors seeking cheap treatment, and there was a waiting list, but he helped me jump the queue.

'We don't have a problem with drugs or racism. Women are equal—' Yamilia snorted derisively at this from the kitchen '—and Cuba has a vibrant culture, a sense of community, a common identity.'

Yamilia danced past the table singing, 'We are the world, we are the people.'


Manolo, at what was probably Tony's prompting, tried to introduce me to Cuban beer rather than rum. I didn't like Crystal, the popular brand, so he suggested Hatuey and then mocked my pronunciation of it. Pronounced *Atway*, it was a bottled beer, best drunk chilled. On the label was a small dark-skinned man against a colourful rural background.

'Hatuey was a Dominican Indian,' said Manolo. 'All Cubans and Dominicans were Indian. The Spanish killed them. They tried to fight but were too weak and didn't have enough weapons or fighting experience or killer instinct. Hatuey came here and organised the few Indians left alive. For a while, they had some success. Then the Spanish caught him and burned him.'

'So he's a hero?'

'Yes. When they were about to burn him, they asked him if he wanted to convert to Roman Catholicism. He asked them why he should. They told him he wouldn't go to Heaven if he didn't. He asked them if the Spanish would be there in Heaven. When the said Yes, he told them he didn't want to go. So they burned him.'

I liked the story and the beer became my drink of choice for a few months. It was good beer, better than Crystal, but hard to find, apparently because of a copyright dispute over the use of Hatuey's name. Anyway, it was the story that attracted me; I don't really like beer and I soon went back to rum.

Manolo's German girlfriend arrived for a visit. She stayed at a *casa particular* in Villa Panamericana. The two of them talked a great deal in German and Spanish but appeared not to have a physical relationship. I met her at Lucia's one day; I don't know why she was even there. We went for a coffee. Blonde with pale blue eyes, she looked rather pasty but exuded Aryan good health.

'You don't see much of Manolo,' I said.

'I'm not really here for Manolo. I keep returning but not now for Manolo. He's just useful. And why are you here?'

Very direct.

'It's fun. Why are you here?'

'Same. It's fun, it's different, it's unique. And the men.'

I remembered a conversation with Yamilia at a baseball game. I had noticed a striking blonde sitting with a crowd of Cubans. I asked Yamilia if the woman was Cuban. She looked her over scornfully and said, 'She is Swede. She come here to fuck big black man. In her own country she would look like this at those men.' She held her nose, lifted her chin and put on a haughty expression of superiority. 'Here she is different; nobody can see her. She wants to fuck black men with big *pingas*.'

'And you are here for Yamilia?' she said.

'Sort of. She was the catalyst.'

She snorted.

'Didn't you find it a bit shocking at first, the sex here?'

'You mean the biting and scratching, the roughness of it?'

'Not so much that: the openness of it, the flaunting of it, the things they say. It amazed me the first time.'

I stared blankly.

'You don't know? Oh, my God,' she buried her face in her hands. 'You're unaware of how basic it is? The way they act? The way they talk?'

I wasn't sure where she was going with this. She seemed excited. I waited.

'It's all, "You fucking whore, I'm going to fuck you until you can't walk straight" or "Come here you whore bitch—do this, do that." You don't know about that? You don't do that with Yamilia or the others? I've heard the women here say that European men are all shy and scared and treat them like glass, as though they might break—that they don't realise how much the rawness is shared. That's it's not just a male thing. That the women want it too.'

'Yamilia can be a bit rough. I don't like it that much—sometimes, maybe, but not that much. I may say some things when I feel like it; things I've picked up.'

'Of course, your Spanish is not good. Why is that? You've been here quite a long time now.'

'I've wanted to learn but they all speak pretty good English —José, Manolo, Lucia, Raúl, even Yamilia. I try, but we always end up speaking English. It's just easier.'

'You have to learn. You won't get the most out of life here until you do.'

'I'd like to and I've tried, but I don't think I'm good with other languages, and they speak so fast. The rough language, you like it?'

'I love it! It's healthy. I give the same back. You learn that here. Get everything off your chest, clear your mind, give what you get. It's such a natural way of living. Full of contradictions but healthy. They're always talking, shouting, moving, living in the moment. It's good for the soul.'

Her face was flushed. I could have had her. I didn't want her.

# 18

# Jealousy

Yamilia was often jealous. If she caught me looking at other women she said, 'You like?' and shook her head at my denials. She was even more annoyed when she caught women looking at me, often completely misunderstanding their reasons. She was extremely rude to a young American woman who only wanted to know how I'd got a phone and where she could get one. In some ways I liked this: if Yamilia was jealous, she must care. But it was tiring and in some cases destructive. She was especially jealous of José: jealous of his hold on my friendship, his hold on my time and the value I gave his opinion.

Because Tony liked José, Yamilia had to tread carefully. Tony didn't yet know about José's problems with the police and his habit of driving without a driving licence. He respected José's knowledge of the underbelly of Havana life, thought of him as protection for me, trusted him to make sure I wouldn't fall foul of the wrong sort of people and hoped he would keep him informed about what I was up to and what I was thinking. So at least for now, while Yamilia wanted to make the right impression on Tony, she had to tolerate José.

I found it rather comical to see the two of them feigning friendship and respect for each other. Her attempts at peace never lasted long, though, and Celia, guilty by association, suffered too.

We had planned to meet José and Celia at the Latin American Stadium for a Saturday night game. At the very last minute she decided she didn't want to go. I'd thought she enjoyed these nights, which involved rum and music and humour, no matter what the quality of the game, but now she insisted she hated them and wasn't going. And if she wasn't going, she didn't want me to be going either. I told her I was going.

'To see your friend José. You fuck José?'

'That's stupid. You were supposed to be coming and Celia will be there.'

'You fuck Celia?'

I called a taxi from my cellular.

'You think me stupid?'

She advanced as if intending to hit me, her face a picture of manufactured indignation.

'You think me stupid?'

She wanted a confrontation.

'I'm going,' I said, and walked into the front garden to wait for the taxi.

I'd worn a suit because we were going to a club afterwards. It was a hot, breezeless evening and I was already beginning to sweat. My intention had been to take an air-conditioned taxi to the game, where the stadium would be cool and I could remove my jacket, then wear it at the club where the extreme air-conditioning would make it welcome.

I hadn't expected to hang around so long for the taxi to arrive but while I waited, Yamilia joined me, put her arms around my waist and smiled at me. As I relaxed, she grabbed my wallet from my jacket pocket. I caught her as she tried to run back into the house but when she struggled and we fell I found I still couldn't prise the wallet from her hands. It crumpled in her grip, bending my passport and cards.

'You no go, you no go' she said, over and over again.

In the middle of all this, the taxi arrived. The driver got out, leant against the side of his car and watched us.

'*Momento*,' I shouted.

He shrugged. I was out of breath and sweating. Just a few minutes after showering and I could already smell myself again.

Yamilia shouted at the driver telling him to go.

'You sure?' he said in English.

'No. Wait,' I shouted back. Much of my enthusiasm for the evening was gone but I wasn't going to let Yamilia ruin it completely. That would have been too easy a victory.

She still had my wallet and without knocking her unconscious I couldn't see how to get it, but there was some money in my back pocket, so I made my way towards the taxi. Yamilia saw my intention and sprang at me. I kept my hand in my pocket to stop her getting the money and she bit me on the arm, hanging on for a few seconds until I shoved her away. Only when I unlocked the gate did she give up.

In the back of the taxi I wiped her saliva from my sleeve. Her teeth had dented the fabric and my arm stung. I tried to hide my breathlessness and anger from the driver, whose eyes studied me in the rear-view mirror.

'Fiery woman,' he said cheerfully, 'strong.'

'Sí.'

'Women, eh? What can you do?'

I turned and looked out of the window. I could hear my breathing, feel my heart beating, my chest rising and falling. The driver turned on his radio and hummed to himself for the rest of the journey.

I had about eighty dollars in my pocket. José would pay in pesos for the game but we didn't have enough for the club, where entrance alone was twenty-five dollars.

'What's up?' said José when we met up.

I told him.

'You are crazy man.'

I took regular sips from our bottle of rum, barely watching the game, sinking deeper and deeper into resentment at Yamilia's histrionics. I didn't want to; I fought against it and would much have been much happier if I'd simply snapped out of it. What I needed to shake off this bad night out was a good night out but the game, the company and the entertainment weren't having the required effect.

'I'm going,' I said.

I gave José and Celia some money for the drinks and left, then took a taxi to central Havana and sat in a tourist bar watching on TV the game I'd just walked out of. I stared at the screen without seeing it, brooding on the ruined evening.

My bad temper made me worse-tempered, my anger made me angrier. I remembered every one of Yamilia's false accusations and each of her tantrums. What had amused or delighted me before became sinister. The good times became bad times. Optimism became pessimism.

The barman tried a little conversation, then gave up.

I drank for hours, moving from bar to bar to avoid conversation. The rum had little effect. I kept replaying in my mind the details of the fight, her spoilt, smug, child-like expression, the crumpled passport, the heat of my body and the smell of sweat. I tried to slow myself down, get some perspective, breathe more slowly; nothing helped. I thought about finding a woman for the night, for revenge if not for pleasure, and for once that didn't appeal either.

I wanted to book into a hotel but needed my passport. The thought of going back to get it hurt me physically.

I ran into a few people I knew. I allowed my expression and my silence to deter them.

When I had only my taxi fare left I headed home. As the taxi stopped in front of the house I caught her silhouetted in the bedroom window. We used to leave the bathroom light on all night and its glow shadowed her as she approached the window and then stepped quickly back.

I felt suddenly calm. I took my time paying the driver and kept my eye on the window as I opened the gate. Dingo barked his warning to the intruder. I unlocked the door. She could have used the latch to lock me out but she hadn't. I walked through to the back patio to quieten Dingo, and glanced into the bedroom as I passed. A solitary foot hung over a corner of the bed.

I hadn't eaten for hours and my calmness caused my appetite to return. I made a sandwich, drank half a litre of water, had some more rum and gave some scraps to Dingo.

She lay naked, face down on the bed, one fan keeping the mosquitoes away. Her eyes were closed, her breath feigning sleep. I cleaned my teeth and undressed. Her legs were slightly parted. I used my knees to push them apart and slid straight into her. She was already wet. Normally I would have been slow and gentle, waiting for her to accept me, but now I moved hard and fast. She raised herself up onto her hands and watched me in the mirror. I pushed her head down again and held her hair bunched in my hand. I leaned back and watched the mirror. She was moaning lightly and smiling at my reflection. I grabbed her hips and pulled her onto her knees. She reached through her legs and very gently stroked my balls. The unaccustomed gentleness, at odds with everything else that had happened that evening, made me climax quickly and, as I emptied myself into her, she came too. My strength drained from me as though I was losing blood and I only just avoided collapsing on top her as I rolled to the side of the bed, tired and weak as death. The last sound I heard was her laughing.

I woke at 11:00 to the familiar sound of Yamilia singing. I wasn't hung over—the water from the night before had spared me that. Unfamiliar smells wafted into the bedroom. She was cooking. The smell of bacon reminded me that I was hungry. Breakfast was rare and was usually accompanied by the accusation that I never made it. Nor did Yamilia. Tony usually cooked when he arrived.

I washed quickly and approached the dining table next to the kitchen. The table was set with a clean white tablecloth adorned with flowers cut from the garden, and plates, cutlery, coffee, bread and fruit. I looked into the kitchen, cautiously, unsure what I'd find. She stood with her back to me at the sink in shorts and T-shirt, busy and still singing. I stood silently and watched, but after a few seconds she wiggled her bottom at me without turning round.

'Buenas dias, mi amor,' she said, 'como esta? Sentado por favor.'

She didn't usually eat in the morning but today she'd set a plate for herself. She stood behind me, reached around and poured coffee. She stroked my shoulder as she moved away. Soon she was back with bacon, eggs, mushrooms and tomatoes. She sat down opposite, poured herself some water and began to eat.

'Eat, mi amor.'

I sat and we ate in silence for a while.

'Big surprise for me in the night,' she said, smiling her most beautiful of smiles and winking at me.

*The reason of the unreason which has afflicted my reason,*
*debilitating my ability to reason, so that it is with good reason*
*that I complain of your beauty.*
Don Quixote

# 19

# The Blue House

The move to the blue house in Guanabacoa came not long before I was due to leave the country again to renew my visa. Tony assured me it would be the last time I had to get a visa from Mexico because once we were settled into the house, he would get my visas for me—at a price.

All the legal work had been completed: lots of documents and signatures, witnessed solemnly in a lawyer's office nearby. With the signing and the handover, Yamilia had been given to understand that she now owned the house, which pleased her greatly, although I was assured by Tony that she didn't, because that wouldn't be wise. It was his name that would be on the deeds, but Yamilia and I would be legally in residence, or would appear to be in residence: I wasn't sure what the actual position was. Would we tolerate the occasional company of Chuchi and his wife? She would cook if we liked and Chuchi could do odd jobs.

The whole arrangement seemed unlikely and suspicious but it was as solid an arrangement as I was likely to find, Tony said, given the legal objections to selling land to foreigners. In my heart, I doubted that the house would ever truly be mine or that I would ever see any money from its sale. I also knew that what I was really doing was buying a house for Tony, and paying rent in advance for it, but I already loved the place, had imagined the fun to be had there, and even anticipated a future in it of domestic bliss. And it was $9,000 dollars—nothing, I thought, at the time. As for Yamilia owning the house, no, of course; Tony's ownership put it in safer hands.

I enjoyed life in the blue house. To begin with, we continued to live by old habits, going out often, even though there wasn't much to do in Guanabacoa and Havana was now a fairly long drive or taxi journey. Gradually, apart from weekends, we stopped going out and people instead came to us. It became a typical Cuban house with people coming and going, day and night—constant noise, chatter and music, constant life. Yamilia even welcomed José as our single guest one evening when she was cooking, a peace offering of sorts—just me, Yamilia and José, drinking rum and watching baseball and talking. Strange how similar life had become to the life I'd left at home: drinking and watching sport on TV. Or maybe not so strange.

The next day we spent a lazy afternoon people-watching at La Catedral in Havana. A group of young, self-conscious, well-dressed young men made their slow way across the square. 'Italiano,' said Yamilia.

José nodded sagely.

'Gay,' he said.

Yamilia gave them her full attention.

'Sí, gay,' she said sadly, shaking her head. 'Ay, beautiful boys.'

She whispered in my ear, covered her mouth with her hand, 'Chris, Raúl is gay.'

'Raúl, mi medico?'

'No.'

She stroked her chin to indicate the brother of our bearded leader.

José nodded conspiratorially.

'Hermano de Jefe,' she said, '*el hermano de Fidel*,' and, looking around the square, she touched a finger to her lips.

We were pestered by a local nuisance. Unlike other, thankfully rare Cubans, who asked for money, she pestered and wouldn't be discouraged. After a few minutes Yamilia reached for her handbag and handed her a dollar. The woman, in a voluminous multi-coloured dress that she appeared to fill quite comfortably, accepted gracelessly and, in her own time, left our table. She wandered over to the other side of the square, then up a small side street and, still in view of the entire square, hitched up her dress, revealing a big, brown, pantless arse and pissed up against the wall, standing, leaning back like a man—a long torrential gush.

'Ay,' said Yamilia, as she and José hid their faces behind their hands.

The woman, oblivious, wandered off to annoy tourists elsewhere.

As night drew in, we went to the bar where I'd been with Yamilia on our first night, two years before. It faced the street, its tables divided from the passing public by a small fence. No Cuban could get past that without the right company or money. Every night, a girl, pretty and a bit overweight, came to dance to the music. She stood outside the fence, dancing alone, oblivious to all but the music, throwing smiles at the musicians as though they were her personal friends. Or maybe just the music was her friend. It could have been sad but it wasn't.

Tonight a new dancer appeared, a tiny man in dirty working clothes but with astonishing charisma. One by one he grabbed the attention of everyone in the bar, including the musicians, who began to play just for him. He performed there in his own world for perhaps an hour, Havana's answer to Michael Jackson, stopping whenever the band took a break. When he ended his act, the entire bar stood for him, cheering loudly and clapping. He smiled and bowed modestly; one or two tourists offered him money. He shook his head and disappeared into the night.

Tony visited the blue house every day, a lordly presence, checking that everything was OK, that I'd been accepted as a neighbour and that no CDR members had reported us. One of his sisters, Silvia, lived a few doors away. She was a malevolent presence. Charming to my face, the dull hardness of her eyes was less welcoming. She tolerated Yamilia with a fixed smile of martyred superiority.

'Is she CDR?' I asked José.

'I no know. Maybe. She don't like me. I think she don't like you; she not want you in this house. Now you have paid the money, I think she want you leave so she take the house for herself.'

'But what about Tony?'

'Sure. Tony control the family. He like you. And he like money. If you make him money, he will look after you. If you have no money … .'

He shrugged.

Silvia, tall, fiftyish, very white with white hair, carried herself as though she believed that, but for the revolution, she would have had her rightful place among the aristocracy. She visited regularly when I got ill briefly, bringing me home-made soup two or three times a day. That was good of her but one day, while I was watching baseball on TV with José and Tony was in the kitchen making coffee, I heard them talking and glanced in their direction. Silvia pointed at José, who had his back to them, made a V of her right index and middle-finger and tapped them against her left upper arm. Whatever she meant, Tony dismissed it with impatience. After she'd gone I asked José to explain. He laughed.

'Is a sign white Cubans make,' he said. 'It mean: he black, he trouble.'

Tony didn't like the car business I'd started with José in Santiago. Having liked him when they'd first met, he'd now changed his opinion about him, perhaps because, like Yamilia, he was territorial and saw him as competition for my attention. He started emphasising how unreliable José was, how he could be distracted at any moment and how he might meet someone else, take my money and disappear. I disagreed. José was young and reckless, though probably less so than me, and I considered him as good a friend as I'd find in Cuba. He was also smart and streetwise, which Tony wasn't. He stole small amounts, but never too much. I wondered whether Tony was projecting onto him his own intentions.

I decided to keep Tony happy and let him come up with an idea for another business. He did. It was the same idea that José had had. Buy three cars; rent them out. The only small differences were they would be kept in Tony's drive and would only be rented to well-off Cubans. This was a neat touch and typical of Tony. His Cuban clientele wouldn't pay so much but it would be safer and Tony would have more control. Nothing with José was ever quite safe.

I enthused as though it was the best and most original idea I had ever heard, giving Tony huge credit for his business acumen. The cars would be neither new nor air-conditioned but since the smartest cars were reserved for foreign tourists, these would do fine for Cuban families on a tour or visiting relatives.

We did it. I didn't make much money out of it but it was better than nothing. How much of the receipts Tony took, I never knew, but as I hadn't done anything apart from buying the cars I felt I didn't have much grounds to complain.

It was time for me to renew my visa again and I decided to go back to Mexico City because the journey was familiar. It was also fast. I wanted to go and return home as soon as possible. That's how I felt; that Cuba was home, where I wanted to be.

Tony's attitude to Yamilia had always been ambivalent. While Yamilia behaved as if the two of them were secretly in cahoots, he'd given me the impression that he didn't trust her, for reasons he never made clear—perhaps only because the idea of their being in cahoots was a fabrication. As time past, his distrust of her was no longer quite so well-hidden and she now behaved as if she distrusted him as well. She obviously felt less secure in the house, watching suspiciously whenever I talked with him. Bizarrely, in her paranoia about the house, she formed an alliance with José, who had also begun to resent Tony, both of them childishly, possessively criticising him for his growing influence over me. I didn't mind at all. I didn't mind being fought over, if it meant my presence was valued, and it meant that José and Celia became more frequent visitors.

We often visited a beach near Matanzas. José had discovered it, a beach for Cubans, free of tourists, on a small bay hidden from the road by forest, about fifty miles east of Havana. Used mainly by local people, it was never crowded. Beer and rum were served from a scruffy hut where they cooked anything you wanted, including freshly caught fish. The atmosphere was unstrained and relaxed. Celia was confident enough to talk to me without fear of Yamilia.

One day we watched as they brought an enormous fish ashore. It was an ugly thing, fat, about four-foot long. They carried it to the hut. The owner said, 'Do you want us to cook it for you?' They cooked it and put it on our table with some salad. We ate what we could and gave the rest to some kids. As we sat eating, Yamilia asked about the eyes: Were they good to eat? Did they give you strength? José curled his lip at the thought and Celia turned away. I wasn't going to try, either. So she speared one of the eyes with her fork, put it in her mouth and crunched it, smiling. Then she did the same with the other one, all the time watching us. The light in her eyes said: 'You know I'm badder than you.'

We usually drove back to Havana in daylight but, today, none of us had any desire to leave. The sun was a fierce orange ball sitting on the horizon, its warmth already directed elsewhere. The silhouette of a lone pelican drifted heavily, lazily across the shallows, full of fish.

'Where do pelicans go to sleep,' I said.

Yamilia rolled her eyes. José and Celia laughed. The downward movement of the sun was tangible, the day turning grey to dark blue and suddenly pitch black. After a few seconds of respectful, eerie silence, as if waiting a while to be sure the sun had really gone, the nocturnal cacophony clicked, buzzed and screeched into life in the woods behind us. We could hear the loud slaps of unseen people dealing with the emerging mosquitoes.

Yamilia shivered.

'If we light a fire the mosquitoes will stay away,' said José.

'We don't have any food or water,' I said. The hut was closed.

'Give me the car keys,' said José. 'I'll find a place.'

And he did., a little further along the coast.

We stayed the night on the beach, sleeping for a few hours in our clothes, although it never got cold. After waking up with a swim we ate breakfast by the now-open hut. For an entire day the four of us had lived in complete harmony—friends. There was no reason why it shouldn't have stayed that way, and I let myself believe that it could. But this was the last truly peaceful day I would have in Cuba.

*Love is like war: easy to begin but very hard to stop.*
H.L. Mencken

# 20

# A New Voice

The night before my flight to Mexico, I was alone in the house when the phone rang. A male voice said, 'Old man, this is not your house, it belong to me. My house, my woman.'

The line went dead. I told Yamilia about it when she returned from shopping. A show of nonchalance failed to conceal the fear in her eyes. She walked to the kitchen and busied herself putting things away. Then she changed the subject. I called Tony. He was cool, dismissive of the call. I may have imagined the tension in his voice.

'Don't worry,' he said, 'I will deal with it.'

Deal with what? Deal with it how? With whom?

Once again I was back from Mexico within forty-eight hours. Once again Yamilia was out. Chuchi and Maria were alone in the house, welcoming me as though I'd been away for a year. Maria fussed about me, gave me masses of food and tried to persuade me to sleep off the journey, although it had only been a two-hour flight. Chuchi was equally attentive, which was very strange. Never exactly friendly before, he hovered around me, asked how I was, assured me that Yamilia would be back soon and told me that everything had been absolutely fine in my absence.

Yamilia arrived soon afterwards on her bike, a bag full of

shopping in the front basket. Food for the evening meal, rum and beer. She fussed around me too and invited Chuchi and Maria to stay for dinner. As we ate Yamilia bared her teeth at me.

'Look, Chris, I fall off my bike.'

She touched a broken tooth with a fingernail.

'I must go dentist. My smile!'

They chattered too fast about how Yamilia had hit a pothole and tipped over the handlebars, chipping a front tooth and banging her head. *Comico, no?* Yamilia was so silly. She should look where she is going. Not so beautiful now, eh? Maybe the bang on her head would do some good. Not be so crazy, *sí?* I smiled with them. They kept my glass full all evening. Yamilia was very giving that night, taking nothing for herself, which was unusual. It didn't help me sleep, though. Something was up.

Yamilia and Maria went to Lucia's the next day. Lucia would speak to Raúl, Raúl would speak to someone and Yamilia would get her tooth fixed. Chuchi pottered about the house, smiling horribly at me whenever we met. When he offered to make me a coffee, I knew something must be terribly wrong. I told him I was going out to buy cigarettes.

Silvia was sweeping her patio. She gave me her thin, joyless smile. Another person sat drinking coffee. A friend, I supposed.

'*Café, Chris?*' said Silvia.

We sat at under a large umbrella, the air thick with malice. They waited. We exchanged pleasantries. Silvia had no English but the friend did, which was possibly why she was there. Nothing of any consequence was said. I considered leaving, pretending that I wasn't concerned. Then, on the point of getting up to go, I asked the most innocent of questions.

'Anything happen while I was away?'

Silvia sighed, as if regretting having to tell me such a tale but relishing it at the same time. She spat out rapid bursts of Spanish and the friend translated. Two nights ago there had been a commotion. Banging on the door of my house and shouting. It was Amado. He shouted for Yamilia to come out. She shouted through the window, told him to leave, but he stayed. He went on banging and shouting. The whole street could hear. They came out to watch. At last Yamilia stepped out into the street. Amado shouted that this was his house, that she was his woman. They couldn't hear what Yamilia replied. She spoke quietly. He slapped her on the side of the face. She took it, standing with her hands on her hips, defying him. He hit her again and she fell down. He picked her up by her hair, threw her down to the ground and kicked her. Everybody saw this. Maria opened the door and shouted at Amado. He would have hit her too but Sylvia had already called for the CDR. While Amado continued to rant, one of the CDR men arrived, smacked Amado in the face and threatened him. Amado weighed up his options, got on his motorbike and drove away, making the watching neghbours jump out of the way. Maria took Yamilia back in the house.

'Chris, this is disgraceful. We cannot have this behaviour here. Everybody knows that your woman brings trouble. The CDR have tolerated your noisy parties but you must be careful here, not draw attention to yourselves. These houses are respectable.'

'This Amado,' I said. 'Is this the son of someone called Lazaro? Or some other Amado?'

'I don't know, Chris.'

Silvia jerked her shoulders and looked away. I didn't think she had anything else to say. I stood up.

'Gracias por el café, Silvia.'

I called José and took a taxi to Havana. While I waited for him to meet me, I phoned Paul.

'So is this guy going to affect you? Us?'

'It's a long story.'

Hmm, why doesn't that surprise me?'

'I'd like him out of the way.'

'Have him killed.'

When José arrived, I reported what Paul had said.

'You want kill him?' said José.

'Can I? Would I get away with that?'

'No.'

*The big difference between sex for money and sex for free
is that sex for money usually costs a lot less.*
Brendan Behan

# 21

# Aftermath

After I'd heard Sylvia's story, I had wanted to kill Amado or, more accurately, wanted him to not be around anymore. As my anger subsided, I put together a plan. It was mad but I had to do something. Not wanting to end up in front of a firing squad and, truthfully, not having that much violence in me, I had settled for breaking his nose with a kid's miniature baseball bat. It was worth it just for the look on his face. The second he opened his door, I hit him; flattened his nose, splattered his white shirt with blood, spoiled his greasy good looks for a while. Easy. And completely dumb.

I didn't go home to the blue house but drove to the white house that Yamilia and I had had stayed in previously. Tony was often there, doing repairs on the place, feeding Dingo or enjoying the company of women who weren't his wife. On this particular evening, he was out so I waited and helped myself to his rum. I got smugly, happily drunk and when there was a knock on the door, I opened it to someone I didn't know. A woman.

Waiting behind her stood Amado and a couple of friends. Pushing past her, they stabbed and kicked me, hit me over the head with a hammer and left me bleeding on Tony's cool tiled floor. I would have stayed there but for Dingo. He created such a racket that the neighbours were forced to investigate. They found me in a spreading pool of my own blood.

I woke up a couple of days later. They couldn't take me to hospital because the security police would have taken an interest, so Raúl came round and patched me up. Again. *Muchas gracias, Dingo.*

After a few days, when I was able to hobble out of bed, Tony drove me slowly to the blue house and Yamilia helped me stretch out on the patio.

José and Celia came round, as well as Sylvia and two or three of the neighbours, but Yamilia ordered everybody from the house because Raúl had said I needed peace and quiet. She took advantage of the privacy and was wearing only a pair of my boxer shorts, though I had trouble appreciating it.

Guanabacoa was a noisy, rough town, just eight miles east of Havana, but here on the patio the sound was muffled. There was rain in the air but it was still a few hours away. Yamilia set the plates on the table under the mimosa tree. It was shady and cool in the yard; a breeze rustled the bougainvillea against the high walls.

I could barely move to eat my food. Everything ached. The light hurt my eyes. My fingers wouldn't work. A fly settled on the wound at the back of my head, I couldn't shake it off. Yamilia sprang at it and waved it away.

'*Hijo de puta!*'

She lightly stroked the area around the bald patch where Raúl had shaved me and stitched me up, then carefully placed a sunhat there. She watched me eat. It was a slow, painful process but I was hungry. She nodded and smiled: if I wanted food I must be OK. She gave me an evil smirk, as if there might be something else I wanted. I groaned inwardly and hoped she was joking.

She cleared away the plates, singing in Spanish as she clattered about in the kitchen. I feared that she might break something; it was a rare day that she didn't. She came to the door drying a plate, fixed her black eyes on me.

'You white, like a spirit.'

I'd lost a lot of blood through the head wound. She reeled off Raúl's instructions, trying to rouse me, in precise English: Lots of sleep, lots of sugar and two tablets, three times every day. No smoking, lots of fruit, lots of water—and no rum.

She went back into the kitchen and the singing stopped, just a banging of pots and pans. She returned and sat down, her lips a tight line, a foot twitching. Serious now, and angry, because she wasn't happy, because something had happened that she didn't want to think about, something that would affect her life.

'You nearly die,' she said.

'Amado hurt you.'

'No esta importante.'

'It was important.'

I drifted off. When I woke up, I told her that Amado had called me a maricon.

'Que?'

'Amado, at Tony's, before I lost consciousness, while they kicked me. He called me a maricon, many times.

Yamilia was silent for a long time, eyes wide, eyebrows high on her forehead. Then she threw back her head and laughed. Her laughter changed everything—her, me, the atmosphere, the world. She had found the funny side and was happy again. I failed to see the joke. She gave me a look that made men jealous of me at fifty paces.

'You? A maricon?' Gay.

'Sí.'

'You no maricon, you fuck me every day.'

She collapsed into hysterics again. I suppose it was funny but laughing hurt my ribs. She went to the kitchen. I heard her opening the fridge, crashing about, the clinking of glass and pouring. She returned with two large straight glasses filled to the brim with rum, soda and ice. She saw my surprise and shrugged.

'Your medicine. I put sugar in and two tablets. I know you. No rum, you die.'

We chinked glasses, 'Fidel'. I took a large swallow; it burned the cuts on my lips and mouth, then, a few seconds later, a wonderful calm. All was right with the world. The miracle of Cuban white rum. I took another sip. Somehow she got me to the bedroom, took the glass from me and put it on the floor.

'Slow down. Later.'

Later, the only sound in the room was the rise and fall of Yamilia's breathing. The pain and solitary rage seeped out of me. Images of Amado, his green eyes as devoid of light as a reptile's, receded and my world contained only the rare, natural force of her. Her eyes clouded, her face grew soft and she slapped my face hard. She dug her nails into my chest, opening one of the cuts, which bled onto the sheet. I felt myself swell and burn painfully and I cried out but didn't resist. And while I was inside the heat of her, and as her sweat dripped onto my face and the smell of mariposa rose from her hair, I was happy, in the only way I can be made happy, with a woman who understood how this was the case.

I slept immediately. When I woke Yamilia was leaning against the doorframe, smoking a sorry-looking joint. She wore my boxer shorts again, back to front this time. She still looked great. She glared at me, her eyes hard and dangerous. I asked for the joint. She ignored me.

'You no die,' she said.

It sounded like a threat, as if she'd punish me if I did.

'Not just yet.'

'No,' she shouted, 'You no die. I want baby. Good baby.'

'OK'.

She puffed furiously on the joint, her eyes unfocussed, lost in her head, a look I knew well, that signalled it was best to keep her away from knives or from anything she could throw or break. Then she changed, snapped out of it and threw the joint onto the patio. She came to the bed, where she seemed to see the open cut for the first time.

'Lo siento.' Sorry. She dropped some saliva over the cut, spread it with her tongue.

'Make good baby. Your eyes, your head and this. She pointed to my legs. She often did this. Once, as I completed a driving manoeuvre, she nodded her head in approval, said, 'Hmm, is good coordination.' She was ticking off her genetic shopping list, creating a beautiful child in her mind. She was quite open about it. There were plenty of faults too.

'You want my legs?'

'Me flaco,' she said, glaring angrily at her own legs.

'Your legs are good.'

'Flaco,' she said, ending it. Skinny. 'You love me?'

'Siempre,' I said. Always.

She smiled.

'You want baby?'

'Sure,' I said, not sure at all. 'My blue eyes, tu corazón negro.'

'My black heart,' she said. As she flashed the eyes and the teeth at me, I wondered again what I was doing here. The web of the black widow. She smiled happily, tried to stroke me into life again.

'Can we start tomorrow, Yamilia? I need sleep.'

'Me too.' It was four in the afternoon.

She took three Diazepam from her bag and swallowed them. They can be bought over the counter in Cuba for a penny each. She lay down next to me.

I woke the next morning. I felt good, although I hadn't yet tried moving. Yamilia was soundly asleep beside me. Odd to think that in just one month's time we'd be finished. And that I would have started a war. Well, that somebody would have.

*I do not cultivate the same tastes as tourists.*
Che Guevara


## 22

# Paul Returns


Paul arrived for his second visit just as I had been passed fit again by Raúl. He brought six detective novels with him. Disappointed by his lack of enthusiasm on the previous visit, we did our best to find better ways to entertain him. He said he liked the blue house, in spite of our having yet to instal a flushing toilet. I wish we had done. On the first morning he blocked our squatting toilet with toilet paper and was mortified when Yamilia had to set to work with a plunger and a bucket of water, showing him where to find these should he be responsible for the same problem again. To flush our toilet, you had to pour a bucket of water into it. It was very basic but it worked; what it was not likely to do was impress a millionaire's son, used to five-star hotels. Welcome to Cuba.

Paul seemed more enthusiastic about our business than he'd seemed to be since his last visit. He talked about chartering tourists from England and, with the help of Rumbos, the tourist arm of the Cuban government, capitalising on the exotic. Sell it with a hint of the Cuba that tourists don't get to see, he suggested. Set it up, pick the right employees, sit back, do very little—and get rich. It sounded great, it sounded easy, it sounded the way ideas sound when you're drunk and they remain dreams. Tony hadn't managed to arrange the Rumbos meeting for this trip, but was working on something for next month, when Paul returned.

Apart from complaining about the rough-and-ready nature of things Cuban, Paul remained indifferent to Havana. Where I saw magic, colour and character, he saw squalor and inefficiency. He couldn't adjust to the casualness about time and service, so our social life revolved around only the handful of top hotels. I like the peso bars; Paul liked the Meliá Cohiba, though this only mattered when he was sober. Most of the time he was drunk and indifferent to what country he was in, let alone which bar or restaurant. And anyway, it was me and not him who wanted to live here. The purpose of the visit was to decide, finally, if we could make money in Cuba.

Paul, surprisingly, struck up a friendship with Chuchi. They spent hours fiddling with my laptop, which I only used to keep a diary and watch DVDs. His booming voice and Chuchi's annoying whine accompanied many an afternoon otherwise occupied by TV baseball and music. Paul was determined to gain internet access, available then only at selected hotels. Even I, a confirmed Luddite, knew this would be impossible, but it didn't stop him trying. I liked Chuchi but he annoyed me with his constant pottering and smugness. He would perform the simplest task, like fitting an extension lead to the stereo, and then fix me with a supercilious grin, implying that, without him, these tasks would never be completed, because the useless Englishman—me—was too dim and too lazy to work it out.

Our water came from three plastic tanks, high up on platforms at the back of the patio. Running water was available for two or three hours in the evening, when we filled the tanks. Chuchi liked to take over the task of filling them with a hosepipe attached to an outside tap. But I liked doing this too. We eventually had a battle over who filled the tanks. He arrived every evening to find me there, contentedly filling the tanks myself. It relaxed me, I enjoyed it but he spoilt my enjoyment by watching, arms folded, his expression one of pity because I wasn't doing properly a job that a monkey could do. After he and Paul discovered their shared interest in technology, Chuchi expanded on my deficiencies.

'Paul very intelligent, you no.'

Maria was different. She was short, round and very hairy; hair on her face, arms and legs and, I presume, everywhere else. Yamilia pointed this out one day in Chuchi's presence.

'Ella es tu esposa, Chuchi; te tiene que gustar mucho.' This is the wife you chose; you must like them round and hairy—roughly translated.

Maria was a great cook and cleaned constantly. I liked the way the bed linen was always clean and fresh, without the chemical smell you often get in hotels. She washed it every day and worked all day, every day: washing, cleaning, mopping, cooking, usually with people and gossip and music to accompany her. I don't remember ever seeing an unclean room or house in Cuba. Daily cleaning was necessary to keep insects at bay and it was the one chore that Yamilia had done religiously when we living at Rosa's and in the white house. Here in the blue house, crawling insects didn't stand a chance; and I'd never seen a cockroach. Maria ruled the kitchen and I was happy to let her. Yamilia would shadow her, mainly gossiping and occasionally doing something to help, but Maria didn't want help. Yamilia was the lady of the house and Maria put up with her intrusions, as she saw them, but I don't think she wanted Yamilia around or even liked her.

During Paul's second week I had a mild fever. On a bad day I stayed at home while Paul, José, Yamilia and Manolo went to the beach. In the evening I joined them around a football game on TV. I thought I could drink myself out of whatever I had. Paul said that they had bought cocaine and taken it to the beach, that he had fallen asleep in the sun and now had lobster legs. Yamilia had said nothing to me about liking cocaine. I was surprised enough when I'd seen her smoking the joint. It was probably nothing but it set off all sorts of fresh doubts about what I didn't know about her.

When I quizzed her, Yamilia said she hadn't taken any of the cocaine and didn't like it but I was in such discomfort, I became incandescent and shouted at all of them, accusing them of assorted betrayals and deceits. They watched me in silence, which made me worse. I accused Paul of cheating me, José of stealing my money and Yamilia of untold infidelities. I paced about, shouting and swigging from a bottle of rum. My cheeks were burning. Then the ceiling receded before my eyes and my head hit the floor.

Yamilia woke me the next afternoon. I allowed myself to be dressed and taken by taxi to Lucia's surgery. I didn't stop my accusations as the taxi door closed. Another taxi waited for Paul, who was leaving. I wanted Yamilia to stay with me but couldn't stop shouting at her.

Paul's taxi must have followed us to Villa Panamericana, because it pulled in behind us when we stopped to let Chuchi and José out. Paul opened the door, leaned in and hugged me. He smiled and laughed, talked to me, an echoing jumble of words. I tried to push him away but was too weak. He kissed me on the cheek. The others smiled as though admiring a new baby. My head boiled; I heard sounds like radio interference. Just fuck off, fuck off and then fuck off some more. Don't leave me here. What's so funny? Am I dying? The lights are too bright. I want to sleep, but I can't. And then they were gone and Yamilia and Lucia took me to the surgery.

I had pneumonia. Raúl had to hunt down the medicines and drugs I needed at various clinics and hospitals. The US embargo gave the health service serious problems, making drugs common to us hard to find. His expression and his hushed conversations worried me more than how I felt, which was just tired and hot or cold. I drifted in and out of sleep, oblivious of time. Yamilia came and went, sometimes staying the night. She was comfortable and welcome at Lucia's anyway.

After a week Raúl declared me fit to leave Lucia's place, but under strict conditions. I was to stop smoking and alcohol was banned until I was fit again. I felt refreshed by all the sleep I'd had and, for a time, didn't want to drink or smoke anyway. I read and reread my books, watched TV and DVDs and slept some more. Yamilia, always good when I was ill, fussed around me while Maria did the work. I slowly started to emerge, as if waking from months of dormancy, slightly baffled as to how I'd got here.

Raúl or Lucia visited every day, sometimes together. Raúl gave me something that made me throw up regularly, to get the phlegm off of my chest. Very slowly I slid into a drowsy contentment, an appreciation of what I had, a different outlook, a sober outlook. Tony, concerned at first—a dead Englishman would have been awkward—was happy to have a calm house to administer, with no problems to have to smooth over. The calmness was catching. The house lost its manic energy, was quieter, more at peace with itself. I heard nothing of Amado or Lazaro, which may or may not have been due to Tony: I still didn't know if he knew who they were or what leverage he might have over them, if any. He had now made an appointment with Rumbos for the next month, when Paul returned. There was plenty of time to prepare.

*When in doubt, risk it.*
Holbrook Jackson

# 23

# Matanzas

I parked the Jeep at the centre of the bridge, the longest and highest in Cuba. It was a tourist spot, so there was room on both sides of the road. Far below, and south as far as I could see, was tropical forest. To the north, behind me, was a clear view of the sea, a few hundred yards away. For the same reason that it was a tourist spot, the bridge also posed a security risk. As I approached I passed the usual Lada up on the slope, with two bored policemen inside, waiting for nothing to happen.

I leaned against the railings and looked at the forest below, while vultures flew under the bridge. I like vultures: without them the smell of death would be everywhere. They don't bother anyone, unless you happen to be dead, and they clean everything up before lumbering off to digest it—ugly great birds doing a valuable social service and minding their own business.

On the slope a motorcycle cop had parked next to the Lada and was talking through the window. They were about two hundred yards away. I knew I should leave, find another place or try another day, but I'd made up my mind. I'd had the box with me for far too long. In it, the urn containing my late father's ashes, something I took with me everywhere: my one link to the past. Yamilia knew what was in it and it spooked her out. She had finally lost patience that morning when a priest of Santeria had come to bless the new house. 'Get it out of here', she shouted. We argued for a while, but she was right; I understood why she was unnerved by it—it was as sinister as voodoo but it also meant I hadn't fully let go of my former life —so to please her, I took the box, bought a cheap spade in Guanabacoa and drove to Havana. I parked and walked to Plaza de Armas, on the west side of Havana Port. I thought I could put the ashes in the ground there among the plants, maybe sprinkle in some seeds, or come back later with a sapling. There were worse places to rest, at the heart of socialism's last stand, with pretty girls passing by all day and night.

One look told me it was impossible: too many people, police on every corner. How would I explain it? It couldn't be explained. So I drove to the bridge, fifty miles from Havana, ten miles before Matanzas and, heedless of what the police might think, decided to go no further. The location was perfect: emptying the ashes onto the forest treetops far below would be the dramatic send-off to past connections.

I looked round at the police on the slope. They weren't using binoculars; they were just talking. I wasn't doing anything wrong. What could they do? I took the box from the Jeep and put it down on the road. I realised that in fifteen years I'd never even opened it. It was still sealed with brown tape. I pulled off the tape, opened the lid and took out the urn. It was plastic, which was something of a letdown, but my gesture would redeem it. I unscrewed the top and shook the ashes into the strong wind. For a few seconds they had shape, like a plume of smoke, and then scattered and disappeared. Goodbye, Dad. I dropped the urn back in the box. There are still worse places to be, I thought.

I tried to summon up a few moments' spiritual meditation —the purpose of life, the meaning of time—but was soon interrupted by the motorcycle cop riding slowly across the bridge. I glanced as he passed: a snapshot of gleaming chrome, blue uniform, black helmet, reflective sunglasses and knee-high, shiny black leather boots. He stared back and carried on over the bridge and parked on the opposite slope. I turned back to the view. I was certain now that at some stage one of the policemen would speak to me. The cardboard box still lay at my feet. They had seen me throw something. If they asked what was in the box, what could I say? Not the truth: I was disposing of a dead body? It was simpler, surely, just to get rid of it.

I picked up the box and dropped it through the railings, watching it take forever to float to the forest below.

They were down on me in seconds. What are you doing here? What have you just thrown? Who are you? Where are you from?

I said I'd been eating my lunch and had thrown away the wrapper after finishing it. I apologised if that was littering. Not very good, but what could they do?

They could do plenty as it turned out.

They leaned over the railings to see what I'd thrown. They took my wallet and passport. I tried to explain again. The motorcycle cop ignored me, lost in his own self-glory. He walked to his bike and spoke into the radio. This was going to get silly. I knew it would get silly because I was nervous and wasn't behaving with my normal self-confidence. Anyone would guess from my perkiness that I was hiding something and had made up a story on the spur of the moment. If I'd told them the truth, they wouldn't have believed me. If they had believed me, what I'd done was probably illegal. Having told them one thing, I couldn't now tell them something else. And I didn't want to tell them what I was doing anyway: it was my moment, for myself alone—the discarding of history.

They told me to drive the Jeep to the slope where I'd first passed them. Motorcycle Man led the way a few feet in front of me. They indicated that I should wait in the Jeep. The two cops went back to their car; Motorcycle Man kicked up dust and sped to the other side of the bridge. The two in the car were no longer interested in what happened. They were leaving it to Motorcycle Man. Whatever I was up to, it was either trivial or too much trouble for them. Or maybe their shift was about to come to an end. Motorcycle Man, however, had decided to call up reinforcements. I hoped to be able to talk myself out of whatever I'd got myself into and get out of there in the next half hour.

While waiting I played music in the Jeep, a compilation tape of up-beat dance tracks what would appeal to whoever happened was sent over to me. But I'd misjudged this too. Maybe I'd turned the volume up too high. The two cops now watched from their car, then came over and asked questions about the music. By the time the security people arrived an hour later, the three of us were chatting normally, as though I didn't really have to be there.

The security people arrived in several cars, not Ladas now, but sleek new models. Motorcycle Man, his lights on full beam, led them across the bridge. I was beginning to hate him.

These were serious people, some uniforms, mostly plain clothes, efficient and energetic. They parked on both sides of the road and spoke briefly to the two cops. Agents were being despatched to check the bridge. They couldn't get down to the forest but they examined the road surface, leaned over to look at the supporting stanchions, scrambled down the banks to see underneath. This was ridiculous. It was Motorcycle Man: he'd seen the box floating in the wind. What did he think it was? I realised that the two from the Lada knew this but Motorcycle Man was having his day and he'd called in the report. Whatever really happened didn't matter anymore. The new people had to deal with what he'd told them.

I stayed in my Jeep watching them, composing my face into an expression of bewildered, injured innocence. Whoever was the boss stopped telling his men what to do and stood by his car watching. This was a serious security call and it had become his responsibility. He was ensuring he had everything covered: he'd get the flak if it wasn't. Traffic was being slowed by the parked cars. I watched as he considered whether to stop it during the check. Then he stared at Motorcycle Man, who was telling anyone who would listen how he'd saved the day. His eyebrows rose, he pursed his lips and I saw, or hoped I saw, a slight, dismissive shake of the head. A good sign. Then he looked over at me. Not such a good sign. I felt a stab of panic.

He ordered me out of the Jeep and looked me over without speaking. He was short, powerfully built, well-dressed and handsome, with piercing green eyes. He shouted an order and two men began to search the Jeep. He spoke to Motorcycle Man and then to the two Lada cops, whom he asked for my wallet. They came out of the Jeep with some cassettes, an address book, cigarettes, a lighter, condoms, a novel, a Cuban-published history of the country, a map of Cuba, a pair of Yamilia's sunglasses, one of her tops from behind the seat and the spade. He looked at the spade and then at me, told me to get in the Jeep. He got in beside me and closed the door. The music was still playing. He was holding my wallet, my passport, my address book and the map.

He opened the passport and confirmed my details, then went through it, page by page. I tried to appear confident. I wasn't worried about the box and the bridge; surely, eventually, they would realise that that was nonsense. What I was worried about was what they would find when they probed deeper. That I owned a house in Guanabacoa. That my ownership was illegal. That I shouldn't even have been staying in an unregistered house: it was through the registering of addresses that the security police knew where everyone was. In addition, that Yamilia's papers weren't legal; and that my friends and visitors were up to all sorts of stuff that was flying below the radar. I imagined the house now. Yamilia was there, perhaps the Santeria priest too, probably Chuchi and Maria. And the deeds to the house—Tony had those. I imagined everyone I knew being arrested, the house confiscated and me deported. I'd been lucky up to now, and protected up to a point. My whole life in Cuba could collapse because of this. I was very, very uneasy and had no idea what to tell them, just a very vague plan: get them to like me, appear relaxed and play it by ear. Brilliant.

'You have visited Cuba four time in three years, Mr Hilton.'

'I love Cuba.'

No reaction, just a hard stare.

'You have been here now for nearly a year. In that time you have made three visits to Mexico and one to Panama. Where have you been staying? What have you been doing?

'I've stayed in lots of places, all over the country. I want to start a travel business with Rumbos. I've been travelling, looking at hotels and planning itineraries.'

That made him think. Rumbos was the government's tourism agency; if you wanted to work in tourism, you needed Rumbos's blessing. I'd met Rumbos only once so far; I hoped I'd be remembered if called on.

He went back to the passport and looked through the other stamps. The USA, three times, just before I started visiting Cuba, the most recent visit lasting five weeks. I'd always liked the variety of stamps in my passport. They were colourful, romantic, evocative. Now, as he studied them, I wished they weren't there.

'You spent much time in the United States in 1997 and 1998.'

'I have friends there.'

'Then you began to visit Cuba.'

'After one visit I didn't want to go anywhere else,'

He lowered his head, studied me over his sunglasses. He sighed with a big movement of his shoulders and, still holding my open passport, turned to look out of the passenger window. He took off his sunglasses and tapped them to the music. The tape would keep repeating until someone turned it off. The searchers were all back, milling around. There was nothing to find.

'Where are you staying?'

'In Guanabacoa.'

'Where in Guanabacoa?'

'I stay at a house there.'

'What is the address?'

'I don't know the address.'

He gave me a weary look.

'You do not know your address?'

'No. I know where I'm staying—I can find it when I'm driving—but I don't know the actual name of the street. It's an old colonial house with a big, blue arched door. I can find it, but I have no idea of the address.'

'You should have a card with the owner's details. All government guesthouses are registered. You are staying at a registered house?'

'I don't know.'

'It is illegal to stay at an unregistered house. You could be deported.'

'I know that.'

He sighed, tapped his glasses a little faster and looked over at Motorcycle Man. Again, I sensed mistrust: that he wondered if this traffic cop was really as stupid as he looked, or whether he was onto something. There was only one way I could play it: as a likeable rogue who was not really up to anything bad enough to concern them.

'OK. Mr Hilton. We have problems with terrorism in this country, particularly from the USA. You have been reported as having a similar appearance to someone we have been looking for. I don't know what you were doing here. We have to check everything. You will be taken to Matanzas police station and questioned. Some people will look over your vehicle.'

He'd said all he wanted to. He called over a colleague, got out of the Jeep, spoke to him and handed him my stuff, then walked to his car without a backward glance. The new guy got in. He smiled pleasantly.

'You drive,' he said.

I drove the ten miles to Matanzas. Motorcycle Man led the way, lights on full beam. As we entered Matanzas he waved at people he knew, the conquering hero. I tried to talk to the new guy. He told me his name was Ramon—Ramon Sanchez. On the journey I tried to mock Motorcycle Man. 'Arrogante,' I said, pointing at his back. He turned to me, smiled his contented smile and asked for a cigarette.

I parked in the yard of Matanzas Police Station. I knew the area. I'd been here before as a tourist. It was a rough place, good fun but not one of the safest places in Cuba. Motorcycle Man, his duty done, was preparing to leave. I felt a sudden surge of hatred, got out of the Jeep and headed towards him. Ramon walked slowly to the door of the police station, unconcerned. I got to within a few yards of Motorcycle Man's bike when, without acknowledging my existence, he gunned it, the screeching tyres spraying dust in my face, and sped off. I watched him go. Ramon stood at the entrance watching. He smiled and beckoned me in.

He had a big office, important man. He took his time, found some notepaper, a pen, and sat down opposite me. He started with my address. I didn't know. He smiled and wrote something down. Occasionally he spoke to a female assistant, who entered information into a computer. Periodically, she fed him information back. They spoke rapid Cuban Spanish. I couldn't understand much of what was said, just odd words and phrases, names of hotels, places I'd visited dates. I wanted to tailor my story to what they knew. Ramon spread some of my stuff over his desk: my passport, address book and a tiny leather diary. He studied them for a long time, stopped, smiled at me and studied them all again.

'You not know where you live?'

'I know where I live. I just don't know the address.'

A charming smile. I thought: He only has to ask me to take him there and I'm fucked. We're all fucked. A one-hour drive and I'm finished.

He was looking through my passport, pausing now and then to smile at me. He asked me a question that I didn't understand. He tried it another way. I still didn't get it. He tried in English. Hopeless.

'I will get an interpreter,' he said. 'We cannot talk like this.'

He stood up.

'I'm going to eat,' he said. 'Come back here in one hour.'

'What shall I do?'

He shrugged.

'What you like.'

I went outside. I was hungry, tired and pissed off. Desperate, too, for a cigarette. I'd not smoked for over a month.

The thunder and noise of traffic was heavy and constant. It made me felt nauseous. I walked to a shop for cigarettes. As I sat on the steps smoking, a man of about sixty approached me, smiling. Handsome with white hair, tall and fit-looking, nimble. He sat next to me on the steps.

'Is that a Benson and Hedges?'

'Yes.'

'Can I have one?'

'Sure.'

'My name is Noberto. Noberto Castro.'

'Castro?'

He shrugged off my surprise.

'Here is like Smith in England. It's nothing. I am your interpreter. I live down the street here; they always call me when an English person is in trouble. So, you are a terrorist?'

'Do I look like a terrorist?'

He didn't reply immediately. His pale blue eyes studied me as he smoked his cigarette.

'No, not like a terrorist. Something else maybe, but not a terrorist. Why do they think you are?'

I told him.

'I see,' he said, 'so there is no problem. Just tell them the truth. People get themselves in trouble when they lie; these people check everything.'

'I was afraid of that.'

'Ah.'

'Where are you from in England?'

'Near London,' I said.

My stock answer.

'Where near London? Oxford? Essex? Kent? Canterbury? I know England. France, too. Fine countries. I lived there when I was younger. But this is Cuba. You may not be a terrorist, but I'm afraid you may have to go through some shit before they realise that, my friend.'

Ramon returned from his lunch. We went through the same questions again, and Noberto translated. Ramon smiled a lot and told me several times that I could be deported. He was interested in the tiny address book. It was full of phone numbers given to me in times and places that I couldn't remember, by people I couldn't remember.

'What are these numbers?'

I stared at the book. He turned it around for me. I studied the page for a few seconds, gave the appearance of deep thought. I shrugged.

'*Chicas*, I think.'

Ramon smiled and winked, Noberto smiled, I smiled—a communal smile—all boys together here. He put the book down, leaned back in his chair, and stretched with his hands behind his head.

'Your vehicle will have to be searched. I have made the necessary telephone calls.'

'What do I do,' I said again.

'You wait. We find you.'

Noberto took me to a bar close by. I bought us both a meal and some beers. I still hated beer but was making a big effort to follow Raúl's fitness regime.

'So what are you doing in Cuba, my friend? How long have you been here?'

'Nearly a year. I'm trying to start a tourism business.'

'Tourism. That's good. You must give me a job. I can translate for you. Tourism is where the money is. Remember me, my friend, when you start your business.'

'I will.'

'So. Do you have a woman here? Cuban women are the best in the world.'

'Yes, I'm with a woman.'

'What is her name?'

'Yamilia.'

'Yamilia. A nice name. A good woman?'

I managed to keep a straight face.

'She's a fiery woman.' He grinned. 'Yes, she's a good woman. So, when will they come to search my car?'

'This is Cuba. It could be a long time, my friend.'

'Why haven't they put me in a cell?'

'They will. This is all part of their games. Be very careful what you say.'

I was already being careful. Since they had planted him on me, there was every possibility that he would report back anything I said and was just waiting for me to drop myself in it. I wanted to trust him but I knew I couldn't.

I also wanted to believe that they knew I was small fry and not a terrorist or a major criminal or an enemy of the state or an agent of the USA, and that they didn't really care about me, and that as long as I was polite and didn't offend them, they'd soon let me go.

There was a public phone on the wall close to our table. They probably listened into it whenever Noberto had sat someone where he'd say me. I didn't want to use it but I didn't see too many other choices.

'Can you call someone for me?'

'Of course. Who do you want me to call?'

'Can I talk freely to you?'

He was offended.

'Of course you can. The second I saw you I knew you were not a bad man. Fucking police. Don't worry. I only translate. I don't tell them anything.'

And so I told him everything—all about the house in Guanabacoa. About Tony. About the deeds. It was like a great unburdening. I rued doing it but felt the blessed relief of confession. Then I asked him to call the house. If Yamilia answered, he was to ask for Chuchi, tell Chuchi I'd been arrested, and tell him to call Tony.

I watched him phone. Chuchi answered. Noberto spoke to him as though they'd known each other all their life. Cuba was like that. They were all in it together.

Noberto put the phone down. He'd enjoyed himself.

'Chuchi will go to Tony and tell him. He doesn't want to talk on Tony's phone. Who is Tony?'

I told him. Said I thought he had some influence, might be able to speed this up. He looked doubtful.

'I hope so, my friend. I hope so.'

We had time to spare, no sign of the inquisition. Norberto took me to his house, a spacious white villa in a row of spacious villas. I sat in his kitchen at a large hardwood dining table while he made coffee. Piles of old copies of *Granma*—the Communist Party's official newspaper—lined one wall, stacked in piles, yellowed and curling at the edges; copies too of *Le Figaro* and the *New York Times*: inflammatory stuff.

Norberto's son arrived, thirtyish and overweight; at his father's request he gave me a limp, sweaty palm to shake. He was sent to buy sugar but did not return. The house had a sad, deserted feel, I didn't sense a woman's presence, nor did I think there had been one for many years. Then the phone rang. My inquisitors were on their way. We had only waited an hour.

Ramon waited in front of the station. Two minutes later they arrived in two cars, screeching to a halt in front of us. A van pulled up behind them. Six people got out, all armed. I had the impression that they'd been disturbed from something important. A game of pool, perhaps. A dog handler released two Alsatians from the van. The men spoke to Ramon, who beckoned me over. We all walked round to the back of the station where my Jeep was parked among a row of other cars. They stood together with Ramon and Norberto. All moustached, all casually dressed, in jeans and shirts.

One of them spoke to Ramon, who spoke to Noberto, who spoke to me.

'You must reverse your Jeep to the centre of the car park.'

I reversed the Jeep and got out.

'Now open the side doors and the back door. Leave them open.'

I opened the doors.

'Now stand away from the Jeep on the other side. Don't come towards us.'

I did as I was told.

The handler let his dogs loose. They leapt enthusiastically into the Jeep and sniffed everywhere. They sniffed the tyres; one crawled underneath and sniffed there. After a couple of minutes they began to whine impatiently. I knew what they were saying. 'There's nothing here, man. We're wasting our time.'

I was fascinated by the dogs, so fascinated that I didn't notice the others. I turned to see six of them, guns drawn, straight-armed, Hollywood style, all pointing at me. I tried not to laugh, looked over at Norberto. He winked at me. The dogs were fed up. Their handler instructed them to repeat the process. They yelped in protest but went through the motions, whining all the time: 'There's nothing here. Waste of time.' They gave up, barked in unison at their handler. He spoke to the others.

'Nada.'

In a moment they holstered their guns, muttered to each other, got in their cars and sped off, leaving me, Ramon and Norberto alone in the car park. Ramon came towards me. Norberto translated.

'Mr Hilton. We owe you an apology. We have a problem with terrorism in our country. You were mistaken for someone we have been looking for.'

I stopped him, shook his hand.

'Forget it. I understand that you have to be careful. Thank you for your polite treatment. Can I go now?'

He said I could. His eyes told me that he knew I was returning to something distinctly illegal involving Cuban citizens. He didn't care, nor did the others; they had more important things to do. I couldn't believe it. They'd ignored all the peripheral stuff. I was free. Ramon smiled his contented smile and walked away. I got into my Jeep.

'Thank you, Norberto. Please take some money. I'm very grateful for all your help.'

'I don't want your money. But if you have more Benson and Hedges, I'd be happy with those. Just give me a job when you start your business. I'm glad it worked out well for you and your friend Tony. He must have some important friends.'

'Yes. I think he must.'

'But let me give you some advice. You have been lucky today, but don't underestimate people like Sanchez. He will smile at you as he locks you away. Don't forget, we learnt security from the Russians. We are not as slow as we seem. Be careful, my friend.'

I stopped at the first shop and bought a bottle of rum, my first in weeks. Driving back I smoked, drank and sang along with the music. I couldn't figure out what sort of day I'd had.

Had what had happened been lucky or unlucky? I thought about my father. Had I done the right thing? Had I shown him respect, throwing his ashes off a road bridge in Cuba? If I'd asked him, he would have settled for Upton Park, the home of his favourite football club. How should I be feeling? I didn't know. I just knew that I was happy and getting happier, that I'd had a little adventure and that he'd looked after me. That would do. I relaxed, took another swig of rum and sang along to the music.

*Què le pasa a esa mujer?*
(What's up with her?)
Song Title / Juan Almeida Bosque

# 24 Cry Out In Your Sadness

Yamilia refused to accept what happened in Matanzas. She insisted that it was a made-up story; that I'd been with José and other women. Tony spoke to her. He told her that he'd spoken to the police in Matanzas, who'd confirmed my arrest, and to some friends in security, who had speeded things up. She accused him of collaborating with us, the first time she'd been anything but polite to Tony. I offered her Noberto's phone number which she refused to call, saying that I could easily set someone up to speak to her. We waited for her to calm down but she didn't. She didn't let up at all, and dragged whoever else happened to be at home into the argument. Her repeated tantrums drove me from the house and I began meeting José in Havana, fuelling her accusations further. He re-introduced me to Aledmis, a friend of his whom I'd met before briefly.

Aledmis's flat at the top of a tenement was so neglected that it seemed to have been condemned. Five flights of dusty stairs, creaking and dangerous, took us to the attic. Concrete and plaster dust floated in the sunlight. Surprisingly, the loft was spacious and clean, partitioned off with curtains in bright greens, yellows and reds, interspersed with cushions, rescued furniture and a mattress. Some of the furniture he had made himself from offcuts. Creative plumbing and wiring allowed him to filch his water and electricity from his neighbours.

The two of them settled into a game of chess. Aledmis was polite but cool. He switched on the afternoon's baseball for me by touching two wires together. A strangely sculpted antenna, assembled from metal rods, coat hangers and wire, provided reception. The aerial barely protruded lest snoopers ask why a deserted property should require one. A DVD provided pirated films—big business in Cuba. I wondered why I'd not been up to his flat before. Perhaps he disapproved of me.

Aledmis gave about a third of his concentration to the chess while beating José several times. José, smarting from the humiliation, began to bait me about Yamilia, a familiar argument. I argued that, contrary to popular belief, she was intelligent. I didn't mean that she was well-read or intellectual in any way; she obviously wasn't: I meant that she possessed an innate wisdom, that she saw through bullshit, that she could sometimes encapsulate in Spanish, English or French, without prior thought, complex ideas and wonderful humour. But it was too fine a point to argue, here or at any time. Neither my Spanish nor Jose's English could handle it. The only person who would understand was Manolo, who hated her too much to be objective.

'Your woman is not intelligent,' said Aledmis, drawn into the conversation, with surprising force. 'She is trapped and she can't break free. You think she's without history? You're wrong. She's a prisoner of her past. The opportunities you have given her, she could have done so much. She could have learned a skill, educated herself, bettered herself, bought a house that would have been useful to you both, that you could have rented out part of. She could have learnt to drive, so many things, yet all she does is buy things and drive you crazy.'

He lay back again, conversation over and, it seemed, our company no longer required. Mabe this is why José had brought me: the hear it from a disinterested third party. As we walked back along Obispo, José was silent. He didn't need to speak; his expression spoke for him. It said, 'I told you so.'

I wouldn't let it go. 'Whatever problems she's got, whatever hold Lazaro or whoever has over her, what she really suffers from is her lack of power. She craves control and it frustrates her that she has none—frustrates her more that those who have control over her are so inept, that they use their control so badly. She's completely dependent on others. Whatever security she has is provisional—never certain, never sure.'

'You talking about yourself, Chris!' said José with a grin.

'I am. I expect her to adapt to whatever I want to do or whoever I want to see or however much I want to drink. I don't know anyone who gives her the honour she deserves. I don't. I lied to her about putting the house in her name because it gave her so much pleasure to think she now owned something. Isn't that terrible? She's left with trying to fuck the love out of me, and the more she does it, the more desperate it is. The fact is, I'm an abusive partner—just like all her previous partners have been. All she wants is respect and it's nowhere. I guess it's a woman thing. Trouble is, it makes her a pain in the backside.'

José squinted at me in surprise.

'Whoa,' he said.


Yamilia disappeared for two days and I didn't miss her. Nobody did; she had become an irritant to everybody, mocking and persistent in her indignation at my supposedly upstaging her for other women. I wondered if this was simply paranoid jealousy or whether it had to do with other pressures that she'd never shared with me. She'd also created a fresh excuse to hate José again—something else that made no sense.

In her absence, I found myself enjoying the strange peace of the house and realising how, even before this, Yamilia had put everyone on edge with her unpredictability. I began looking forward to Paul's next visit and our appointment with Rumbos. I read books, went shopping, smiled at girls in the street. I sensed a different life from the different life I thought I was happy with.

I had arranged to meet José and Celia at the Latin American Stadium for the baseball. As I was preparing to leave, Yamilia arrived in a taxi. She smiled and kissed everyone in the house, oblivious to the baffled stares.

'Where you go?' she said.

'To the baseball.'

'Who playing?'

'Industriales and Pinar del Río. I'm meeting José and Celia.'

'I come too.'

I held the taxi.

She was bright and happy at the game. We ate nuts, drank rum and enjoyed ourselves. I slipped right back into it, forgetting what had gone before. When she was happy, I was happy. When Yamilia was looking away, José shook his head, raised his eyebrows and chuckled at what he considered her performance.

'You are crazy man,' he whispered to me.

Even Celia was at ease, such was Yamilia's cheerfulness. She invited them both back to the house. We watched a movie, drank some more and stayed up talking until late.

In the morning Yamilia wanted to go to the beach. Not one of the local beaches, but the one near Matanzas, where we had spent the night. We did the same things as we'd done then but this time the atmosphere was vaguely tense and Yamilia drank too much.

As I drove home she fell asleep, her head lolling from side to side in the front seat. We took it in turns to support her head, so floppy that it seemed her neck might break. I was tired and wanted a drink or two to complete the journey. We stopped at a little roadside bar in the middle of nowhere. A surly barman gave us a bottle. Two old men sat at one of the tables. The three of us sat at another. Yamilia slept on in the Jeep. We drank and talked to the accompaniment of cicadas and the noise of passing traffic.

A door slammed. The door of the Jeep. Yamilia stood looking at us, blinking. Then she walked to the bar and ordered a beer.

'Ay, *por dios*,' said José, 'Oh, my God.'

Celia shrank as Yamilia sat down opposite me, next to José.

'You want drink more?'

'I was tired, Yamilia, and you were asleep.'

'You and your friends, you want drink more?' She turned to José. 'You want this man drink too much?'

She jerked her head at me. José said nothing. She turned to the barman, shouted something at him in Spanish. He ambled slowly to our table and put another beer in front of her. She laughed and said in English, 'Something wrong with your legs?'

He looked at her and then at me. His expression said: Are you going to do something about her?

She shouted something at the two old men. They stared back at her without expression. She looked over her shoulder at the barman, who was lazily cleaning a glass and watching her. His watching her upset her. She leapt from her chair, knocking it over, and moved to the bar. She leaned on the bar, sticking out her ass at the rest of us. She asked him questions, which I couldn't understand and which he ignored, cleaning glasses and staring at a space above her head. She answered for him, shrugging her shoulders, staring into his face. His blank eyes met mine. Are you going to do something? She gave up and walked unsteadily back to the table. She noticed the two old men again. She spread her arms. 'Ay, *viejos*. *¿Cómo están?*'

She sat back next to José, nodding slowly at me.

'Chris,' she said. 'My husband. You stop to drink more with your friend José. He is your good friend. José, the knife man.'

She thumped José on the arm.

'José. You friend of my husband. You good man, José. My husband think you are good man.'

She turned to Celia.

'You, you fuck my husband?'

She slammed her beer on the table. It frothed and spilled over her hand. Her head drooped forward and, for a moment, I thought we might be able to pick her up, carry her to the car and take her home. Then she looked up at me, eyes wild. She pushed back her chair, nearly fell over it and staggered to the old men's table. She spoke rapid fire Spanish at them, laughing at her own jokes. They stared back impassively, waiting to see what she would do next. She staggered into the next table, kicking a chair out of her way. They had metal bases and it must have hurt, but either she didn't feel it or chose not to show any pain. But she *was* showing pain. She turned and stared at our table.

'Me no crazy,' she said and, pointing shakily, '*you* crazy.'

She screamed at us. She kicked tables and chairs. She broke glasses and bottles. The barman and the two old Cubans didn't say anything. They hadn't been so entertained in ages. But they wondered why I didn't just hit her and shut her up. José wished he could but he knew he couldn't, because of me. And she knew that. She knew I wouldn't and she knew he couldn't and she screamed out her hard life and her determined enjoyment of it. She took it out on us and I let her, because I hoped she would be happy again the next day. And she knew I hoped so. And she thought I would love her despite of it. The most honest, ballsy, don't-give-a-shit person I've ever met, and she thought I would love her forever. And at that mment I did love her. I didn't care what José thought of my machismo or what the barman and the two old men thought of my ability to control my woman. I loved her more than ever. But I knew we were finished, because life cannot be lived in this way.

# 25

# Breaking Up

Many of the problems with Yamilia stemmed from *malenten-didos*, misunderstandings. In spite of our various faults, the age difference, our instability, the weight of popular opinion against her, I still think we could have made it. But misunderstandings happen. They happen often enough with people of the same nationality, from the same culture. Add the language problem, a woman of gale-force temperament and a lazy, middle-aged dreamer sliding into alcoholism, and the potential is limitless.

She stayed for a few days, quiet and subdued, the memory of her performance at the bar hanging heavy over everything. We didn't smile or laugh, couldn't smile or laugh, but skirted each other like two wary animals forced into the same cage. One night she suggested we eat at the Nacional, maybe for old times' sake, but she was sulky during the meal and I was no better. Conversation between us had dried up; we had everything and nothing to say. Still, she seemed in no hurry to leave, pouring frequent measures from our bottle.

'I want to fly,' she said.

'Fly? Fly where?'

'Fly with you, any place.'

She'd had enough of Havana, the way I'd had enough of England. She'd had enough of the battles she had to fight, the people she didn't trust, the inevitability of the days that were to follow. And she wanted me to take her away from it all. Surely if I loved her I'd do that? But I didn't want to leave Havana. And where would I take her? England? And whoever might be waiting for me when I touched down, wanting a quiet word? She waited for the answer that didn't come, drained her glass and rose to leave. The evening was over. Maybe that was when she decided to give up the struggle.

That weekend I walked into the house to find Yamilia on the patio with some girlfriends I hadn't seen before. She didn't acknowledge my presence or introduce me. We passed each other a few times as we moved around the house. She gave me a look I'd seen so many others receive: scornful, unpleasant, unwelcoming. There was nothing I could say or do, nothing she would understand. This wasn't like other times, other rows; something was ending here.

More new friends appeared at the house. She stayed away for a couple of nights. Two hundred dollars disappeared from my wallet. While she was away I spent time with Manolo. He didn't attempt to disguise his dislike for her, partly, I knew, because the feeling was mutual.

'This is the beginning,' he said. 'She is making her move. They will be here soon to take everything.'

They?

He took me to see some of his friends. One lived in a small palace with marble floors, a mix of antique and modern furniture, expensive art and a large pool. Where did money like that come from? I didn't ask. We got drunk and talked about Yamilia. The friend's wife said, 'She is losing a good man.' Right.

Manolo fed the insecurities that had never really died.

'She has been setting you up. Now she's back with Lazaro.

He wants the house. Amado wants her. They'll come for you. You have to speak to Tony. You can't deal with this alone.'

'Why have they waited so long? They could have done this at any time.'

'Because she hadn't left you. They needed her on their side. If she'd married you, then they'd have had a problem.'

'Why a problem?'

'Beause she'd have all the power. They'd be out. Now she's their toy again.'

'That doesn't make sense.'

'Why should it?' he shrugged. 'She's crazy.'


Yamilia returned one afternoon while I was watching football with José and Manolo. They got up and said goodbye. She sat in the other armchair and picked up watching the game where they'd left off. She drank a few beers. We talked a bit about nothing very much. It got late. She stood up, stretched and yawned. She stroked my neck as she passed behind my chair on her way to the bedroom. I was tired but waited until she was asleep before joining her. As I settled down she put her arm round me. I jumped at her touch, not wanting it. I got out of bed, went back to the living room, sat and lit a cigarette. After a minute she followed me and lit a cigarette too. She watched me in silence. I couldn't look at her. I looked straight ahead and finished my cigarette. Then I got up and went to a drawer and took out two diazepam. I swallowed one and offered the other to her. She looked up at me and we held each other's gaze for a few seconds, then she took the tablet from my hand and swallowed it. I let her go first. When I eventually followed, she appeared to be asleep. I got into bed and lay with my back to her.

I woke late the next day. Yamilia had gone. Maria gave me breakfast, let me finish my coffee and beckoned me to the living room. She pointed. Yamilia had taken the DVD player. Chuchi stood in the background, arms folded, nodding stupidly. I checked my wallet. There hadn't been much there but she'd taken what was there as well. I asked Tony to come over. The war had started.

When Tony arrived, he poured himself a glass of rum and lit a cigarette. He told Manolo to ask me if I agreed with his plan. José and Chuchi were there too. We had two cars, he said. We were to move all my stuff now. He suggested we take it to his other house, where I would stay. I said I wanted to go to Villa Panamericana and Rosa. It would be safer: they would not expect me to be there. It was easier for José to reach and Raúl and Lucia were neighbours. He was a little offended that I'd turned down his hospitality but said OK. Later he, Manolo and Chuchi would return to chain and padlock the house. Don't worry, Chris, he said; if they want to fight, we will fight them. It all had the feeling of a military briefing. Everybody was a little pumped up and excited.

We moved my possessions in one trip. Rosa welcomed me in with an 'I-told-you-so' look on her face. Once I was settled in, Tony, Manolo and Chuchi went off to secure the blue house, Rosa left for her alternative accommodation and José and I got to work on a bottle of Silver Dry. When we'd finished the bottle, José left too. I said he could stay but Celia was expecting him. I wanted more rum but only to knock me out; then decided against it. I trudged to the bedroom I'd shared for four months with Yamilia. It seemed ugly and desolate. I tossed and turned for an hour, then got up and tried to read. I couldn't concentrate. It was early morning in England, so I phoned Paul.

'When you arrive in three weeks you'll be staying at a different address.'

'Again? What have you been up to now?'

I told him the story.

'OK, pal: it doesn't change anything.'

But it did. It changed everything.

*If this is dying, I don't think much of it.*
Lytton Strachey (last words)

# 26

# Trouble

The blue house was locked. Chains and padlocks secured its arched doors. People were looking for me, including Yamilia, apparently. Friends stopped me and asked after her.

'*Se acabó,*' I'd say. It's over.

They'd say: 'Sorry: you were a good couple,' or 'You looked happy.' It didn't help.

Lucia set up a meeting for Yamilia and me. She wanted us back together. When I told José, he called me a fool but didn't try to stop me. Tony would have been furious, had he found out. Rosa tried to make me consider the alternatives.

'Chris, this women have bad friends. She no good for you. Forget her. Make a life for yourself. Find a nice woman. There are a thousand women here who would make you happy. Yamilia is bad news. She will pull you down. I will marry you. You will be legal. You can live here and fuck who you like.'

José was still laughing at her brazenness as we left.

'Do you think she's right? Maybe I should marry her.'

'Rosa? No!' he said, shaking his head. 'Don't believe her. You never leave her house. She lock you in!'

Lucia took me to her surgery where Yamilia was waiting.

'I know you two,' she said. 'Every time you fight, you get back together. Every time.'

She smiled and left the room. Yamilia glared at me.

'Why you close the house?

'You know why. Too much trouble.'

We went around and around.

'Where you stay?'

'I can't tell you.'

'With Tony,' she said.

'No.'

'Sí, you stay with Tony. You think he help you? You think José help you? You think they your friends?'

'José is my friend. Tony too, I think.'

'Tony,' she spat the word. She mimed someone stepping on an ant. 'He will do this to you.'

'You introduced me to him.'

'Sí. Look what he do to me. Now I'm nothing to him. He only like your money. He will take the house.'

She moved away.

'I no understand you, Chris.'

I turned to look at her.

'I good character for you. What you want?'

Her voice had changed; the challenge had gone out of it. Suddenly I just felt very, very sad.

'What I want is peace, Yamilia. Tranquillity. Calm.'

'I want too. Come to Camagüey. We can stay with my mama. Before, there, no problems.'

'No, there were no problems then.'

'Come to Camagüey. No need money there. No Tony, no José, no Havana, no trouble.'

I thought I was going to say, 'Yes, let's go,' but I didn't. I said, 'We do need money, Yamilia. You like money. I like money. I need visas. I need to phone England. Your mama's house is too small. There's no privacy. We'd have to find somewhere else. It won't work. We'd fight.'

'"We'd fight"? In Camagüey we never fight.'

'True, but I didn't come to Cuba to live in Camagüey.'

'No, you come to find perfect woman. Make business. Fuck. Drink. OK. So go to Tony. Go to José.'

She had gone as far as she was prepared to go. Further, in fact. She got up, opened the door and called Lucia. As soon as Lucia appeared, Yamilia started. The hurricane built in strength as she detailed the injustice and ridiculousness of the situation to Lucia. As she shouted Lucia looked sadly between the two of us.

'I can drop you off in Havana, Yamilia,' I suggested as a peace offering.

She looked at me scornfully,

'You think I can't get to Havana?'

She slammed the door and was gone.


A few days earlier, a Dutchman who lived in Miramar had phoned me.

'You need to be careful,' he said.

'Of what?'

'Rosa told me about you. She's a friend. You know too many things, too many people. This woman of yours, she can damage you. She's out of control. They'll use that to get at you.'

'How?'

'Believe me. In Cuba it happens.'

'What happens?'

'She only needs a piece of your hair, anything of yours.'

'Santeria? Yamilia?'

'Listen to me. I've seen it happen. That's all she needs, some hair, some clothing, anything. Don't laugh at this. She can damage you.'

'Yamilia doesn't know anything about that.'

'Yes, she does. They all do. You are well known. You have enemies. I'm telling you, take this seriously.'

He gave me his address and told me to visit him, urgently. I promised I would, to learn how to avoid being cursed or doomed or whatever. I didn't go.

The fact was, though, that the weight of opinion against Yamilia was almost unanimous. From the first moment we'd been together, José and then nearly everybody else had warned me off her. I had ignored all of them, defended her, tried to figure out what vested interests they might have that prejudiced them against her. And now we were finished. Had I been wrong to defend her? No. She was the product of a predicament that she couldn't get out of and I was sorry for her, but I also couldn't deal with her—we'd established that now—and I had other priorities. I still had most of my money, or so I thought—I never checked—and I had what seemed like a viable business plan with Paul. The car rentals in Santiago were bringing in good money; the ones that Tony was operating were bringing in a litle more. I was in good shape.

But. Cuba can be exhausting if you don't go with the flow. If you're a foreigner, alone, without fluent Spanish, it's hard. Yamilia was gone and I was tired. Tired of all of them. Tired of reading between the lines and watching my back. I couldn't find the space to think clearly. Maybe I just needed some time away. The trouble was I couldn't go near an airport. Not unless I wanted to spend a week or two in the company of the security police, while they questioned me and caught up with whatever I'd been doing in the year since I'd last seen them.


José was watching the French Open Tennis when I got back. He poured me a drink as I sat down.

'Capriati,' he said. 'Good game.'

I sat and watched, finished the rum and poured another.

'José,' I said, 'I know you don't like Yamilia. I know things would be better for you if she weren't around. Really, what do you think of her?'

'You know what I think. I think she is bad.'

We watched the tennis and finished the bottle.

'You want more?' said José.

'Not here.'

'You want to play pool?'

'I need a woman.'

He brightened. He'd been trying to fix me up with a woman —'a good woman'—since I'd come to Cuba. A woman, who would love me and look after me and not be any trouble.

'The woman I introduced to you,' he said. 'You remember?'

I didn't.

'In Chinatown. Is a good woman; she like you. All the time she ask about you. Not beautiful like Yamilia. You don't need another beautiful woman. This is a good woman.'

'I don't want a good woman tonight, José.'

He gave me a look that said, 'She's not *that* good.'

We drove to Havana in my Rentacar and parked near José's flat. He told me to wait and went off into the crowds. Ten minutes later he was back. She was with him.

'I see you tomorrow,' he said.

She got into the car. I recognised her but couldn't remember why. I asked her name. Marita. Mid-twenties, white, very pretty, in fact. I asked if she'd like to go for something to eat, a drink, maybe a club. We could go to Villa Panamericana later.

'Sí,' she said, nodding eagerly and smiling.

She settled back into the seat, her body turned towards me as I drove. She laughed happily, leaned over and put her tongue in my ear. I turned off the Malecón and into Zueleta, slowing down for the car in front. I noticed movement from the corner of my eye. A car coming from the left, leaving the tunnel roundabout. A bit fast, I thought. I turned to look. It *was* fast. I waited for it to slow down. It was bound to. It didn't. I had nowhere to go. It hit me just at the back end of the driver's door. I felt a flash of pain in my left arm before I was thrown forward and rightwards at the same time.

I remember thinking: this is a stupid way to die. I remember thinking: I wish I'd had Marita first. I remember seeing the lamppost coming towards me. I remember my face going through the windscreen and the breath going out of me as my chest hit the dashboard. I remember my right knee hitting something. I remember looking over at Marita as I was thrown back into the seat. She was sitting and watching, sheer horror on her face, but still in the same position. I remember thinking: I'm glad she's not hurt; that would be too much.

Then I remember hands on me and lying in the road with people all around. I tried to get up but I was a mixture of rubber and pain and blood. I remember one face, a man staring down at me; I watched him as I sank beneath the tarmac into a deep black sea.

I woke in a white room, a bright light in my eyes, faces peering down at me. Something had woken me: it was pain. A nurse was stitching my upper lip back together. I tried to move. A male voice shouted and hands gripped my shoulders. I looked around. There were eight of them, mostly nurses, watching me curiously.

'Buenos noches,' said a female voice.

With effort I lifted my head an inch, looked down at my body. Another voice.

'Take it easy.'

A white towel covered my middle, a tube protruded with yellow liquid draining into a bottle. Another tube taped to my arm from a bottle above the table. The nurses were pretty. I lifted my left arm a little. It felt light.

'Where's my fucking Rolex?'

Some chatter. One of the nurses jangled her wrist. Among the bracelets and bangles was the Rolex. She shook her head and laughed.

'Don't worry,' she said. 'Give you later'.

A doctor was talking to me.

'You were in an accident,' he said. 'You have been drinking.'

'I haven't.'

'Your blood result says you have.'

He held up some x-rays. '

You have cracked some ribs. Your knee and shin are damaged, and maybe your spine too. Many cuts on your face and head, the rest of your body, some scars. We need to look at your head and neck, take some more x-rays. You will have to stay here for some time. You have other injuries. Have you recently been in another accident?'

'Sort of.'

He stared at me and shook his head.

'The security police will want to talk to you.'

The nurses were cleaning me up. One picked pieces of glass from my face and forehead with tweezers, another behind me shaved my head carefully. A new face appeared. He didn't look like a doctor.

'Mr Hilton. You have had a serious accident. You have been drinking.'

'I haven't.'

'The tests say you have. Listen to me.'

I listened.

'Do you have insurance?'

'No'

'This is not a tourist hospital. Some Cuban people brought you here in their car. You will have to pay. How will you pay?'

'Do you have my wallet?'

He brought it to me. I showed him the cards.

'OK,' he said.

'We checked with the security police for your hotel. They have no record of you. Where have you been staying?

'At the Ambos Mundos.'

'The last record is eleven months ago. Where have you been since then?

'Travelling.'

'Where?'

'All over.'

'Where did you stay?'

'Many places. Please, I'm tired. I can't remember.'

'OK, but the security police will want to see you.'

'How is the girl?'

'What girl?'

'The one who helped me from the car.'

'No, Mr Hilton. The girl was in the car.'

He studied me for a few moments, decided to let it go.

'Is my cellular here?' I said.

'Yes.'

'Can you call someone for me?'

'What is the number?'

I showed him, told him what to say.

Twenty minutes later she was there. She was furious.

'Who you with?' she said.

'Nobody. I was alone.'

'You? Alone in Havana? Me no stupid.'

She looked me over, saw the tube, lifted the sheet and smiled.

'*Se ha encogido*,' she said. It's shrunk.

She walked away and spoke with one of the nurses, demanding information like a ward sister. Back at the bedside she studied my face.

'Señor Frankenstein.'

The nurse behind me said that I needed more stitches. Yamilia went round to watch. The nurse sprayed something on my head and I yelled and nearly leapt from the table. Then I felt the pain in all the other places. Everywhere. The nurse who was wearing my Rolex brought a syringe, spoke to me gently in Spanish as she wiped my arm and pushed it in. I slipped beneath the black sea again.

I opened my eyes to more pain. It was dark. I tried to move my head but I couldn't lift it or turn to see where I was. I could hear light snoring, somebody moaning in their sleep, a woman. Street voices and music floated up from somewhere.

That was no clue. Havana never slept. I tried to remember. The doctor said something about my neck but I wanted to move, see where I was. I closed my eyes, braced myself, lifted and turned my head. I yelled with the pain. José stirred in the chair by the bed. The noise had woken him. He smiled sleepily.

'You OK?' he said.

'I'm alive.'

'You look terrible. Your face, she is cut to pieces.'

'I know. Yamilia said I look like Frankenstein.'

'Yamilia was here?'

'I called her.'

'Why?'

'I don't know.'

'I do. You are crazy man.'

He said Tony had been, looked me over, established that my injuries were 'superficial' and gone off to deal with Rentacar.

José got me a private room and brought in some cigarettes and rum. Yamilia appeared once more with some food and then disappeared, not to return. Apart from occasional checks from the bad-tempered doctor and nurses peeping in, we were left alone. On the third night José brought Celia.

'You stink,' she said, and took me into the bathroom where she helped me to wash.

As we drank and smoked and talked, my pain eased,

'Let's get out of here,' I said.

'Do they know where you're staying?'

'I don't think so.'

With a white gown over my bloody, torn clothes, I hobbled to a waiting taxi and we went home.

# 27

# Payback

I hardly moved for two weeks, mostly lying on my back while my ribs healed. I read, watched TV, allowed Rosa to fuss around me and Lucia to remove my stitches. I managed to get outside once but was put off by everyone staring at me—my face, a mass of scabs. I had been lucky though; in time the facial cuts healed. It was the top of my head that took the main impact and beneath my hair there remains a mass of scars and dents. If I ever go bald, my head will frighten small children.

'Look,' said José, 'they park here when we come to Havana. From here they can see you waiting, see Marita come. You drive to here—he pointed to the junction—here you always wait. They have 100 metres to make some speed, and then bang, they hit you from the side.'

I was never convinced of this. If Lazaro and Amado wanted me dead, there had to be easier ways. Why would they risk injury to themselves? Even Amado wasn't that stupid. I didn't like paying for the damage to the other car. But I got away with the damage to the hire car, which was a write-off: Tony had seen to that. And I had been drinking. I wasn't drunk, but that wasn't important; by being over the limit I had put myself in the wrong, despite the fault being with the other driver. The police and security forces were involved and they wanted a score on their charge book. If they didn't get it, I would be escorted to the airport, at best.

Tony chaired the meeting with the police at Rosa's flat; he told them I wasn't yet fit enough to visit the police station. The police had been to Rentacar, who told them where I lived. Tony told Manolo to tell me to keep quiet—that he would conduct negotiations.

Rosa stood in the kitchen doorway, arms folded, surveying the whole bunch with disdain. The police tried to conduct the meeting with an appropriate gravity but Rosa was smart. She had spread the table liberally with beer, rum and snacks and despite their attempts at official disapproval, something of a party atmosphere slowly developed. Rosa, already popular, kept this going with good-natured cajoling. Tony tried to keep matters on a more serious level, purely business, but even he could see that perhaps her approach wasn't a bad idea. I did as I was told and kept my mouth shut. I was referred to, pointed at, argued over, accused and defended. Rosa finally addressed me directly.

'Chris, drinking is good while you drink but it is doing you harm. Especially you. The next day you are not yourself. Your health has been bad. Drink is no good for you. Drink is no good for anybody.'

'Everybody knows that,' I said, 'but not many people do anything about it.'

The room was silent while they waited for a translation and then, apparently because this was the funniest thing they'd ever heard, the entire room erupted in laughter, regarding me as if I was some mischievous little boy who'd just said something cute. Final attempts at officiousness evaporated. The police left when the drink and food was finished. They didn't take me with them.

They had agreed on a price. The car owners wanted $5,000. They got $2,000. The traffic police got something, and the security police, and the tourist police and everyone present.

The people who had taken me to the hospital didn't ask for anything but I gave them something anyway, and the guy at Rentacar got something too because I felt sorry for him. The hospital charged me $1,200, which I didn't begrudge. There had been a lot of x-rays and tests and I'd had a lot of free help in the past. In total, Tony needed $6,000 to secure my freedom. I didn't have it but I could get him $800 a day from ATMs. I told Tony he'd have it in a few days. Don't worry, Tony. Todo control.

Later, José produced an x-ray. He said it was of Marita's thigh. It showed a clean break, the pieces of bone touching with the joins an inch apart. She was OK, he said, but her family—who knows? Perhaps a thousand dollars would quash any litigious tendencies.

'José,' I said, 'She phoned me. She's fine. She asked me how I was and suggested we try again, by taxi this time.'

Although he was suitably sheepish, I was a little disappointed. This was by far the worst scam he'd ever tried on me that I was aware of. And why now? Did he think I was on the way out, so what the hell? Whatever, it removed any residual guilt about the blow job from Celia while he slept in the back of my car.

*Living with lust is like living shackled to a lunatic.*
Socrates

# 28

# The Bad Woman

I celebrated my recovery by going often to the Villa Panamericana Hotel and playing pool. I would play for money, a few dollars a game. I would play for hours there because I enjoyed it. I was pretty good and my play improved with alcohol—up to a point. Before I reached that point I usually won, beating all-comers and racking up some bucks. But once people got to know me, some of them hung around, waiting until I had passed my tipping point. Then I tended to lose.

There was a woman in white who played a good game. We played a couple of times and then she offered to play me for five dollars and first to three. She smiled constantly: that's one of the few things I remember. I also remember the struggle I had to beat her, and the playful grin when she handed over my money—her ballsy, don't-care attitude. Maybe she reminded me of Yamilia, I can't remember, but I had to have her. And she seemed amenable.

She spoke no English and merely smiled at whatever I said in Spanish. About ten of us had been playing. On seeing my intentions they warned me, one by one.

'Is very bad woman.'

And then, 'is lesbian,' which was apparently much worse.

Making no headway with me, one of them fetched Dayan, a

friend and a professional dancer. He was well-travelled, highly intelligent and spoke fluent English and French.

'Chris, seriously, I have to advise you against this. This is a woman with a very bad reputation.'

He didn't add that she was a lesbian. I suppose being well-travelled and highly intelligent, he was sophisticated enough to consider it unimportant.

'What can she do to me?' I said. I couldn't see the problem.

'It's your decision, mate,' said Dayan, patting my shoulder. 'Nobody here will force you to change your mind. But think again.'

I did think again. I remember thinking that if she was a lesbian, I'd need to get enough rum into her to get myself into her. And that's about all I remember.

I listened to José as he spoke into my cellular phone, patiently explaining in reasonable terms to Tony that my credit cards had all gone and that I wouldn't be able to make today's meeting. There was a pause while Tony digested the news. He was obviously nervous. He had nominated José as my legal guardian—and this thing had happened. He must have asked where the cards had gone because I heard José reply, quite openly and honestly, that I had insisted on sleeping with a lesbian the previous night, despite many warnings not to, and that, unusually for me, I had fallen asleep straight afterwards and could not remember anything when I woke up.

There was a brief pause, José flinched and held the phone away from his face. I could hear Tony shouting from the other side of the room. When the shouting died down, José told Tony not to worry. I had cancelled my cards and new ones were on the way. She hadn't been able to access any cash, not knowing my pin numbers, and had only had time to spend a hundred dollars on shopping before the cards became unusable. He would have his money shortly. Tony's answer was apparently brief and to the point.

'What shall we do?' said José.

I had no idea. I was still hung over and trying to take it in. I had a few hundred dollars in cash. She hadn't bothered with that, nor my watch, nor anything else, which was strange. Perhaps she had left in a hurry. Perhaps I had woken up and disturbed her. I thought not. I'd clearly been unconscious and she wasn't the worrying kind.

'Woman like that, she should leave alone,' said José.

I knew that now.


Tony got money I owed him two weeks later after the new cards arrived. He asked again if I would move to his house, where he thought there'd be less scope for trouble. I refused. A few days later Yamilia called my cell phone. She wanted me to meet Lazaro.

'Why?'

'We want speak with you.'

We.

'He want your house,' said José when I told him. 'He think Yamilia own the house but she don't. They try to take it, now he want "negotiate". Don't meet them. He try to frighten you. You both use violence: you on Amado, Amado on you. Is not good you meet.'

'I can't give him the house. I don't own it either. It's in Tony's name.'

'But you have the authority. Tony protects the house for you.'

'So they can't threaten me. It's Tony they need to talk to.'

'Chris, they can talk Tony any time.'

'They can? How?'

'He is brother of Lazaro wife.'

'What?'

'They have very bad relationship. Is *una enemistad*. A feud. Lazaro rape Tony's sister, *hace muchos años*—many years ago. Tony force him to marry her. Now he keep her like prisoner in his apartment. Is very bad blood.'

'Fascinating. I want to meet him,' I said.

'Why? Is dangerous.'

'I've met him once before. He's caused me so much trouble. I want to face him down.'

'Don't do it.'

We spoke to Tony. For the first time I think he doubted my sanity. Acknowledging my own culpability, I said that without the interference of Lazaro and Amado, life could probably have worked out differently and for the better. I didn't want to fight him, just show him that I wasn't going to run away.

'Life can work out differently,' said Tony. 'You can still do everything you want, just not with Yamilia and her *camarilla*— her clique—and not here. They're desperados. They're reckless. They have no reserve. Lazaro is dangerous. He's using Yamilia to reach you. Do not let her work on your feelings. She will, if you let her. She's a woman of the street. She protects herself the only way she can. She cannot put your interests above hers.'

'You only saw the bad side of her,' I said. 'Sure, she could be wild, but do you think I was easy to live with? She hoped I would make her happy but she never felt safe. In the end, she was torn. Who would be better for her: me or them? They are nasty people but they were her only security before she met me. I accept that it's finished, but I want the best for her. She deserves it. I want to meet him.'

They stared at me. 'You have no idea,' said Tony.

'Don't meet anywhere they suggest,' said José, when it became obvious I wasn't going to change my mind. 'Meet them in a place of your choice. Old Havana, somewhere public, somewhere unexpected. Do not agree to anything and do not let them take you anywhere. Chris, it will be like meeting the mob.'

'You must take José for translation,' Tony insisted.

'No. I want Yamilia to translate.'

We met at seven in Cathedral Square, full of light and

tourists. There were just the three of them: Lazaro with Amado beside him and Yamilia slightly behind. I watched as they come closer, the father powerful and authoritative, Amado expressionless, Yamilia dwarfed and prim. They came to my table, waited stiffly for me to invite them to sit and then took their seats. Lazaro refused my offer of drinks.

'This woman is like a daughter to me,' he said in Spanish.

'That's why she was beaten up in the street,' I said in English.

Yamilia repeated the sentence in Spanish. Amado glared at me as if already preparing for a fight but Lazaro rested a hand on his arm and smiled the same thin smile I remembered from the night at his house—Magic Night. Then, with a helpless shrug, he turned abruptly from the others and pulled his chair closer to mine. He leaned forward, as though he wanted to take my hands in his, then placed them on his knees instead. His grey eyes seemed unnaturally pale, filled with anger despite his tolerant smile.

'Listen to me,' he said in Spanish, rejecting translation. 'You are rich. She is not. You don't need this house. You can buy another house.' He touched Yamilia's arm. She flinched. 'Give her the house. Buy a house somewhere else.'

'Is this what you want?' I said to Yamilia.

'Sí, Chris.'

'But you know the house belongs to Tony. I'm not in residence anymore.'

'But your name is on the documents,' Lazaro hissed.

'Tony—tu cuñado—can fix that. I'm not your problem. You're your problem. Your family is your problem. You have a lot to sort out. Don't let your household rubbish spill out on the street.'

I glanced at Yamilia briefly as she turned, nervously, and translated. His shoulders twitched and he looked at the floor. His breath came noisily as he rubbed his hands together.

'Will you stay in Havana?'

'Yes.'

'Then give us the house.'

'No.'

The metal chair screeched against the cobblestones as he pushed it back with his legs.

'Vamos,' he said to Yamilia and Amado.

I watched them walk across the square and disappear down a crowded street. None of them looked back. As they went, it occurred to me that beyond posturing, I'd achieved nothing except to establish that I was going to be unhelpful. That was not a good result.

*All history is sex and violence.*
Ian Fleming

# 29

# Jared

With Yamilia gone I began to spend time with Celia, especially when José wandered Havana in search of business. She was easy company and wanted nothing from me, often visiting the flat. One day we were due to meet José after she'd been to see Lucia in her surgery. José was not alone when we arrived at the Ambos Mundos.

'This is Jared,' he said, introducing me to a short, slightly overweight tourist. 'He is from Jordan.'

Jared had small, black, close-together eyes. He looked past me at Celia and kissed her on her cheek, too enthusiastically, which made her wince, then kept his gaze on her in a way that made us all uncomfortable.

When I came back with drinks, Jared accepted his without a thank-you glance and kept ogling Celia's breasts. She had a hair and manicure appointment later and was wearing old jeans and a T-shirt. She turned away from him and José, perhaps to avoid a scene, wound up their business. Another scrap of paper, another name, another number for his collection.

'He fuck me with his eyes,' said Celia.

Not in a pleasant way either, I gathered. Celia and José had a quick exchange about the quality of his company. I caught the word vulgar.

'What's your business with him?' I said.

'Not much. He want to buy something. I give him name.'

Celia left, saying she would be three hours. Hair and manicure appointments were social occasions too.

'Three hours English time?' I said when she'd gone.

'No.'

'Three hours Cuban time? That's seven hours?'

'About that,' he said.

We each made some calls and José gave me my takings for the last week, a little short as always. As long as it stayed at a little, I ignored it and he was smart enough to understand. We spent the afternoon at a rooftop bar, shaded, in a strong breeze, chatting and watching the ferries chugging back and forth across the harbour.

José told me a story of the ferry. On one occasion some passengers hijacked it and took it to Florida, including those who didn't want to go. Most of the passengers returned to Cuba. Now the ferries were only allowed enough fuel for a single crossing to prevent it happening again.

Celia returned eight hours later, her nails shiny and black. She was still angry about Jared.

'You want me to fight him in the hotel, Celia? Forget it.'

She wasn't impressed and played footsie with me under the table. José tried again.

'It's just business, Celia. He not my friend.'

Business or not, Jared was dead within the month.

# 30

# A Trip To The Bank

The ATMs in Havana were out of cash. At a bank I asked for five hundred dollars. The cashier, a brunette with a sinful smile, slowly counted out my twenties, licking her fingers before peeling off each note, holding my eyes with a gifted twinkle. I walked to the Ambos Mundos, ordered rum and settled down by the window to read my book.

I must have had a busy night because I woke in a room at the Hotel Florida near the port. I didn't have much money left so I returned to the same bank. The same cashier greeted me, and raised her perfectly sculpted eyebrows as I asked for a further five hundred dollars.

'*Por esta noche?*' she said. For tonight?

'Sí.'

Can I come?'

'OK.'

The eyebrows relaxed, the eyes shone, the smile, promising much, widened.

*Nobody knows anything.*
William Goldman

# 31

# Paul Again

Paul arrived for our appointment with Rumbos. He was more relaxed this time, more open to Cuba, less irritable. We had probably evened out at similar levels of alcoholism and clashed less than before. Rosa eyed him with mistrust, convinced that my drawn-out fall from grace was all his fault. It wasn't, of course, but she could no longer blame Yamilia. Tony enjoyed Paul's company, while mistrusting anybody who drank so much. Paul had arrived as a drunk; I had contrived a slower descent and many people still saw in me the bright-eyed hope of the previous year.

The meeting with Rumbos was for the following week. Paul said he had now got the ABTA licence and was well on his way to recruiting customers. He favoured City of London investors as likely takers of our Cuban experience. Encouraged by José, he also dared himself to approach a Cuban woman at a bar. Afterwards, we asked him how it went.

'She offered me $5,000 dollars to take her out of the country,' he said. 'I sense a business opportunity!'

'Let's bring people in before we start shipping them out,' I said.

We made our plans and once we'd reached a certain hour in the evening and a certain level in our intoxication, we'd persuaded ourselves completely of our Rumbos plans. We drew up lists of prospective employees: I set their wage levels, Paul cut them back. He also crossed out most of the women I added to the tally.

'With men we can expect a low level of embezzlement and allow for it,' he said. 'But women cause chaos.'

I told him that was sexist.

'So enlighten me about your smooth, rewarding relationship with Yamilia and all the success it brought you.'

'That's not fair,' I objected.

'Really? How much money have you got left?' he said.

I told him I'd been living on my income and not spending too much. 'I got through about $50,000 in the first few months but it's settled down since then.'

'It might be an idea to check.'

'No. Facts are unlucky. Anyway, we'll all be rich soon.'

'And Cubacell? You made rather a lot of early-morning calls. And not just to me, I gather.'

'Not that many. Not a problem.'

'Sure you remember them all?'

I had been sleeping badly and started using diazepam to help me drop off, then found I was using it to deal with anything uncomfortable, which extended to getting up in the morning. It added to a general sense of unreality and disassociation and a continuing stubborn refusal to review my finances. I began to drive around alone, finding different bars, talking to strangers, wanting something to happen—trying to make something happen. Paul stuck to the big hotels, with José as a guide; withut a chaperone; he could get lost in his own house.

José called me; Paul got panicky if I was away too long. They were having a late drink; did I care to join them? I left the bar I was at and drove to meet them. They were at the Habana Libre, the airy lobby of which was full of men with young women at their sides. At the far end, a group of women and girls sat together, nursing single drinks, hoping to attract interest.

Paul and José sat by a window, giving them a clear view of the entire entrance area and the elevators and overhanging walkway—all the comings and goings of the hotel. This was Paul's favourite pastime, people-watching, especially dodgy-people-watching, speculating on the nature of desire and the corruption that surrounded us. Whenever I went there I felt that, despite the large numbers of tourists and the shopping precinct, the hotel couldn't shake off its historic air of criminality and rebellion.

'This is more like it,' said Paul. 'Why didn't you bring me here before?' Corrupt to the core, this was his world.

In the centre of the lobby, by the circular bar, sat a group of six men, each accompanied by young Cuban hostesses sitting decorously and demurely beside them. The men spoke loudly, in English, of television and films, of producers and fixers, of money and of deals, too arrogant to keep their voices down. They name-dropped, laughed loudly at each other's jokes, and ignored their female companions.

I recognised one of the faces from TV. He leaned forwards, a big man, emphasising his words with expansive sweeps of his hands, garnering laughs from the others. The young woman next to him was black and pretty, and seemed to possess more energy than the other escorts. She wanted to say something and kept repeating a phrase, but her partner merely talked over her, which only made her more insistent. The other girls lowered their heads in embarrassment; the men became silent, no longer laughing on cue. A fug of tension, tangible as the clouds of their cigarette smoke, hung over the table.

Paul and José watched the scene, as the girl began to tug at the man's sleeve.

'Don't do that, love,' muttered Paul to himself. 'Not a good idea.'

The black girl continued to tug, oblivious of the

atmosphere that had built up. Finally, without looking at her or interrupting the flow of his conversation, the man backhanded her across the face. She looked around her, wide-eyed, aware for the first time of the stares and the other girls' lowered heads. A trickle of blood ran from the corner of her mouth. She said nothing after that, lowering her head and fumbling in her bag for a tissue, which she held to her mouth to keep the blood from her clothes.

I imagined what might happen if the men found themselves alone, without hotel security or police or money to protect them, and came across José and his friends. I didn't think their self-adulation would last long; at least, I hoped it wouldn't.

We met Tony at his house the next day, so he could brief us ahead of our meeting with Rumbos. We sat quietly as Manolo translated his more complicated instructions. Tony seemed encouraged by our silence, taking it as a token of our concentration.

'*Todo control*,' said Tony smiling, as we walked to the taxi.

I gave him the thumbs up.

'*Todo control*, Tony.'

I wasn't in a good way. I had swallowed two diazepam washed down with rum before leaving my flat, but at least I could operate. Paul was a walking corpse, white-faced and red-eyed, and clung to my laptop like a lifebelt.

The taxi dropped us off at Rumbos, where we were shown into a large office. Alicia, a pretty, smiley woman of around thirty, introduced herself. She was very pleased to meet us and said she would do her best to help us with our ambitions. We told her we were pleased to meet her too and would be honoured to receive her help.

She had a pile of brochures and documents on her desk and, while she talked, I tried to listen while Paul tapped at the keyboard, his hands shaking behind the screen. Welcoming and cheerful, Alicia glanced at him occasionally but focused more on me, treating him more as the financial man, the silent type, the one who was timid with people but good with figures. I looked down at what he was typing and saw that the screen on his laptop had gone blank. He continued to tap away, though, refusing to meet my eyes. Alicia continued unperturbed, smiling and chirpy, fastidiously explaining every detail to me, perhaps thinking that all English businessmen were like this: remote and weird.

I listened but heard nothing. The angel on my right shoulder said: This is fantastic and easily possible; you'll walk out of here millionaires. The devil on my left should said: You had diazepam and rum for breakfast. Your partner is incapable of speech. This is going nowhere.

At one point I became aware of her telling me that this was a great opportunity. Rumbos would do most of the work if we supplied the tourists. There was money to be made for us. Fifty-fifty with Fidel, of course, and unlimited scope for the future. I concentrated on her cleavage; it felt like the only way to stay sane.

Eventually we got up to leave, apparently with Alicia's blessings. I had an armful of documents. Alicia called us a taxi. As it drove off, I turned to Paul.

'What do you think you were doing?' I said.

'I was trying to find the inspiration that I wasn't getting from you.'

'Typing at a blank screen? Were you mad?'

'I was hiding from your magnificent negotiating skills.'

'I think I held up pretty well.'

'You spent the meeting staring at her tits.'

'It was preferable to staring at your shaking hands.'

'I think we need to stop at a bar.'

'So you can erase all memory of your performance?'

'Todo control?'

'Oh, you remember Tony's words, do you? Yes, todo control.'

In the bar, Paul had a meltdown.

'This is pointless,' he said.

'It can work,' I insisted. 'We just need a plan of action.'

'I don't want it to work. I hate this fucking country. I don't want to work here. I don't want to work, full-stop.'

'You don't have to work here. I'll do that. You just find the punters.'

José joined us.

'I have to call Tony,' he said. 'What happened?'

Paul snorted.

'Tell him it went well,' I said. 'Tell him Paul will set everything up in London and then we'll meet them again to confirm everything.'

'True?' he asked Paul.

'No,' Paul replied. 'Cuba is impossible. Nothing works here. You can't get anything done here. I hate it. I hate the people. I hate the food. I hate the music.'

'You like the rum.'

'I can buy that in Oddbins.'

'Maybe it will grow on you.'

'Fuck off.'

We took another taxi, this time to the Ambos Mundos. With a fresh splash of rum, Paul began to reconsider. I went to the bar for drinks. Next to me was an American, doing the same.

He said he was a baseball coach and visited Cuba regularly, arranging games between American and Cuban kids.

'They let you do that?'

'By invitation of the Cuban government, yeah, I'm allowed. I work for a charity. I spend three or four months of the year here. You on vacation?'

'I live here.'

'You live here? That must take some arranging. You got real estate here?'

'A house in Guanabacoa.'

'Guanabacoa, where's that?'

'A few miles, just the other side of the harbour.'

'I'm Rob,' he said and extended a hand.

He was about my age, short, in a too-tight shirt that hugged his paunch, and sported a black, untidy moustache on his round, red face. At his table, a woman, black, sleek, expensive and bored, sat gazing through the window. With her sat his government minder, slick, well-dressed, menacing and attentive. Rob stayed chatting at the bar with me, not hurrying to get back.

'I'm looking to buy a house here. Need a base. Save on renting. You interested in selling?'

'Maybe.'

I described the house and he asked if he could look it over.

I guessed that Tony would help with the conveyancing, if there was money to be made, so I asked the American when he'd like to visit.

'Soon as,' he said. 'Tomorrow good for you?'

'We can do that.'

I drove Paul and José straight to Tony's. He wasn't enthusiastic but his appetite for a profit won through. He'd open up the house tomorrow. Tony, Manolo and I would wait at the house while Paul and José went to fetch Rob in a taxi.

I arrived the next day with Tony. The blue house, which Tony had padlocked and chained and which I hadn't seen in six months, was clean and tidy. The furniture I'd bought with Yamilia was still there. It all looked the same.

I'd had some rum and diazepam before leaving home, and asked María for another rum at the house. She served me morosely.

'Slowly, Chris,' said Tony.

'No problem.'

'And how is the she-devil?' said Manolo.

'You're so funny, Manolo: you should be a comedian. Oh— you are.'

Chuchi arrived and exchanged brief words with Tony. He was angry about something. Then he left hurriedly.

'Problem, Tony?'

He shook his head. Manolo said nothing.

Paul and José arrived in a mini-bus taxi. Rob had brought his entire entourage. I sat them down in the large entrance hall and offered them rum, beer and coffee. They turned everything down. Rob looked uncomfortable. His minder stood impassively by the door. He spoke only to Rob, occasionally coming forwards to whisper in his ear and then stepping back. He made no eye contact with anyone else. The woman looked around her in undisguised disdain. The body language wasn't good.

Tony had asked that he should do the haggling, with Manolo's help. We were going to pitch for $15,000 and accept $12,000.

José beckoned me to the kitchen.

'The tunnel was closed,' he said.

The tunnel under the harbour was the quick way from Havana to Guanabacoa and, on a good day, made this a twenty-minute drive. This morning, the taxi had been forced to go the slow way, in heavy traffic, and it had taken forty-five minutes.

'And Paul never stop talking,' José said. 'He talk too much.'

Back in the lobby things were not going well.

'It's too far out,' said Rob. 'I need somewhere with quicker access.'

Would a better price tempt him? If I threw in the furniture? He didn't say no outright.

We were still discussing terms when Chuchi returned with a local CDR guy, who directed a tirade at Tony. While Tony tried to play it down, Chuchi stood to one side, smiling horribly and nodding at everything his new friend said. The

CDR guy ended with a flourish and the two of them left.

The situation was obviously irretrievable.

'Well, I'm outa here,' said Rob, and he and his entourage were gone.

'*Mi otra casa*.' said Tony. '*Ahora*.' My other house. Now.

They locked up the house again and I drove with José, Paul and Manolo.

'That went well,' said Manolo.


At Tony's house, I shared a bottle of rum with the others. Even Tony joined in, and puffed at a cigarette too.

'That was not clever,' said Manolo. 'Your moves lately, Chris, they are not clever.'

'He was never going to buy it,' I said. 'Tony, is there a problem with the CDR?'

He dismissed the idea with a wave of his hand, as though shaking off an insect. His drinking and smoking, though, said something else.

'Chris,' said Tony in his biggest voice, and spoke to Manolo, asking him to translate. 'Your drinking is a problem.'

'My drinking is a problem?'

'This is not the way to run a business. Too much rum and too many women and too many pills. You're going to drive yourself crazy. If you want to make a go of things, it has to stop.'

I glared at José. He shrugged.

'You need to leave Rosa's place. Live here. Pay minimum rent. I'll keep an eye on you. We can work together and make sure that our plans—your plans—succeed.'

'I like it at Rosa's.'

'Of course you like it at Rosa's,' he shouted. Tony had never shouted at me before. 'So do the hospitals and the doctors and the nurses and the police and the security cops and the Rentacar people and the insurance companies and every *chica* in Havana! Your life is making trouble for me. It can't go on.

You want my help? You stay here and you only drink beer. No more rum.'

'I don't like beer.'

'Then drink mojitos. No more straight rum. And stop the diazepam: you don't need it. José, don't give him any more. You're his friend. Keep him out of trouble or don't come back to this house.'

José nodded. Paul giggled.

'Fuck off.'

'And find yourself a good woman. I know you suffered when Yamilia left but you're through that now. Find a good *chica* who won't be any trouble.'

'No more she-devils,' said Manolo.

'You can shut the fuck up, Mr Happy.'

'*Que?*' said Tony.

José translated. Tony laughed, stood up and ruffled my hair. He ignored Manolo and used José to translate.

'Chris, Chris. It's OK. I'm on your side. But you have to slow down. At Rentacar you have a reputation: they say you've got more lives than a cat. You've used up enough already: don't use up any more, please.'

He laughed and asked for more rum and cigarettes. I agreed to the conditions, except for leaving Rosa. Everyone sat around drinking, chatting and smiling. Except Manolo, who didn't smile at all. He was silent, staring at me with bare hatred.

*If we knew the truth about each other we could take no one seriously.*
*There isn't one among us who could afford to be caught.*
*That's all life is. Trying not to be caught out.*
Willie Donaldson

# 32

# José Goes To Prison

I slowed down. When Paul went back to London I gave him a list of books to buy for me and when they arrived in Havana, I spent my days at the pool, reading. Anxious not to lose me to Tony, Rosa spoiled me. She cooked in the evenings and made us weak mojitos and we watched DVDs. Lucia started bringing her family again and life began to feel the way it had when I'd first come to Cuba. Only Yamilia was missing. I knew she stayed in touch with Lucia, who, as one of the few people who thought we were good for each other, tried to set up another meeting. I said no, but I thought about her all the time.

Celia called my cellular phone.

'Is José. The police take him.'

'Why?'

'I no know. They come for him today.'

I took a taxi to José's flat. I'd never been there before, which was strange. It was very small but was all his. Most Cubans live with several family members. To live alone takes effort and resources. His clothes hung on a wooden stand-alone rail. I recognised some of the stuff I'd given to him.

'First we need to find out where he is,' I said.

It took a full day of phone-calls. José had been arrested with over twenty others in a massive swoop. He was in prison, and no, we couldn't visit.

We still had no idea what he was supposed to have done. I didn't want to ask Tony for help at the moment—he was still getting an income from my cars but, other than that, I wasn't pleasing him very much these days—so I went to the British Embassy. I don't know what I thought the Queen's representative in Havana could do but the embassy staff spoke English, which made them seem like a welcome port in a storm.

They received me with icy politeness. The situation, whatever it was, was not something they wanted to get involved with. The fact that I was even associated with people arrested in a police raid made me on the way to being *persona non grata*. The Cuban authorities could do as they wished with their own people; what the embassy didn't want was my getting dragged into it and dragging them into it after me. I left with a stark warning from the secretary to the British Consul that was only barely diplomatic. 'Watch yourself,' I was told. 'Do you seriously think you're immune? Hang around with these people and you'll be rounded up too—and we won't lift a finger to help you. Have you got it?'

Reluctantly, I went with Celia to a police station. They asked me, but not her, to leave. I waited for two hours.

In the taxi, afterwards, she spoke in a flat monotone.

'The Jordanian, he dead. Some people kill him and they hide his body under their patio. José's phone number, it was in his wallet. All the contacts of that horrible man, they arrest.'

She hadn't liked Jared alive; she didn't like him any better for being dead.

'Three people, they strangle and kill him. The American cut him here.'

She drew a line across her throat.

'The American? Which American?'

'Andy,' she said.

A marked patrol car trailed us openly until we got to the flat. When Celia got out of the taxi, I asked the driver to take me to the Inglaterra, where I sat on the terrace, nursing a drink until the police got bored and drove away. Then I walked back to the flat.

She repeated what she knew in a voice, dull with shock: the death of a man, an idiot abroad, who played at being a gangster and had the bad luck to run into Andy and José; shocked too at José's having had the bad luck to run into both of them. She struggled to speak as the repercussions for José began to sink in. I poured her a drink. I thought for a moment she was going to refuse. In fact, she finished it in two gulps and asked for another.

'Can we see him?'

She shook her head. 'Impossible.'

We went to see Tony.

On the Malecón, a pelican, blown ashore and lumbering desperately to get airborne, flew directly at our taxi as it waited at a traffic light. Two boys chased it, making grabs for its legs, as it tried in dreamy slow motion to escape. Finally gaining some momentum its feet brushed our windscreen as it rose, and in leaping for it, the boys landed on our bonnet, giggling at us through the windscreen. We laughed back at them. Two policemen were standing at the crossroads. They were laughing too.

Tony went berserk, Manolo translating as he shouted at me in Spanish. The police's net of inquiry would spread out and José's arrest would hurt him. He didn't want them poking around. He didn't want to be involved. 'They'll take an interest in you too. Even more interest. You're a foreigner. You've got to break with your friends. With all of them. Especially this one. He's not worth it. He's a gofer. He's unreliable. He's stupid.'

'But he's a friend, Tony. And a business contact.'

'A friend?' Tony jabbed me in the chest. 'His trick with the x-rays was the work of a friend?'

Celia didn't know about the x-rays and asked me to explain. She shook her head. Tony seemed to notice her for the first time.

'Ay, *chica*,' he said.

He sat down next to her. In his soothing baritone he repeated to her what he'd just shouted at me.

'Ay, *chica*.'

'Her name is Celia,' I said.

'Celia,' he repeated sadly. He stood up and put a hand on her shoulder, shaking his head.

I told Manolo to translate my words exactly.

'The first time I met you, Tony, I gave you $100. As a gesture of faith. Every time we went for meals with you, for pleasure or business, they charged me tourist prices and you took half the bill as your cut. When your sister Loli helped with Rumbos and advice about the business, I gave her $500 and you took a cut. You're making at least $200 a week from the cars I bought and I'm hardly seeing any of it. The wardrobe you sold me wasn't worth even half what I paid you. Everything I do you take a percentage of.'

Tony fixed me with his pale green eyes, hands on his knees. Celia tried to disappear. Manolo tilted his chin at me: You through yet? I wasn't.

'You took your cut from the house, from the police, from Rentacar. And the $15 rent you charged me each day when I was here with Yamilia? Behind my back you gave her $5 of it, without telling me. You were overcharging me to pay her. Why would you do that?'

'She insisted,' he said.

'Why would you agree? You didn't even like her.'

'He hated her,' said Manolo.

'You're telling me that José, my friend, is a danger because I don't know what he's up to and who his friends are and that he's on the take?' I said, ignoring Manolo. 'You're a friend too —and you're on the take and I don't know what you're up to or

- 238 -

who your friends are. Who isn't on the take? José is where he is because he gave his phone number to the wrong person. That's all it is. I know you don't like him, but he doesn't deserve this and we're going to get him out. I'll pay but you have to use your contacts. Just tell me what it costs.'

Manolo started to speak but Tony hushed him impatiently.

'I will talk to some people,' he said, 'and see if I can find out what's happening.'

'It's not just money this time,' said Manolo.

'Don't speak,' said Tony, making a zipping motion across his mouth.

'It's José who has to keep his mouth shut, not me' said Manolo. 'They'll want him to admit something so they can exploit it. That's how they get their power. That's what makes him a danger to us.'

'And *chica*—Celia,' said Tony, ignoring Manolo and nodding at me. 'Keep him from trouble. Please.'

In the taxi Celia breathed a long sigh. José would not be around for a while and that was that. Freed from uncertainty, Celia quickly adapted to the new reality if my presence.

We had a few drinks at the flat and, for a change of scene, went to see Salome at the Havana Theatre. As we walked home, Celia said, 'Yamilia is Salome.'

'But I still have my head.'

Back at José's flat she poured our drinks. Her taste for rum would not help my efforts to reform.

'Even if Tony help José for nothing, this cost you much money.'

She pronounced 'nurthing' and 'murney' in her slow, smoky drawl.

'I know.'

I wondered what freeing José would actually cost, and then, for the first time, how much I had spent during my time in Cuba, and then how much I had left.

'Celia,' I said.

'Sí?'

'I don't think I have much money left.'

She threw her head back and laughed.

José's flat became home because, for now, Celia didn't want to be alone, and I didn't want to be alone, and we could be of more help to José together. So we told ourselves.

I found it odd how uncomfortable Celia seemed in Havana, never fully at ease, as though expecting something awful to happen at any moment. In José's flat, she relaxed and became herself but on the streets, in bars, or anywhere public, she became quiet and timid. Having seen the confidence she displayed in Santiago, this was baffling. Baffling and attractive; it drew me powerfully to her. I could never be sure if it was my predator's instinct for female weakness or the need to protect her. Both, probably.

She rarely wore makeup. Her eyebrows were trimmed, she had one stud earring in her left ear and she did nothing with her hair other than keep it very short. It was like a form of brutal honesty—this is me: take it or leave it. She wasn't beautiful, nowhere near, but I felt a strong attraction. She wore only jeans or short skirts with skimpy tops, but carelessly, not in any look-at-me way. When we went dancing she wore a sort of soft trilby and a man's jacket. I found myself looking at her often, not looking away easily, thinking about the rest of those lovely slim legs and her small bra-less breasts. She looked straight back, laughing her smoker's, knowing laugh, delighted at the weakness of men. Her brown eyes were warm and amused, sometimes frightened. She was gentle, seemed to yearn for gentleness in the macho, biting, scratching, swearing world of Cuban sex. Tears sometimes appeared in her eyes—she didn't sob—and would just roll down her cheeks. She wept without knowing.

We lay on José's bed. Through the blinds, the evening sun

dappled the dark and off-white of our bodies. I felt a twinge of conscience and said as much to Celia. She smiled.

'Chris, José not here,' she said and kissed my chest. 'You worry too much.'

'OK, no more worrying.'

*Reality is merely an illusion, albeit a very persistent one.*
Einstein


# 33

## Isabel Visits


The ringing phone woke us early. Celia picked it up, listened and replaced the receiver without speaking.

'Isabel is here,' she said. 'She wants talk to you.'

'Isabel? The security guard's daughter? Where is she?'

'Here. We can walk. Five minutes.'

She was sitting on the sea wall of the Malecón, her back to the sea, staring through, rather than at, the teeming crowds. She had just hitched from Santiago. Some Mexican tourists had crashed one of our cars, which was a write off. No serious injuries and they would claim on their holiday insurance, but the police had got involved. They'd traced the car, found it was being hired illegally and had impounded the others. It should have meant big trouble but Isabel's father had smoothed things out. We'd escaped, for now, but it meant that the hiring business was finished, and with it the money we were all making. Isabel had travelled the length of Cuba—500 miles— to tell and warn me.

'So you are all OK? Nobody's in trouble?'

'We all OK.'

'Do they know it was me who bought the cars?'

'No'

'So they don't know my name? They don't know who I am?'

She shook her head but exchanged the briefest of glances with Celia.

'OK, so what now?'

'Nothing now. Is finished.'

So why had she come? A phone call could have covered this.

'I come give you this,' she said.

She handed me a bundle of notes, maybe $500. 'For the cars.'

I offered some back to her. 'For your journey.'

'You keep. You need more than me.'

Then she asked something of Celia. They spoke rapidly but I caught Yamilia's name. Isabel turned and studied me for a few seconds, the usual severe expression, dark eyes bright with calculation. I held her eye. She jerked her head and turned away, as though I'd made an obscene suggestion.

She joined a queue waiting for lifts. After a few minutes, a truck stopped. A few men were already standing and sitting in the back. A small crowd spoke to the driver, some walked away, others climbed up. Isabel joined them. As the truck pulled away she stood in the front corner, her hands on the back of the cab, her long black hair blowing around her as she stared at the sea. She didn't look back.

Weeks later I saw her on television, part of a group of young Cubans off to Columbia to lend their medical skills. She spoke confidently to the camera, explaining their task to the Cuban people. They were filmed at a farewell dance to celebrate the trip. The camera panned across the faces of the dancers, whose smiles filled the screen. The view widened. Isabel, alone, stood in isolated bafflement at the jollity around her.

*It is agreed, then, that I shall not kill myself till two or three days hence.*
Candide

# 34
# Broke

Tony said I could do nothing for José concerning the charge he was facing—accomplice to murder—but that $1,000 might speed up the process, get the case to court quicker. As for Santiago, it was all over, which gave Tony the cue to wind up our own car business and pay off the staff, to make it harder for the police to trace us. I told him to sell the cars, since they were now unusable, and take whatever rent and visa money he was owed. He didn't want to sell but I needed money fast and so he agreed to do what I asked. For the first time since I'd arrived in Cuba, I wanted to gather all I had, put it in a Havana bank and keep a close eye on it. Then I could take stock. Make a new plan.

Since having lost money to the United States Treasury, I had found another route for transferring funds from London. It all went into an offshore account, from which I could transfer lump sums of £5,000 at a time. The commission was extortionate but at least it arrived. I hadn't checked the account in months, merely taking what I needed from ATMs, and I didn't want to close it, because I was expecting to need it in the future, but I did need a large sum of money right away to pay for my own costs, and José's and whatever else Tony might need.

I phoned the bank from my cellular while Celia slept, and asked them to send me the equivalent of £5,000.

'You don't have £5,000,' said a voice.

'That can't be right.'

'I'm sorry, Sir. You have £2,576 left in your account.'

I argued with the voice. It had been a polite voice when I first opened the account; now it gave me the impression that it couldn't be wasting its time on someone who was worried about a few thousand pounds when it had rich customers to deal with. I reminded the voice about the $27,000 that had been confiscated in transit by the Americans, blaming it for its incompetent stewardship but the voice denied responsibility. It said the change in law was an anti-corruption sting and that banks hadn't been alerted in advance, precisely so that launderers could be ensnared. Since I wasn't making any headway and my chest was hurting, I told the voice to send me the £2,576. It said it would.

The sudden realisation that I'd blown everything started to enter my consciousness. The car racket in Santiago was over. The police had impounded the cars. America had impounded my £27,000 in a sting operation. And Paul had had enough of Cuba. What was I going to do?

I made coffee and topped it up with rum.

Isabel had given me $500 in compensation for the cars in Santiago. Tony would give me some money for the sale of the cars here in Havana. Then I'd give him a thousand to keep him sweet and another thousand to resolve José's case. With the last of the Jersey money, I'd have about $10,000. I took a coffee and some toast into Celia. She ignored the toast and sipped the coffee.

'Is rum in here,' she said.

'You'll need it.'

'Why? What happen?'

'My money has gone.'.

She showed neither concern nor surprise.

'You be OK. You live like Cuban now. You make money before; you make money again. This was your education, Chris. Many people who comes to Cuba goes crazy, lose their money, get deported. You still here.'

She poured two tall glasses of rum.

'Here. One glass only, too early for more. So, we have no money?'

'Maybe a few thousand left.'

She spat out her coffee.

'Chris, is enough for me to live for years with that!'

But not for me. And nor for her, either. Not living with me.

We tried. We bought from the markets and cooked in the flat, but it was hard. We still drank rum, which was cheap, but found that the cost mounted up when you drink it every day. When I had to meet Tony, I tried hitching rides but it took hours and I soon reverted to taxis. During the week I'd stay in and watch DVDs with Celia but on Saturday nights we'd go out. Then rum, and sometimes coke, made us invincible and money drained away even faster with the night.

Tony was pleased to hear about my attempt at frugal living and was keen to get back to business with a new car rental operation somewhere else: perhaps Cienfuegos or Holguin, or even something much more clandestine here in Havana. I didn't tell him how broke I was. Instead, I said that I was waiting for a large payment from England and couldn't do anything till it came.

I did tell all to Paul, however, conscious for the first time of the cost of my calls.

'What have you done with it all?'

He sounded like an indignant parent, scolding a child for going through all their pocket money. I didn't say anything. When the lecture was over, I said simply, 'So I'm short of cash. Can you help?'

'I'll see what I can do.'

'Bring a card I can use or some cash. I'll pay you back if you want out. I just need to get started again.'

'OK. Will do.'

'And will you call my mother and the others at home, and tell them I'm OK?'

'Absolutely.'

*I believe we have had all the fun we can expect here.*
Charles Ryder: Brideshead Revisited

# 35
# Trial

José had been in prison for six weeks when, on a Friday, Tony phoned to say that the case was going to court. The trial would begin the next Monday. Tony was uncharacteristically optimistic. José, according to his sources, had said nothing, so he could be charged with no more than having someone's phone number in his wallet—a very, very minor accessory, if that. Possibly a light sentence or some form of probation. The trouble was that José was quite well known and far from innocent in other areas, so there was always a danger of his being punished for other crimes, real or imagined. There was public access but Tony asked us, particularly me, to stay away. My money had helped to speed up the process, but there was nothing else I could do. I could only wait.

Celia and I sat at a roof-top bar overlooking the harbour, sheltered from the summer sun by a canopy and grateful for a tiny breeze from the sea. It was so hot that even thinking sapped the energy. If you weren't in the shade, Havana was unbearable. It was Saturday, late afternoon, and we were waiting for the evening, the cool and the dark, the time to drink, dance and forget. We both enjoyed watching people and inventing lives for them. Celia was a good drinking partner, talking easily but equally comfortable with silence. She never really got drunk, would just decide at some stage that she'd had enough and she'd drop off, just like that.

We had been sipping slowly for a few hours, drinking water too, and were just ordering food. Neither of us had much appetite but rum on an empty stomach was sure to end in nausea.

'Chris, how much money you have?' she said, emerging from thought.

'Not much: I'm down to a couple of hundred dollars.'

'And after that, you empty?'

'Yes, until Paul sends more.'

'Let's go out tonight, have a good time. Finish it now.'

And forget Monday and José for a few hours.

We took a taxi to Tony's house to pick up my best suit and shoes. We bought a long, low-cut, blue silk dress at the Habana Libre. Celia never wore high heels and settled for some white-leather sandals. At home she gelled her short hair and combed it flat. She tried on the dress, twirled in front of the mirror, the evening sun revealing glimpses of her body beneath.

'Can you see if I wear anything under the dress?'

She wore the briefest of thongs and no bra but I couldn't tell. At certain points, the light seemed to reveal all, a tantalising hint of nakedness and promise which vanished in a second as the silk became sheer. I stared as she twirled, waiting and wanting further glimpses of her, despite her availability to me.

'I can't see,' I said. 'Sometimes I think yes, sometimes I think no.'

'Perfect.'

When I was ready, too, she adjusted me to her satisfaction and stood beside me in front of the mirror.

'Mmm, elegant. We are ready.'

At La Catedral we were the object of disapproving glares from tourists. I'd been used to it with Yamilia, but this was the first time with Celia. She noticed too.

'Why they stare?'

'Because I'm exploiting you.'

'Exploiting?'

'Old man with beautiful young girl. I must be doing something illegal.'

She laughed until tears ran down her cheeks, looking directly at the tourists until they turned away.

A new club had sprung up in the narrow warren of streets around Obispo. Derelict a few weeks ago, it had now been fitted with a long narrow bar, colourful murals on the lower walls and low multi-coloured lights to hide the emptiness above—there was no roof, just a hastily erected canopy. There was a small dance area and a pool table, for which two bouncers demanded a three-dollar entrance fee to keep it exclusive. The place was full and it all felt new and wicked and exciting. We danced, played pool and got slowly very drunk.

Celia was stared at constantly by other men, teasing them as, trapped by their own nature and desires, they tried to see through to what the silk dress hid. And all the time, she smiled happily, feigning obliviousness and unconcern.

As my money vanished, I yearned to prolong this life: the crush of people, the sharp reek of tobacco and perfume, the brilliant smiles, the smell of rum and sex.

'Let's stay at the Nacional,' she said, at two in the morning.

'OK.'

In the taxi I watched clothes drying on the balconies along the Malecón. They were blowing horizontally. The air had cooled, the sea angry and spraying the wide path and one lane of traffic. We slowed as a policeman diverted us into the far lane. He looked into the taxi, shone a torch at me and then waved us on. I asked Celia for a cigarette. She didn't answer, her face between her knees as she sniffed from the tiny mirror she kept in her bag.

It cost a ridiculous amount to get Celia into the hotel. It didn't matter. If I was broke today, tomorrow or the next day—

what difference did it make? We ate to keep the drunkenness at bay, the rooftop restaurant almost empty. I recognised an actor with three girls: he was passing round cocaine, smoking, laughing, drinking, secure in his affluence. He didn't give us a glance, although the girls did. Who was I? Who was the skinny girl? What were we doing here?

We were spending the last of our money and tomorrow we would be poor.

A slow ballad began. Cuban ballads always sound beautiful, breaking your heart even if you understand not a word, the guitars insistent, the voices full of yearning. As my Spanish had improved, and I was able to translate what I heard, I was often surprised at the discover meanings that I'd never guessed at: 'Ay, my beautiful Maria, when you walk along the beach, the way the cheeks of your ass move makes me feel horny,' or the popular song of the moment, played everywhere: 'Papaya con dolor': vagina of pain. Celia hummed and sang into my shoulder as we held each other upright. In the background the sea lashed the sea wall and the road with explosive cracks. The sky was low, the night grey and black, the lights of a tanker just visible as it made its slow passage along the horizon. Parts of Havana were blacked out with the usual power cuts in the poorer areas; the tourist spots and the hotels alone shone on in the gloom.

I felt as free as I thought anyone could be. I had more freedom than the Hollywood actor with his nose on the table. He couldn't leave the hotel because he didn't know anybody or know what to do. I did. I could go and join his group or I could leave and find the cheapest of peso bars and spend the night with a real señorita. Or I could just go home—with Celia.

*The face is familiar, but I can't remember my name.*
Robert Benchley

# 36

# Where Am I?

My head felt like a beaten anvil. It was already uncomfortably hot and heading for intolerable. Normally, if I drank too much, the most I'd suffer was an attack of nausea and a nasty, queasy feeling that put me off eating and drinking. I never got headaches but this time, I felt that a blacksmith was shaping hot metal inside my skull. It was bad. The only answer was sleep, but dread, dread in the pit of my stomach, kept sleep at bay. Clogged with phlegm and wanting to throw up, I reached for my cigarettes, only to realise that I didn't recognise the room.

I moved my foot backwards and touched warm flesh. I turned with difficulty. It was Celia.

'Where are we?' I said.

'The Nacional.'

'Do we have any money left?'

'Some.'

'Can we stay here another night? I need to sleep.'

'I think so. Then it is finished. Chris, you fall over in the night. You never do this before.'

'I'm sorry. I won't do it again.'

'Chris, no get sick again.'

'Don't worry, I can't afford to now.'

*I think crime pays. The hours are good, you travel a lot.*
Woody Allen

# 37

# Verdict

They all went to trial on the same day. The three killers got life. Of the others, only those who'd admitted to anything got prison sentences. In two months José had said nothing. My money may have got the case to trial sooner, that's all. José was on his own. Fifteen to a cell with one pot to piss in. No visitors. Heat and stench. Occasionally the arrival of a new inmate.

'They put him in our cell to get me to speak to him,' said José, 'but I know what they do. They want me to say him something. I no say nothing. Other times they take me to their office. "Say something about the others and it will be good for you." I no say nothing.'

After two months they gave up. José got a form of probation involving community service.

'Aledmis, he say something,' said José.

Aledmis, his friend from the loft, had talked. He'd been given thirty years. Clearly he had nothing to do with the murder. Maybe he admitted to other things. Maybe the police knew he'd done something else. I didn't know. I remembered his lovely loft space, his skill at chess and his thoughtful nature. Thirty years.

'He cry,' said José, without obvious emotion or concern.

The implication was that Aledmis should have kept his

mouth shut. And that he shouldn't have cried. José shrugged: that's life.

What about Andy? José said he thought they would shoot him. I disagreed. Andy was far from a model citizen but he was an American. If Fidel could have made political capital out of him, he would have done: the awful Yanks coming to Cuba and murdering tourists. But this had been a drugs deal. Drugs were coming through Cuba, not staying long, and being shipped out. There was no mileage in shooting him—if there had been, they'd have done so while the story was still hot. Instead, they'd quietly deport him later.

José was a hero in his barrio. He came out thin and grinning, with a thick black beard. Girls wanted him and got him. Celia looked on with amusement until they got bored. Then she went back to him.

I asked José what exactly had happened with Andy and Jared.

'The time you see me in the Ambos Mundos with Jared, he ask me where he can buy cocaine. I tell him about Andy: that's how he makes his money. Jared give me his phone number, that's all.'

'And Andy killed him?'

'Andy and two other men. They take his money, $30,000. They never had no cocaine.'

'How did the police know?'

'One of the men get scared. He want speak to the police. They shoot him and throw him in a ditch, but he don't die: the gun was no good.' José shrugged. 'This is Cuba. The man get to a hospital and they call the police. He tell them everything.'

José's release coincided with my fiftieth birthday. In celebratory mood he threw a party at his expense for the two of us and Celia. We had gallons of illicit rum, served in small jars —lethal but very enjoyable. The party was half in the street, half in what was really just a coffee bar, adapted for the day. Later, he showed me a photo of the party. Of me with Celia. I was sprawled on the sofa, an empty rum bottle at my feet. I had my arm round Celia, whose head was nestled into the crook of my neck, one arm draped across my chest, the other round my waist. Both our heads were back, mouths agape. José laughed,

'You were like this for hours. Both snoring. Very comical.'

Comical, yes, but sort of right too.

I went back to Tony's. I had no choice. I had no money to pay Rosa's rent. I doubted she still wanted to marry me.

*The best way to die is sit under a tree, eat lots of bologna
and salami, drink a case of beer, then blow up.*
Art Donovan

# 38

# Paul's Last Visit

Paul had promised to bring funds. He arrived fairly sober, smiling nervously. He waved his shoulder bag at us.

'Wait until you see what I've got in here.'

My heart sank. I turned and walked towards our taxi. José got in the front.

'Don't you want to see?' he said as we set off.

I couldn't speak. He rummaged in the bag and produced some books of travellers cheques and guarantee cards.

'These will get us anything we want.'

'Cheque guarantee cards?'

'OK. They won't get you cash but you can buy goods. You can stock up.'

'In England, not here.'

'Why not?'

'Is anything backing them up? Is there any cash anywhere?'

He stared back and said nothing.

'This is Cuba,' I said.

We travelled in silence for a few minutes.

'I've got around £500,' he said.

For a week we circled the big hotels buying only drinks. We bought food at the markets and ate at Tony's. I knew that Paul had funds; I also knew that he'd decided I was a lost cause. He'd brought just enough money to last for the two weeks of his trip. I was morose and sulky while Paul was more cheerful than I'd ever seen him. His travellers cheques had worked so far. That was OK as long as we had cash to back them up, but the cash was slowly dwindling on supplies for the house.

After a week the cash was gone. Paul was unconcerned, confident that the cheques would continue to work. I doubted that: there was always a cut-off point and we were approaching it.

On the second Saturday Paul wanted to eat out. Although his money was gone, José and I had just enough dollars to eat in a peso restaurant, maybe get some drinks somewhere else, so we took him to Chinatown. It was cheap and cheerful, but they served good food.

Paul didn't appear to notice where he was until our food arrived. He stared at it in disgust.

'What the fuck is this?'

'It's your dinner.'

He pushed it away and looked around the bar, caught someone's eye.

'What the fuck are you looking at?' I said.

A well-dressed man of about forty was staring calmly at our table. Not unusual, I thought. People stared everywhere.

José nudged me.

'Eat quickly,' he said.

In the street, José said he thought the man was police of some kind.

'You sure?'

'No, but he look like that. That is the way they look at you.'

'Who the fuck cares,' said Paul. 'Now can we go to the Melia and get something edible?'

José and I looked at each other; José shook his head.

'We don't have any money Paul, I keep telling you.'

'We do have fucking money.'

He flashed the guarantee cards again.

'Put them away,' I said.

I pulled him into a shop. Cuban women were milling around, buying fabrics, towels, toiletries. They looked at us drunken Englishmen, showed brief embarrassment for us, then went on with their business. I propelled him gently into a corner of the shop. José stood by the door, watching the street. I put my hands on Paul's shoulders and stared into his red-rimmed eyes.

'Listen to me. The cards are dodgy, right? They've worked so far but they might stop working at any time, yes?'

He was angry, shaking with temper beneath my hands.

'Every time we've used them until now, we've had enough cash to pay if the cards failed. If the payment hadn't gone through, we only had to shrug and smile and say, "Oh, I am sorry, I must have reached my limit on that one. Have some cash instead." Even if they thought we were trying it on, it wouldn't have mattered. They'd got their money. They didn't care. No harm done. Do you understand?'

He breathed rum fumes into my face but didn't say anything, his lips a tight sulky line.

'Now things have changed,' I said. 'We don't have the money to cover the prices if the cards fail in a top hotel. We can afford to eat in the peso places. We can still buy gallons of rum. But we can't live the way we have been doing. We have to slum it for a while. You only have to put up with this for a few days; then you can go home. I've been living like this for three fucking months. Has it hit home yet? That's why I needed more from you. That's why the *exactly* $400 you sent for my visas left me high and dry every time. You didn't even get the exchange rate right. You left me short. I had to borrow the rest from Tony.'

The women in the shop were staring now. This was more than they'd expected from an early-evening trip for essentials. Paul looked back at them, his face red with anger.

'Don't say anything,' I said.

José was trying to look casual in the doorway. He didn't like this. Neither did I. I'd been determined not to let things get personal but I still needed Paul and he'd be gone soon. I had to convince him that buying some new cars with Tony was an investment, not wasted money. I took a deep breath.

'We can go and talk about this over a couple of drinks in the Melia and that's about all. OK? Shall we go?'

He nodded. We left a bunch of disappointed women to their shopping and headed off for a taxi we could barely afford.

We sat in silence for a while in the lobby. Rich people came and went.

'I'm going to use this card,' said Paul.

José and I exchanged a look. How can such a clever man be so stupid?

'You can't,' I said.

'Who dares wins.'

'Who dares gets us arrested, Paul. Honestly.'

'I've done this all over the world. I'm not stopping now.'

'And if the card doesn't work?'

'We'll do a runner.'

The lobby was massive. We wouldn't have got as far as the door.

'Run where?'

'Out,' he said,' as though talking to a fool. 'Out there.' He waved his arm vaguely in the direction of the sea.

'And then?'

'Then we're gone. Who dares wins,' he repeated.

'This is Cuba, Paul.'

'I know it's fucking Cuba and I'm fucking pissed off with it.'

A group at the next table stared at us; a woman shook her head and tutted. All three of us glared back at them. They looked away. A couple of the hotel security staff watched us from a distance, speaking occasionally into their short-wave radios. José caught my eye, tilted his head in the direction of the door.

'OK,' I said. 'We run. We get away from here. Then what?'

'Then that's it, we're out of here.'

'When you get to the airport, they will stop you. Tourism is their livelihood. You do not rip them off. Nobody does. They will stop you and you will pay them. If you're polite they will deport you and you won't be able to come back. If you behave as you normally do, they will lock you up for as long as they please. You should feel right at home.'

'Shit.'

Paul wouldn't leave. We couldn't abandon him so we sat, a black cloud of alcohol fumes floating above us. The atmosphere was horrible. Half the hotel and most of the security people were staring at us. I was worried for José. They would only deport me; he could get thrown back in jail. Paul got unsteadily to his feet.

'Watch this,' he said.

We watched.

He wobbled away in his too-tight swimming shorts, his ankles swollen from mosquito bites and too much sun when he'd fallen asleep on the beach. His beer gut strained at his white Viva Fidel T-shirt. Wth his beer gut ahead of him, he looked as if he was about to topple over, and only kept upright because his legs kept scurrying forwards. He ran into a few sofas, snagged the odd chair and table and collided with hotel guests, to whom he turned and smiled apologetically in what he imagined was a display of old-world charm.

He staggered on towards the reception desk, convinced in his own mind that he was the embodiment of James Bond after a couple of dry martinis, a true professional at work, and was going to show us how it was done—me, José, Cuba. So we sat back and watched. It was excruciating. We sank back into the soft sofas and tried to disappear. How had it come to this? How had it got this silly? This was so not *todo control*. I could take beatings and car crashes and threats and crazy women, but a drunken Englishman ... ? No.

Having somehow reached reception, Paul propped himself up by the counter and remained there, grateful for something to steady him as he tried to cultivate the attractive female receptionist. Her response was astonishing. She gave him a beautiful smile, listened intently to his patter and smiled some more. Then she examined his card, started scampering back and forth and made a few phone calls. Eventually she came back to him, smiled again and handed him back his card. He took her hand, kissed it and gave a little bow. She laughed. He blew her a kiss, turned away and started back, but had forgotten where we were. He looked around helplessly. A security man guided him back to our table, nodding politely to each of us in turn.

Paul flopped heavily into the cushions of a sofa and grinned at us.

'And that's how it's done.'

What he'd managed to do in the time he'd been working the front desk was to buy another round of drinks. The card had stood for it. We could have got them ourselves in two minutes from the bar. I looked at José. He just seemed relieved that it was over.

'Well done, Paul,' I said.

I patted him on his shoulder. José stood up and patted him too.

'You amazing, Paul. How you do it?' and he sat down and laughed. We all did.

In the taxi back to Tony's white house, I said, 'Can we make that the last one, with that card? Let's eat at home, watch some TV. We have plenty of booze.'

'Of course,' Paul said. 'Now I've shown you guys how it's done.'

We stopped at the usual place, and bought three litres of

Silver Dry and a hundred Hollywood Red cigarettes. I thought they might last us until Paul left. They didn't last the night.

We watched two movies and then put on some music. A bottle had disappeared and José was as drunk as I'd ever seen him. Paul was laughing at everything—the films, the stories, our situation. I needed to talk to him about the money I felt he owed me: not so much, maybe, but a few thousand, at least, to get me on my feet again.

I asked José to explain to Paul why buying three more cars was a good idea, how it would keep me here, keep Tony happy and get everything going again. José was well gone. He slurred his speech, got his English and Spanish mixed up and talked nonsense, not something I'd heard from him before. He stood up to demonstrate where we could keep the cars, swung his arm in an expansive sweep, and lost his balance, falling with a loud slap on the tiled floor.

'Hmm,' said Paul, 'can't say I'm convinced.'

Neither was I. José giggled on the floor. I poured another rum and considered my options. Nothing came to mind.

'Why do you want to stay here?' Paul said. 'My first visit was a novelty but you can't get anything done. It's a shithole. They smile while you talk, then go out dancing, and the next day they've forgotten everything you'd agreed.'

'Is a shithole,' giggled José from the floor. 'Everyone forget everything.'

'He's right,' Paul said. 'Come back to England. I'll pay for your ticket.'

'You're not even paying for these drinks,' I scoffed. 'We paid for them.'

'I'll send you the ticket when I get back.'

'I'm staying here.'

'But why?'

'Yamilia,' I said, surprising myself as well as them.

'No, Chris, no!' groaned a voice from the floor.

'There couldn't be a worse reason, old man,' said Paul.

José managed to get to his hands and knees.

'Chris, Paul: I go to bed.'

'Night, José,' said Paul.

He crawled slowly along the corridor. He wasn't supposed to stay here: it was one of Tony's rules. But it was late, we were drunk and I didn't care. And how would Tony know anyway?

'Night, José,' I called after him. 'Use the bedroom at the back.'


I woke at midday to the sound of someone using a hammer in the corridor. Bang, bang, bang. It could only be Tony, I thought. I didn't want to move; my body was desperate for more sleep and oblivion. But I wanted to find out what the noise was all about.

I staggered into the back bathroom and threw up. As I crouched over the floor, a brown female tarantula stared up at me, about a foot away from my face. Just try it, I thought; I'll fucking bite you back. We'll see who's the most poisonous today.

From there I made it to the kitchen and drank a litre of water from the fridge. I found Tony kneeling in the corridor, fiddling with a fan. I had to face him.

'Buenos días, Tony. Como esta?'

He looked up at me, sad more than angry, and didn't reply. He rose creakily to his feet, sighed heavily,

'Café, Chris?' he said.

I sat in the living room while he made coffee. The floor was littered with a dozen beer cans, some squashed, as well as ash and fag-ends from two overturned ashtrays. One of the litre bottles of rum that we'd bought the night before stood by a chair, maybe a third full; the other two lay on their sides, empty. The black fan lay on its side in the corridor. It was badly dented and, evidently, no longer functional.

Tony returned with the coffee and handed me a cup. He looked at me and opened the patio door. I must have stank of rum.

'*José aquí*, Chris?'

I assumed he was, although there was no sign of him, or of Paul.

'*Sí*, Tony.'

He shook his head sadly.

'*Malo*, Chris, *muy malo*.' This is very bad.

He gestured to the fan.

'*Que problema el ventilador?*'

I had no idea at all, but it must have had something to do with me.'

'He hit me with it ,' said Paul, emerging from into the living room.

He made his way unerringly to the remaining rum and poured himself a glass.

'Morning, Tony,' he said.

He showed us a red-and-blue welt, stretching along the top of his shoulder and down his back. Tony picked up the fan, held it against Paul's shoulder and nodded. Mystery solved. He scratched his head and smiled, despite himself.

'You were aiming for my head,' said Paul. 'You chased me round the garden. There were—I don't know what—snakes and every fucking thing out there.'

José appeared, looking ill. He apologised meekly to Tony, who nodded and shrugged. José grabbed the bottle of water I'd been drinking from, took a swig and, looking at Paul's glass of rum, shook his head, in awe. Then he stared at the bruise and Paul explained.

'You seemed to think I owed you twenty grand because of the Amex card and the disappearing transfer,' he said, as José translated for Tony. 'We had a difference of opinion. You were resentful about the cash for visas and exchange rates, and you used words that compared me to female genitalia, which was unkind.'

'And I hit you because of that?' I said.

'Not entirely. I called Yamilia an unreliable tart and told you

you were mad for getting involved with her. You went berserk, like a whirling dervish. I had to hide in the street until you gave up and went to sleep.'

José was giggling now and a smile forced itself onto Tony's face. Soon we were all laughing. I poured myself some rum and Tony couldn't be bothered to disapprove.

'Can we get some more booze?' said Paul.

Tony cleaned up. We tried to help but we weren't up to much. Paul nursed his rum. When we were done, Tony spoke to José and me in the kitchen. He would go out for some food. We needed to eat, he said; he would cook for us. We could have some rum but we weren't to get drunk. His eyes slid towards Paul in the other room, acknowledging that, in his case, it might already be too late.

Then he asked for a meeting, the four of us; José could translate. Something had to happen. This situation could not continue. We needed to make a plan and see how we could get everything straightened out. Paul didn't understand the situation we were in and didn't understand Cuba. We would explain it to him. Good idea, Tony.

Tony addressed himself to Paul. He gestured around him. 'This my house,' he announced. Paul sipped his rum, smiled and waited for Tony to tell him something he didn't already know. Tony noted the expression—cocky, bored—and changed his tone slightly. This was his house and also his business. He could put tourists up here every day of the week: four at a time, six at a time, maybe more. That was twenty-five, maybe thirty dollars per person per day. A possible $1,000 weekly.

Paul tended to judge people by their appearance. Tony drove an ancient Lada, as did many Cubans, and dressed the same way every day, in light chinos and a white shirt that soon became grubby with sweat and food. Paul didn't take him any more seriously than he took any Cubans. He regarded them as a fickle, annoying and substandard. They had their novelty value, especially the women—the white women, anyway—but he didn't listen to them, didn't get them, didn't know where he was with them or what they were up to. But this was interesting.

Tony listed some of the ways we could make money. Forget Rumbos and tourism, he suggested; that's history. And there are easier ways. Things hadn't gone well so far, mistakes had been made, but it was a learning curve and it could still work out. And I was still here. Surely Paul would value my presence here as a contact—a friend who was secure in a nice house, in a country with no extradition treaty, and where visitors, as long as they weren't completely stupid, could get away with almost anything?

'You are criminal, Paul,' said Tony, bringing his discourse to a head. 'You no serious, you no violent, but you on wrong side of the law. Havana could be safe haven for you. No?'

'Done,' said Paul, 'if you put it that way. Why not? I'll get right onto it as soon as I'm back in the UK. You'll have funds within a week, two maximum.'

We drank to that.

*Do you suppose I could buy back my introduction to you?*
Groucho Marx

# 39

# A Phone Call

I'd had another bout of pneumonia, was convalescing again and was required not to move. Tony had banned me from drinking, said if he ever found any rum in the house again, he'd throw me out.

He wouldn't, of course—not while he still believed I could come up with the sort of money that had brought us together in the first place—but until then I was broke and he was making the rules. Besides which, we'd become friends of a sort; the fact that I was still in his house after several rent-less weeks testified to that. First and foremost, Tony was a businessman and I'd become an investment. The question was: how long before he decided I was a bad one and cut his losses? That depended on Paul. And where was Paul? He had said two weeks, maximum. This was the third week and we'd still heard nothing.

I watched through the wooden shutters. Tony was due soon. He came every day to check on my health and cook breakfast. Dingo would hear him coming and go crazy; then, thirty seconds later, Tony's car would pull up in front of the house. As soon as I registered Dingo's excitement, I sat down on the sofa, two fans moving the hot air around, and tried to look innocent.

'*Bueno, Chris,*' Tony said, entering the room with a broad smile. '*Como esta?*'

'*Bueno, Tony. Muy bien.*'

We shook hands, a daily ritual. He studied me and smiled again. He ruffled my hair.

'*Ay, Chris,*' he said laughing and went outside to give Dingo some food. Dingo slobbered at his scraps while Tony picked fruit in the garden. He'd juice what he found in an ancient blender, add about a pound of sugar and hand it to me.

'*Bueno para la sangre,* Chris, *fuerte, mucho fuerte*'—good for the blood, will make you strong, very strong—and he'd flex his muscles and stick out his chest. We'd both laugh, as we'd done yesterday and the day before that.

Tony prepared breakfast and brewed coffee. He always ate with me, shovelling food into his mouth like a mechanical excavator. His stomach was testimony to a life-long love affair with food. I'd be barely three mouthfuls into my breakfast and he'd already have finished eating, resting his chin on his big hands and watching me with his sharp green eyes. He watched for signs of lack of appetite—lack of appetite brought on by drinking. He thought I was dangerously thin. But my appetite was fine. I finished in my own time.

'*Bueno, Chris*'?

'Very good, Tony. *Gracias.*'

He handed me the pack of ten cigarettes that he rationed me to each day. I'd hustled five dollars from the Cubans playing pool in the local bar the night before, and for a few nights before that. Each time, I'd use the money to buy a half bottle of rum and a packet of cigarettes for José and me to treat ourselves to. Tony knew most things that went on in Bahia, but not that.

We talked about nothing for a while, uneasy because we both knew there was only one topic that interested him now.

'Paul?' he asked, eventually.

I shook my head. I didn't have the Spanish to invent an

excuse. I told him that I was sure that something would arrive in the next few days. He shook his head sadly. Paul. The demon alcohol.

'Lentamente, Chris, lentamente.' Slowly. He looked me in the eyes. 'La vida. Mucho rapido. No bueno.' Living too quickly isn't good.

I nodded sagely at this advice. He ruffled my hair and rose to do the washing up, laughing as he cleared away the plates.

The phone rang. I hurried to the other room.

'Hello, Paul?' It was unlikely to be anyone else.

Silence.

'Is that you Paul?'

'Is that Mr Hilton?'

A pause.

'Yes.'

'This is James Ferguson. Sheffield CID.'

'Yes.'

'And you are Christopher Hilton, previously of Fir Cottage, Leighton Buzzard?'

'Yes.'

'Are you acquainted with a Mr Paul Sant?'

'I know him.'

'He says he knows you too. We have him in custody. He's been incoherent all night. It's hard to believe anything he's been saying. At one stage he was talking about stuffed birds.'

'You're phoning me in Cuba to ask me about stuffed birds?'

'There's rather more to it than that,' he said.

I thought there might be. Tony put his head round the door, mouthed 'Paul?' at me. I nodded, smiling, and gave him the thumbs up. He said 'mas tarde', later, and indicated that he had to go, would phone me tonight. I continued to smile idiotically until I heard the door close.

'Sorry, that was my landlord,' I said.

'So, you have business interests in Cuba?'

'Yes, I live here.'

'Very nice.'

'Yes. It is.'

'What kind of business?'

'Am I in trouble?' I asked.

'Not as far as I know. Do you think you are?'

'No—and I'm not sure why I need to be talking to you.'

'Because unless you corroborate Mr Sant's story, we'll be charging him, keeping him here and refusing him bail.'

'What is his story?'

'Beyond stuffed birds, I'm not able to tell you that.'

'If I don't know what he's told you, how can I confirm it?'

'By answering my questions.'

'I need some time to think about this.'

'You don't have any.'

'Hang on a moment—my landlord wants to speak to me.'

I put the phone on the table, lit a cigarette and went into the garden. Right, I thought. I'm in Cuba, they're not. Whatever they might know abut me, they can't do anything because there's no extradition treaty. So what might Paul have told them? I don't know. It doesn't matter. I'm here. They're there. I have nothing to lose. Stuffed birds? He must have been paralytic. OK. Tough it out.

'I'm sorry about that.' I said. 'What did you want to know?'

'Did you give Mr Sant permission to use your credit cards?'

'Yes.'

'Generous man.'

'Kind of guy I am.'

'Including a platinum Amex card.'

'Yes.'

'Very generous.'

'Thank you.'

'Did you know that Mr Sant has run up a bill of £28,000 on your American Express card?'

'Yes.'

Bastard.

'I see,' he said. 'Why?'

'Why what?'

'Why give him permission to use it?'

'I have a business in Cuba. I need a representative in England. Transferring money to and from Cuba is difficult. I let him use my cards.'

'What kind of business?'

'Tourism.'

'That would be Eternity Travel.'

'Yes.'

He laughed.

'And Mr Sant is a director of the company.'

'Yes.'

'And you're not?'

'No.'

'I see.'

What did he see?

'And is John Freedman also a director?'

'I don't know. I don't know how the business is set up.'

'And was Michelle Lewis the witness to a £40,000 secured loan on a property in Leighton Buzzard?'

Oh dear. An ex-girlfriend.

'I can't answer that.'

'Then Mr Sant stays in his cell.'

'Michelle has nothing to do with this.'

'We need to confirm that she was a signatory.'

'How?'

'Tell us how we can contact her.'

'I don't know.'

'We just need to confirm Mr Sant's story, nothing more. A phone call would be enough.'

'I need to think about this. Give me half an hour.'

'I'll give you ten minutes. I'll call back. If you don't cooperate, Mr Sant stays in his cell.'

He hung up.

I paced the garden, smoking. Dingo sat watching me, his head tilted to one side, emitting occasional little yelps, as if to say: 'Now what have you done?' He saved my life once; I didn't think he could help with this. Not unless they came to the house to get me. Then he'd help.

Right, I thought. Slow down. I'm being irrational. I haven't done anything illegal. A bit naughty maybe but not illegal. Not in England anyway. What Paul might have done is his business. But what did he do? How did he get himself arrested? I'll ask. But what about Michelle? She doesn't know she was a signatory. We forged her handwriting. That's not going to go down well. Doesn't matter. She's done nothing wrong. But if I don't tell them, they'll get find out and that could be worse. I'm going to have to tell them. I'll phone Michelle first, before they get to her. OK.

I must have been talking out loud because Dingo let out a loud bark of irritation.

'Don't worry', I said to him as I walked back into the house. 'It must have been that last bang on the head.'

The phone rang.

'Mr Hilton.'

'Yes.'

'James Ferguson here.'

'I realise that. Why was Paul arrested?'

'He was at a Sheffield hotel, with an escort.'

'If you arrested everybody for that, half the country would be locked up.'

'He didn't have any money ... '

'Some people don't.'

' ... and he didn't have any cash, so he called a taxi to take him to an ATM.'

'And?'

'Then he wanted some cigarettes, so he got the taxi driver to take him to a garage.'

'Still don't see why he was arrested.'

'According to Mr Sant, when he left the garage, he forgot about the taxi and walked back to the hotel.'

'And the taxi driver called the police?' I said.

'Yes. Actually, that's the only part of his story that makes sense.'

He paused. 'So, have you made a decision?'

'I've only got her number at work. Please be discreet.'

'We will. A female colleague will make the call.'

I gave him the number.

'Mr Hilton?'

'Yes?'

'The stuffed birds?'

'Ten years ago, a friend of mine moved to Chicago. He left some of his things with me, including some stuffed birds. He's an ornithologist. They're still in my garage.'

'So it's true,' he said.

'Yes.'

'But why did he keep going on about them?'

'I've no idea,' I said. 'He must have thought they proved something. Perhaps he thought they were valuable.'

'Are they?'

'No.'

'Incredible.'

'Yes.'

'Well. Thank you for your help, Mr Hilton.'

'You're welcome. Call any time.'

Incredible.

An hour later, José arrived. He had hitched a lift from Havana. It had taken him hours. He took off his sweat-soaked shirt and hung it over a chair in front of one of the fans. I was watching TV. He asked if Paul had phoned.

'No,' I said. 'The police did.'

I told him the story. He thought about it for a while, then put his head back and laughed. I laughed with him.

'Your friend!' he said. 'Will he get out?'

'I don't know. Probably. But there's no chance of any money for a while.'

'Is shit.' He laughed again. 'If we get out of this, they say we heroes.'

Something like that.

*We are all as God made us, and many of us much worse.*
Narrator / Tom Jones

# 40

# A New Enemy

I heard nothing from Paul, had no idea if he was in jail or out. More weeks passed and with it the hottest, most humid weather of the year. It stuck to me, heavy and exhausting. I fought against depression, found it hard to lift my mood. The morning journey to buy bread left me drenched in sweat and exhausted. There was no air to breathe. Every breath was a struggle. Clouds of dust circled, disturbed by every passing car, then fell back on the leaves of the trees, on the parked cars, on the shop windows, on the potholed streets. The hurricane season would wash it all away, clear the air and bring new life but for now, all was lifeless, cloying—hopeless. I didn't have the energy to raise a smile at the bakers. I was surly and impatient. I just wanted to get back in the shade, watch TV, read a book—shut everything out.

José visited every day now. Sometimes Celia came too, but not often; she was always much quieter around him, perhaps inhibited because she couldn't speak freely. On one of her visits she looked around Tony's house, examined the empty fridge, saw the plate of rice and beans that he'd left for me and the few cigarettes I had salvaged.

'Chris, how you live like this?'

'I don't have any choice.'

She nodded slowly, as though it had only just occurred to her. When José went to the shop for cigarettes she said, 'Come to the flat on Monday. José away in Guantanamo for few days.'

When they left I picked up the book I'd been reading— reading for the second or third time. I read and then re-read the books I'd accumulated, rarely watching TV except on Fridays and Saturdays, which were movie nights when current films, presumably taken from a Florida satellite, were shown. If I could manage a few pesos for a quarter bottle of rum, this became a weekend treat, as enjoyable as anything I'd done when money was unimportant.

The book had been given to me by Manolo. It was about a rabbi detective in New York, one of a series of straightforward whodunits. I can't remember the title. It was a little daft, but interesting and intriguing enough to pass the time. I got to the last page and noticed something written on the inside back cover that I'd missed before: 'For translation services: $500.'

I tried to remember when Manolo gave me the book. It was many months before, certainly. So he'd been resentful of me all this time.

Tony had told me not to worry about him. I didn't think of his translation as a service, just something he did when Tony needed him. I thought of him as Tony's gofer, not mine. Manolo clearly thought differently. Well, too late now. I couldn't offer him even fifty pesos, nor would I if I'd had it. The message left me vaguely disturbed, though, and I read it several times before putting the book away and starting a new one. There was an implied threat.

I kept an increasingly manic diary, full of plans and solutions to my predicament. I had to believe I could get myself out of this. I'd never really believed that Paul would come through with the money, and now that he'd been arrested, it seemed stupid even to hope. But hope I did. The contrast between my feelings of freedom and power when I'd first arrived in Cuba and my present condition were hard to bear, let alone acknowledge. Self-deception was necessary just to get through the day. Tony was losing faith and patience. José and Celia's belief in my was now essential. If I lost that ... .

One night, the movie I was watching was interrupted by a massive storm. Electricity wasn't cut but reception was down, so I read instead, my back sweating against the plastic of Tony's furniture. I felt a light caress on my shoulder and brushed at it. My fingers entwined with thick bristly legs, lots of them. I leapt to my feet as the large, black male tarantula scurried to escape—bad weather tended to bring them in from the garden. I like tarantulas and often shared my shower with one, usually female, as it watched from the corner of the stall. The females were the more dangerous, the males much bigger, and black rather than brown, but for those few moments my skin crawled with panic and I took off my sandal and smashed it to pieces, legs flying everywhere.

I no longer slept well. Sleep only took me when I was exhausted and then only lasted two or three hours. When I finally dropped off, it was usually getting light, neighbours were stirring and traffic noise was beginning to rumble in the street. A fan directed at the bed kept hovering mosquitoes at bay. I watched them for hours, diving at me and blown back, diving and blown back, constantly frustrated. During power cuts I got up and sat in the garden.

José once told me that he had saved $5,000, the product of many years' painstaking hustling on Havana's streets. It was for when he got permission to travel to the US—if he ever got permission. He didn't want to stay there, just earn enough to come back and live comfortably in Cuba. Like many of the young he was slightly schizophrenic about Cuba, expressing hatred and resentment of the way it barely worked but fiercely proud of it other ways. I once asked him what he would do if the US ever invaded.

'We don't want them,' he said. 'We would fight them.'

On Monday I went to see Celia. I left early, before the worst of the heat, and stood in the queue of Cubans waiting on the sliproad to the motorway. A taxi driver recognised me and stopped. I put my head through the window.

'I don't have any money.'

'I know,' he laughed. 'I hear. No problem. Get in.'

Celia opened a new bottle of rum when I arrived. We watched the street from the balcony for a while and let the rum do its work. She took a healthy gulp from her glass and disappeared. A few minutes later she called me in. She knelt in the middle of the floor, a cardboard shoebox at her knees, secured with elastic bands. She released the lid and tipped the contents onto the floor. A pile of banknotes lay spread out between us. Her dress rode up to the top of her thighs as she leaned back, supporting herself with her hands on the floor behind her.

'Look there, not here,' she said, pointing at the money. 'This will improve your life.'

It was a big pile, mainly ones and fives, a few tens here and there. It wasn't much, a few hundred dollars, but that wasn't the point.

'Where did it come from?'

She shrugged

'It's mine. Now it's yours.'

'What about José?'

'Don't worry. He has money.'

'Thank you.'

'No—not thank you. Before, you buy everything. All drinks, all cigarettes, all food, all dancing, all music, all the time. You pay. Not thank me, I thank you. Now I help you. Finish.'

She shouted the last word with a slap of her hands.

'Celia. I need books.'

'Books?'

She said this as though I'd asked for a new dress.

'Yes. All that time at Tony's. You said you didn't know how I could live like that. Well, I like to read. It makes my time more pleasant. More happy.'

'Like *Salome*?'

'Yes. I can get them from the market. Old books. They don't cost very much.'

'OK. I come with you. They will ask you pay too much.'

I went back to the stall where the guy had sold me the ancient copy of Plutarch's *Lives*. He recognised me immediately.

'Ah, my classical friend. What would you like today? I see you have a new girlfriend.'

I chose a couple of thick Len Deighton paperbacks, just to annoy him. Celia knocked him down to nothing, which annoyed him further. I stayed with her until José returned. Her gentle companionship, her touch, revived me. Black moods can be beaten.

*Mr Kane was a man who got everything he wanted and then lost it.*
Citizen Kane

# 41

# Rita

The local bar provided rum, hamburgers, pizzas and a pool table. On the occasions that I had a few dollars or won at pool, I bought a quarter or half of rum at the counter of the small shop attached to the bar. Rita, who served there, progressed from grumpy practicality to smiles and then outright curiosity. One day she demanded my passport before she would allow me the rum, supposedly to add to the meticulous records she was meant to keep of every transaction. She studied my passport, enjoying her authority. At my date of birth she smiled and nodded. If this meant it had corresponded with her guess, higher or lower, I couldn't tell. I told her that I was staying at Tony's house and explained who and where he was. She cut me off; she already knew. She knew my whole story. She just didn't know me.

I became a regular, often with José, buying rum for when we played pool or to take away. She made no secret of her distaste for hard liquor, and gave us a disapproving glare when she slapped the bottles down on the counter, which was odd for someone who had dedicated her life to selling alcohol. She was a busty, voluptuous, natural blonde, an unusual combination for Cuba. She always wore tiny denim shorts and skimpy vests, not in showy manner, but because it was always hot in the un-air-conditioned bar. Serious and rather severe in manner, she changed when she smiled, shedding years in the curl of her lips. She began to watch the pool games, sometimes singles, sometimes me and José against the locals, until they refused to play us anymore. She seemed baffled by the pursuits and interests of men, the pool, the sport and particularly the drinking, and watched with almost pained confusion as to what the fuss and noise was about.

As we sat waiting our turn at the table one night, a soggy note appeared on our table. The handwriting was uneven and childish. José tried to decipher it. He said it was signed in Rita's name.

'But she no write this,' he said.

'Why, what does it say?'

'It look like love letter, but is terrible, the grammar, the spelling. Is impossible a Cuban person write this.'

It hurt his pride that a Cuban could be illiterate, even in a lowly working-man's bar such as this. Then he laughed as he caught someone's eye.

'Now I understand.'

We were joined by the local drunk, ruined by rum but harmless and funny. He had written the note as a joke. He shoved his unshaven face close to mine and breathed fumes over me as he explained, completely unintelligibly, before laughing, slapping me on the back and staggering away.

'What was that about?' I asked.

'He say Rita like you. He play joke on you, write this note.'

'Do you think she likes me?'

'I don't know.'

'You think she'd like to come out with me for a night in Havana?'

'Ask her.'

'I don't have enough money.'

'Ask her first. We will find some if she says yes.'

She said yes.

José arranged an unofficial, cheap taxi to Havana, an ancient Chrysler that roared and rumbled its slow way along the motorway, blaring music that couldn't quite drown out the arthritic engine, and we sat in the back, slightly uneasy with each other, on opposite sides of the sumptuous, worn leather seats. I didn't have much money or any idea where I was going to take her. The taxi dropped us by the Ambos Mundos, where Jorgé, catching some late-evening sun, called to me from the doorway. We went in for a drink.

Rita hadn't been to Havana for over two years, seemed less familiar with it than me and had never seen the inside of a hotel. I was acutely aware of the restrictions ordinary Cubans had to suffer, not allowed into their own hotels and clubs or onto their own beaches—not without someone like me to accompany them; someone like me who was broke.

We looked at the photos of Hemingway in the lobby. I explained that he had written one of his most famous books here, in between visits to the docks to find his women. I watched for her reaction to that, but she just laughed and studied the photographs again. The lobby was fairly empty; the pianist, absent of tourist requests, played classical music. Cubans and tourists mingled as they passed the windows of the lobby on two sides. Rita, wearing a light cotton dress, sipped her Cuba libre and seemed happy to watch. I desperately tried to drink my mojito at the same slow speed as her. Jorge asked us if we would like to eat on the rooftop bar. She watched my response as I said I wasn't sure, maybe.

I wanted to drink faster because I felt uneasy. If she'd been more talkative or demonstrative I'd have been OK, but I couldn't read her, even though she smiled a lot and seemed happy in my company. Her hair, as always, was pinned up and she wore minimal make-up, with perhaps a little more attention to the eyes than usual. She seemed to regard me with some amusement. Shorn of my image as Mr Irresponsible

Man-About-Town, I wasn't quite sure how to behave. She was well into her thirties but there was still a large age gap. It didn't usually bother me, but now I was surprised that I was even thinking about it. I was tongue-tied.

'You look very beautiful tonight,' I heard myself say.

She laughed, as though I'd just cracked a joke, and put a hand over mine, rubbing it as if trying to warm it.

'Thank you,' she said. 'Don't worry. I happy.'

She finished her drink, which gave me the opportunity to regroup while I ordered some more. Jorgé, with nothing to do, came behind the bar to serve me.

'New girlfriend?' he said.

'I don't know.'

His moustache twitched.

'Why you don't take her to the roof garden to eat? You impress her there.'

'Can't. Don't have enough money.'

He put down the two drinks he was mixing and leaned his hands on the bar. He blinked in time with the twitch of his moustache.

'Your money finished?'

'Yes. I have some, but not much.'

I had fifty of the dollars that Celia had given me. It wasn't enough for the whole evening if we ate at the rooftop restaurant. I took some notes from my back pocket.

'What will you do?'

'I don't know. Go to England, I suppose, and get some more.'

'Can you do that?'

'I think so. I have to.'

Jorgé nodded thoughtfully at that and went back to mixing the drinks. He pursed his lips, took a deep breath and exhaled slowly, noisily. He finished the drinks, but left them on the bench in front of him. He looked around the lobby. His two colleagues stood at the door chatting. The piano player had gone. He gave me a long stare, trying to determine if I was faking it. I looked away, unable to hold his gaze.

'Put your money away,' he said. 'So, you can take her to the roof garden. I take care of your drinks. Pay me next time you come in.'

'I don't know when that will be.'

He looked over at Rosa, who was watching us.

'You will be back. It's only rum.'

He turned away from me and started washing glasses.

We ate on the lovely roof terrace. It had been hot downstairs but up here there was a cool breeze from the sea. We walked to the stone parapet surrounding the terrace. We leaned over and watched the street, dark now, voices and music rising up from the bars below. I watched her face as she gazed out at the lights of the city. She was smiling. I gave up on conversation. She just didn't talk much. I rarely saw her speak to the locals in the bar. She lived alone. She was a loner, like me. Before we sat down again she took my hand.

I started staying at her house some nights after she finished work and she cooked for the two of us on her free days. She spoke only a little English and I worked hard on my Spanish but we hardly talked at all and she didn't seem to need conversation. She revealed nothing about her past; if ever I asked, her smiles and shrugs indicated that it was past history and unimportant. She was completely unimpressed by my recent experiences, merely incredulous at the money I had wasted. For the first time since coming to Cuba I started to drink moderately—partly through necessity and partly to gain her respect and not spoil things.

If she worked during the day, I went to see her as soon as Tony left the white house. She stopped charging me for my rum and cigarettes, which was risky, and I responded by drinking and smoking even less. She also got me the odd pizza from the bar, if she could salvage one without being noticed.

I wondered why, now that I was down and out, Rita took any interest in me. She didn't appear to expect much, perhaps knowing I would be temporary. There were no signs in her house of previous men: photos of husbands, children, relatives. Just one picture of her mother. As we ate one night she said she was going to visit her mother in Holguin; that she would be back in two weeks. I never saw her again.

*Me that 'ave been what I've been*
*Me that 'ave gone where I've gone*
*Me that 'ave seen what I've seen*
*'Ow can I ever take on*
*With awful old England again.*
Rudyard Kipling

# 42

# Enough

Later that evening, walking back to the white house from Rita's, some clods of earth and stones bounced around me and hit my legs with some force. Someone shouted '*maricon*', queer.

I looked up as an open truck passed me with several people in the back. A young boy, about eight or nine, stood at the back, throwing anything he could find at me, gesticulating and shouting '*maricon*', again and again. Someone stood next to him, arms folded, watching calmly. It was Manolo. The truck rumbled on and disappeared round a bend.

A few minutes later I heard shuffling and giggling behind me. I turned to see Amado, Manolo and the young stone-thrower walking fast towards me. Amado had a knife, a nasty-looking old plastic-handled thing, long and so often sharpened that I could see the mauve and purple shades of the metal where it had been ground and the thin, chipped, sharp edge, gleaming silver at its point. Amado had wrapped different coloured tapes around the handle.

They stopped in front of me.

Manolo stood leaning against a fence, one knee drawn up, relaxed and indifferent. The boy, bobbing up and down on his trainers, stood alongside him—an odd face. A Down syndrome face. And now I recognised him: the boy in Lazaro's apartment, asleep in the playpen, on the day of our visit. He was very different now, couldn't stop moving, giggling at Amado in excited anticipation. 'Maricon,' he kept shouting at me. 'Maricon.'

Amado squared off in front of me, holding the point of his knife to my stomach and pushing it slightly as he spat insults at me. I felt it but it didn't hurt. They're not going to do any serious harm, I thought; they can't. I looked at Manolo. He was too smart for this. He knew what the consequences would be, from the police and from Tony. Unlike the other two, he could think ahead, consider consequences. This was just an exercise in humiliation.

Amado held the edge of the knife against my throat. He jutted out his chin, comically I thought, and hissed at me through gritted white teeth. There wasn't enough pressure to injure me, let alone cut me.

Manolo watched; he could see that I'd figured this out and that the fear they wanted wasn't there. I put a hand in my back pocket where there were a couple of dollars that Rita had given me for coffee. Amado moved the knife to the right side of my neck, sliced lightly and jumped away, watching my hand. I pulled out the dollars, crumpled them up and threw them at Manolo,

'Thank you for your translations, Manolo. They were very useful. You're a useful guy to know.'

That was not a clever thing to say. He pushed himself away from the fence with his raised foot and rushed at me. I'd never seen him move so fast. His face was contorted as he tried to kick me between the legs. He missed his target and caught me in the stomach, hard enough for me to fall down. The meal and the rum spewed out of my mouth. It was acid, foul, awful and full of thick brown mucous and, even then, I noted with some gratitude that it wasn't bloody or black.

I lay there, the breath gone out of me, and this stuff, still somehow ejecting itself from my stomach. The sight of me made them back off. I was sure they didn't intend to kill me. Amado, needing the last word, aimed a kick at my hip—no, they didn't want to kill me. Well, they *wanted* to, but they were too scared to do it.

They walked away, talking too loudly and laughing. The young boy danced around them in excitement. Amado got off one more '*maricon*' before they were still in earshot. I lay there, taking in the stench of my vomit, my breath coming slowly back to me. I felt no pain.

I walked home, trying to take deep breaths from the airless night. At Tony's I checked myself in the bathroom mirror. A tiny cut on my neck had bled onto my T-shirt. A black bruise was appearing on my right side.

I sat on the sofa and vomited over the floor. The tiny black insects that lived in Tony's house converged on the mess from all sides. 'They are crazy,' José had said of them, and he was right: they looked crazy, now, as they fed on what I had brought up.

I cleaned my teeth and walked to the kitchen. A quarter of Silver Dry was hidden behind the fridge. Rita had given it to me earlier in the day. I placed it in the freezer and went out to talk to Dingo, who was barking. I fed him some old bread and let him off his chain. He usually shot off round the garden but tonight he just ambled over to the patio door and lay down.

I got a brush and swept the vomit onto the patio. I was going to sweep it from the patio into the garden but Dingo leapt up and devoured it.

I took the Silver Dry from the freezer, poured it into a glass and sat back down in the living room. Tony's ancient TV gave me the usual electric shock as I switched it on. My hands began to shake and I felt terribly hot. I retched but nothing would come. I could smell my own horrible breath. I felt dizzy, rolled onto the floor and lay on my side, a cheek to the cool tiles. Dingo watched, his head on his front paws, whimpering and barking quietly.

The static of the TV woke me. It was 8:00 a.m. and Tony would be here soon. Dingo had taken himself back to his chain. I walked over and tied him up. The tiny insects were all over me. I scratched my head and hundreds of them tumbled out. I showered them all away and shaved. Then I cleaned up the house and mopped where I'd been sick.

Michelle had phoned me two weeks before. I hadn't contacted anyone in England after I'd run out of money because I couldn't afford to and I didn't want them to worry. I had asked Paul to tell a few people that I was OK and that I'd be in touch soon. It turned out he hadn't called anybody and they'd all thought I was dead. My ex-wife Liz, however, had tracked me down. She said she'd left me an open one-way ticket if I needed it, to Gatwick via Madrid. A friend had phoned soon after that. If I came back, I could stay at their new place in the country and chill out for a while, just in case anybody was looking for me.

I didn't have any coffee. I'd thrown my last two dollars at Manolo. I poured myself what was left of the rum: a full shot glass. In the bedroom I rummaged everywhere and found two diazepam. I knocked them both back with the rum and cleaned my teeth twice.

Tony arrived a few minutes later. He slouched through the house and fed Dingo. He'd brought some coffee with him, just enough for two, in a plastic bag. He was sullen as we drank, letting me know again how I was imposing on his hospitality. I enjoyed the coffee, feeling the caffeine mix nicely with the rum and the pills.

'I'm going home, Tony,' I said.

He stared at me, not understanding, but recognising something in my voice.

'To Inglaterre.'

I told him about Liz's ticket and said I'd go to England for three weeks, cut my ties with Paul, get some money and come back. I had no idea if any of that was possible or if I was even telling the truth. He beamed and shook my hand, told me it was a good idea. When I returned we could start a proper business and not have to rely on my alcoholic English friend.

He found a bottle he'd hidden somewhere, the bastard, and poured us both a generous glass. And then another. He was in a good mood, like the old times, because he could smell money again. Even if I didn't make it he could rent his house again. He wanted me to make it though. He left happily two hours later. He didn't want to clash with José, who he knew would be over soon.

With the extra rum I felt great. With diazepam, if you don't lie down and sleep immediately, they wake you up and make you think that all is fine—or, at least, not terrible. I didn't tell Tony that twenty minutes before he'd arrived, before the rum and diazepam, I'd been shaking; that the nausea and fear in the pit of my stomach were so bad that I could barely stand, that I didn't know what to do anymore, or where to go, or what to say, or how I would eat, or even how I would stay alive—that my head had been spinning with the confusion of it all. All I knew was that I had to get out of this place. I'd had enough.

*Keep away from sharp swords,*
*Don't go near a lovely woman.*
*A sharp sword too close will wound your hand,*
*Woman's beauty too close will wound your life.*
Meng Chao

# 43
# Finding Yamilia

I gave up on Paul. I no longer waited on the phone for news about him or checked at the bank for the funds he had promised to deposit. The leg that Amado had injured began to fail and I found the long walk to the bank too much of a struggle, especially when there was only bad news at the end of it. Raúl had advised me to get x-rays in England, where they had better equipment. He thought a cartilage was damaged.

The night before I was due to fly out, José and I sat outside a restaurant near The Capitolio. We'd eaten and now we were passing the afternoon with a bottle of rum, watching the teeming crowds—all the chaos of everyday life in Havana. I was down, so José was down—that's the way it worked with us. He fed off my moods, the good one and the bad dones, but was always there. I felt Cuban now. I didn't want to stay in England, was determined to come back. Whatever it was about Cuba, it suited me. I was at home here, comfortable with all it could throw at me, but couldn't survive here without money. Not without doing things I wasn't prepared to do.

'I want to see Yamilia,' I said.

I hadn't seen her in many months, had no idea what she was doing.

José shook his head. He tried to persuade me out of it, said she probably wasn't in Havana, that she wouldn't want to see me and that we wouldn't be able to find her.

'I want to see her before I leave. In case I don't come back.'

'You will come back!'

'In case I don't.'

He had no choice. I handed him my cellular phone. He began calling people. I cheered up at the idea of seeing her, began to see more life and happiness in the streets. Thirty minutes later he had an answer.

'Well?' I said. 'Did you find her?'

'I know where to find her.'

'Where is she?'

'She is working.'

'Working? Yamilia?'

'In a shop,' he said. 'She working and staying with her relatives.'

'I don't believe it.'

'I know where the shop is. You want go and look?'

'Yes,' I said, 'let's go and look.'

We walked to the shop, about a mile away. It was a convenience peso store, some food items, some clothing, some electrical goods. A bit of everything and not much of anything. Big, old-fashioned and understocked, like hundreds of others. I couldn't see Yamilia.

José spoke to someone.

'She not here,' he said. 'She work alternate days'—the miracle of full employment—'and today is her day off.'

'But she does work here?'

'They say she work here. I have her number.'

I gave him the cellular.

'Call her.'

'What shall I say?'
Good question.

We walked to the Ambos Mundos. We decided on what now
seems like a pretty silly plan. José would call her and say he
wanted to meet her about something important. They would
meet in the lobby of the Ambos Mundos, while I waited across
the street in a bar. Later he would suggest another place and
he'd bring her to me. Big surprise.

The bar was full of tourists and various Cubans who'd
latched onto them. I watched an intense European couple listening, starry-eyed, as a version of José impressed on them the
virtues of the revolution, the absolute perfectness of life under
Fidel. And could they just manage twenty dollars for some new
shoes? The embargo, you know; the wicked Americans. I felt
like an old hand, the cynical old-timer in the corner—and even
sadder about leaving.

Yamilia walked in as though the place belonged to her. She
saw me immediately, smiled a knowing smile, stopped ten feet
away and said loudly, completely without concern for the room
full of tourists, 'Who dance like this? What man dance like
this, so silly?'

She began to dance with an exaggerated swinging of the
arms and clumsy foot movements. Everyone in the bar watched her. She didn't take any notice of them, just continued with
her crazy dance, making me love her again instantly and telling
me, in her funny way, that meeting me was OK, that she was
pleased to see me, that she remembered our dancing, that
even I didn't dance that badly. She sat down. Her eyes bore
through me. She picked up the menu and ordered a beer.

'So, how you are? You married? You have babies yet?'

'It's only been a few months.'

She shrugged. Months, years, decades—what was the
difference? Time was liquid in Cuba. She had no idea how long
it had been. She didn't care.

The smile in her eyes suggested that her life went on the same way, no matter what happened. It wasn't an act. It was the way things were—the way they were with her.

And she was lean, not an ounce of fat on her. She'd never been overweight, but at the height of our high living she'd put on a few pounds. Now she'd shed them and she looked great; evidently, she was better off without me.

She gave me a long once-over.

'Your eyes are tired.'

She looked at some fresh grazes on my arm, the result of a night out with José when, with Celia's money, we'd bounced off a few walls, fallen into a few gutters. She shook her head. That sort of thing didn't happen when she was around. But then José wasn't around when she was around.

She took out her mobile and called someone. She chatted for a few minutes. I could tell it was another woman, maybe a cousin, and wondered why. I thought I caught the name Clara.

We finished our drinks and walked to a peso place. We sat at the bar, facing each other on high stools. José sat behind her, facing the other way. Sometimes he'd listen to us, but most of the time he watched the games of pool, chatted to others.

Yamilia told me about her job in the shop. She got eight dollars a week, a good wage. With enthusiasm she said she could get goods from the shop very cheaply and, at the end of the week, for free. I said I was happy that she was happy; her contentment seemed genuine. I also knew that it was a novelty that would soon wear off. She'd met José tonight, hoping for an angle. Eight dollars a week and cheap food wasn't going to keep Yamilia in nice clothes from dollar shops. José looked at me over her shoulder, shaking his head in amusement. I didn't care. When she was happy, I was happy.

I told her I was leaving on Friday. That I was out of money and had to go home to make some more. That I'd be back in two or three weeks.

'You can go to England?' she said, surprised.

'Why not?'

'You don't have trouble with the police?'

'No. Why?'

'Rosa say if you go home you have trouble with police.'

'Rosa? What does she know?'

'You not a criminal?'

'No.'

She lowered her head, looked at me from under her lashes.

'I think you un poco criminal, Chris.'

'Poco. Maybe.'

'Tony say you washing money.'

'Tony said that? When?'

'Back then,' she said. 'When everything was loco.' When everything was crazy.

Our relationship was difficult for her. When we were away from Havana, we got on OK, we were happy. In Camagüey. In Pinar Del Rio. In Matanzas. In Guanabacoa, at the beginning. When everything was crazy.

'When the house was quiet, we got on OK,' she said.

We did.

'You drank too much.'

I did.

'Paul was crazy.'

He was.

'I no want much.'

You didn't.

'I cooked and cleaned for you.'

Not really: you got someone else to do it, but that was OK.

'I look after you when you sick.'

You did.

'I gave you good love.'

You did.

She took my hand gently. Not like Yamilia. She put it between her legs and clamped them shut. Very like Yamilia.

'I loved you.'

'No, you didn't.'

'You think I not love you? I take you here, here and here.'

She pointed between her legs, her mouth, her behind.

You think I not love you? You think I do this for anybody? You think I do for money? I live with you, cook for you, clean for you. I look after you when you sick. I happy with you. Just was too many people. José. Tony. Everything was crazy.'

It was.

'What you want, Chris?'

I don't know. Everything?

The barman was watching us. He raised his eyebrows at me, shook his hand as though it was burning. She didn't notice. She rarely noticed or cared what others thought. It was no concern of hers. What others thought was their problem.

'One thing no crazy,' she said suddenly. 'Me. Me no crazy,'

And I thought: Really? Weren't you crazy? I remember so many times. When you flew at people for some imagined offence. Your moments of generosity followed by moments of extreme cruelty. The time in the hospital when you pretended your leg was hurt so they'd run around giving you attention when they should have been attending to all those people who really needed help. When you screamed at José and me in that roadside bar that night—screamed at us for hours, with two old Cubans watching. Pacing about and screaming at us, kicking over tables and chairs, breaking bottles and glasses. Needing attention—exclusive attention—furious that other people had come into our lives.

Why were you like that? What really lay behind it?

'Lazaro and Amado,' I asked, cautiously. We'd never actually talked about this before. 'Must they be a part of your life? They're not good for you. They're not the safety belt you want. What they offer isn't security.'

There was a very long pause and I saw something I'd never seen before: tears in her eyes.

'You know nothing, Chris.'

She paused again, trying to decide how much to say.

'You think I am friend of theirs? You think I two-time you when we together?'

'I know you used to see them. When I was away in Mexico, you'd go and stay with them even though you said you were staying with a *girl*friend.' I hammered up how she put the emphasis on *girl*.

'OK, Chris. I go to their apartment. You think I go see them? I go see my boy.'

A very long pause followed while I took this in. What did she mean?

'You meet him, Chris. I hear about it. With Manolo and Amado. He throw stones at you. The night Manolo kick you.'

'The boy in the playpen in Lazaro's apartment? Your son ... ?'

'He no right in the head. Brain no work good.'

I blinked.

'How?'

She tapped out a cigarette and lit it. 'When I first come to Havana, I had fifteen—*was* fifteen, OK? I know nobody. I sleep in park. I find young boyfriend. Amado. He look after me, bring me food from his parents' kitchen. He no tell them we meet. No one want son with girlfriend who live on the street. We ... .' She indicated with her hands that they slept together. 'Before I get sixteen, is my boy born. Is very hard, Chris. Lazaro find out. He no angry. He take baby. Wife look after. She good friend. Hard woman. They all hard. My boy grow up with them. He eleven now. When you go to Mexico, I go see boy. Give wife a break. So. What you think?'

I didn't know what to think. I knocked back my rum.

'But why keep all this a secret. Why didn't you ... ?'

'Why I no say? Big English businessman want fuck street-girl mama with crazy boy? Chris! Get real!'

We sat and looked at each other and I thought, what now?

'So,' said Yamilia. 'I think is time you fly back to London.'

I sat completely immobile.

'Chris.'

She took my hand and sucked one of my fingers.

'I want to stay.'

'No, is good that you go.'

I took her head in my hands, pulled her to me and kissed her face— tenderly, in a way we had rarely kissed before.

She was right. It was good that I go. But I no longer wanted to. And I loved her more than ever.

'I'm going but I'm coming back.'

'You come back?'

'Yes.'

'You sure?'

'Yes.'

She took a deep breath, then gave me a surprised smile.

'OK. Let's go.'

We left José sitting at the bar and walked up Obispo. When we'd walked fifty yards, Yamilia stopped and shouted up to a window.

'*Ay, Clara!*'

A middle-aged woman appeared on the balcony. A *casa particular*. We waited while the woman made a room ready.

Before everything went bad at the blue house, Yamilia had tried to get pregnant. It was her theory that the more excited she got me, the more potent I would be. She would play with me for an hour before letting me inside her.

'Now you have much juice, much power here.'

She went to work on me again, now, determined and methodical. Talking all the time: what she was going to do to me, what she wanted me to do to her. I came inside her quickly but she wouldn't let me stop. With her legs wrapped around my neck she urged me on, slapping my backside hard, pushing me deeper. When I came a second time, she relaxed. Whatever I had left would be too weak to make anything.

'In fifteen year, when you old man in Havana, will be a

beautiful girl here with green eyes. Every man want her. You will follow her everywhere, to stop the men having her, because she is yours and you love her. You will be so jealous and angry with those men. You will want to kill them.'

'What if it's a boy?'

'He will fuck every woman in Havana.'

The woman banged on the door. Time to go.

I walked her to the top of Obispo. One of a crowd of boys said something as we passed. They all laughed. So did Yamilia.

'What did they say?'

'They say I am so small, you must put me on a box to kiss me!'

It was 4:00 a.m.

'I have to work in four hours,' she said.

I kissed her on the forehead. The boys laughed and shouted. I lifted her up and kissed her on the lips. They cheered.

'I will see you in two weeks.'

'OK.'

I started to walk away, shaking my head in disbelief. Then I stopped and turned back.

'Your boy: what's his name?'

She smiled.

'Che.'

Of course.


José and I got a taxi. He had been sitting behind Yamilia the whole time we were in the bar. I waited for him to say something. He said nothing.

'Did you hear everything she said?' I asked him, as the taxi pulled away.

'Sí.'

'And you're not amazed? You have nothing to say?'

'Is not news, Chris. I know this already.'

'What?!'

'Everyone know.'

'I didn't know!'

'She didn't want. She always afraid she lose you. Afraid, one of us tell. Afraid of us all, all the time. Always high drama with her, in case you find out.'

I sat back against the leather seat, stunned for the second time this evening, trying to fit the pieces together.

'So, Tony ... ?'

'Brother of Lazaro wife. Yes, he help his sister care for the boy, but in secret, in background. He and Lazaro ... .' He smacked his fists together. 'He think of Yamilia like ... daughter. No daughter. *Hijastra*.' Step-daughter.

After dropping José off in Havana, the taxi took me to Bahia and Tony's white house. I fell into bed, happy for the first time in months.

*Am I ever going to see your face again? (No way, get fucked, fuck off!).*
The Angels (song title)

# 44

# Leaving

The next day I realised I didn't have my phone with me. I wanted it in case Yamilia phoned. José turned up with Celia at 3:00 pm. He had it.

'Yamilia phone, maybe ten times,' he said.

'What did she say?'

'She want talk to you.'

I called the number she'd been ringing from. It was a communal phone, shared by everyone on one floor of a tenement. A woman answered in rapid, bad-tempered Spanish. I passed the phone to José.

'She says she isn't there,' he said.

'Why didn't you give me the phone back last night?'

'Estaba distraído.' I was distracted.'

I'll say.

I was leaving on a night flight so José and Celia spent the afternoon resting with me at Tony's white house. They had come over every afternoon since the attack, and they'd stay late into the evening. After they left, I'd sit up reading or writing in my diary as the night went on. Sometimes I sat in the garden until dawn, watching the neighbourhood come to life.

I didn't really like the place. It didn't suit me: Bahia was too hot and lacked the breezes I was used to in Villa Panamericana and Havana.

But I would have stayed if I could. I would have stayed anywhere. I even considered calling Yamilia and suggesting we live in Lugareno, but despite her previous assurances I didn't think she could live without money. I knew that I couldn't.

I phoned Tony and told him I'd see him in two weeks. I would have called Rita but she was still in Holguin and I had no way of contacting her. I wanted to phone everyone I knew. The strength of my attachment, even in such circumstances, surprised me. Cuba used to get a bad press and most people were taken in by what they read. I wasn't blind to Cuba's bad points but I found the hatred of Castro baffling. Media commentators queued up to criticise him for a multitude of sins. Why? Why was so important to them? Why was he worse than the nasty little dictatorships of Central and South America, torturing and killing to protect US business interests —why didn't those concern them? Is that what they wanted for Cuba—exactly what it had had before Castro threw the Americans out? Or was it the idea of Cuba that so concerned them, the idea of an alternative to mass greed? Admittedly, the idea hadn't worked—what idealistic utopia had done?—but it still might. Without the crippling fifty-year embargo, who knows? Perhaps that was the cause of the hostility, the fact that the *idea* of Cuba—the *ideal* of Cuba—was still alive somewhere, threatening the size of all the Americans' pools and cars and fridges: the possibility that instead of owning ninety per cent of the world's riches, they might have to make do with just eighty.

José and Celia came to José Martí airport with me. I checked in: Gatwick via Madrid. We had a few hours to kill and enough money for food and rum. I wanted to buy some farewell presents for them but I didn't have the funds. More in hope than expectation I wondered down to an ATM. Five minutes later I was back. I threw $800 on the table. Celia looked around nervously.

'Paul,' I said, flatly. 'He sent five thousand.'

José shook his head disbelievingly. Celia did her disappearing act. Five thousand at any time in the last three months would have got us started again.

'Fucking Paul!' José said.

I bought them presents and gave them some money. I left José something for Yamilia.

'Will you give it to her?'

'I'll give it to her, Chris!'

'No, I mean, will you give it to her?'

He nodded. I looked at Celia who nodded too. Could she make him? I hoped so.

At the gate I turned to wave. With the unexpected money from the cash machine, I'd upgraded to first class. I felt fine, a bit choked maybe, but was sure that this wasn't goodbye.

I also didn't think they would stop me leaving. There were a couple of security people who were curious about what I'd been up to, where I'd been, but I was fairly sure I didn't warrant an airport alert. Besides, I'd come and gone before. And I spent lots of money, which was all that really mattered. They'd let me go and expect me back.

At the gate a uniformed security man studied my passport. He flicked through the pages, stopped and looked into my eyes, giving me a hard stare. I smiled. He stamped my visa and waved me to the ticket barrier.

# 45
# Madrid

At Madrid airport I had a four-hour wait for my connecting flight. This was the old airport, just before the magnificent structure they have now. I remember that Paul hated it, refused to take any flights connecting there. My stomach was churning with butterflies and, despite not sleeping on the flight, I was wide awake. I knew rum was a bad idea but that's exactly what my body said it needed. I settled for a mojito. Cut down slowly, be sensible. I was on my third and quite mellow, when I took out my wallet to check how much English money I had.

I stared at what was left of what I'd taken out of the ATM at José Martí, then counted it out on the bar, just to be sure, heedless of the stares of the barman and fellow drinkers. Nearly five-hundred dollars left. But $4,200 was still available from ATMs.

I looked around me, suddenly confused at where I was. This was Madrid, yes? What was I doing here? Why had I boarded that flight? Because I thought I had to. Because I had been building up to it for days, preparing myself, steeling myself. But that was before I had money. Now I had money again. I could have bought a car with it. I could have got myself a small income from renting the car out. I could have given something to Tony to keep him happy. I could do all those things now, start again, build up slowly, try to not make the same mistakes as last time. But would they allow me back in?

My hands were shaking. And something more. Something pleasant and, at the same time, very uncomfortable. I wanted to lie down. Suddenly I wanted to sleep. I put my wallet away, took slow sips of my mojito and tried to think.

Be calm, body, please be calm: help me out, here.

How many times had I asked that of it—asked my body to perform for just one more day? Get me through this and I'll look after you, I'd say: I'll stop smoking and drinking, I'll exercise and eat well—I promise. I bought another drink and concentrated on my breathing, drawing slow deep breaths in through my nose and deep into my lungs, out slowly, then hold. I had a coughing fit.

I called Paul's mobile. He was at Heathrow.

'So they let you out?' I said, 'What are you doing there?'

'Yes, The Man They Couldn't Hang. I'm thinking about a trip somewhere. No, not fucking Cuba. I'm in the bar. Haven't made up my mind yet. Having a look at what other people are up to. Might follow some silly tarts somewhere nice. Where are you?'

'Madrid. The airport.'

'You always end up in my least favourite places. Why aren't you in Cuba?'

'I didn't know you'd sent any money until I was about to take off. I might have stayed if I'd known. How much money did you make?'

'Enough to send five to you and have a little break for myself.'

At least twenty, I thought. Another five for me would have been nice: enough to set myself up properly. I asked him for ten and we argued about it for a while.

'Alright,' he said eventually, 'I'll let you have another five. Where shall I send it?'

I thought about it. My flight to Gatwick was in two hours.

Or I could just stay at the airport and get the next flight back to Havana. I didn't know what to do.

'Can you send it here,' I said, 'to one of the banks at the airport?'

That would give me a choice: London or Havana.

'I suppose so,' said Paul, 'but what's so great about Madrid Airport?'

'It's my fastest route back to Cuba.'

'Is that wise?'

'Undoubtedly not,' I said.

THE END

# Other titles from EnvelopeBooks

www.envelopebooks.co.uk

## Belle Nash and the Bath Soufflé

WILLIAM KEELING ESQ.

In the first volume of The Gay Street Chronicles, bachelor Belle Nash attempts to navigate bigotry and corruption in Regency Bath without compromising the nephew of Immanual Kant or the legal talents of Gaia Champion.

BB1

## Postmark Africa

MICHAEL HOLMAN

Made an Amnesty Prisoner of Conscience while he was under house arrest as a student in Southern Rhodesia, the author went on to document Africa's emergence from colonialism as Africa Editor of the Financial Times.

EB1

## Why My Wife Had To Die

BRIAN VERITY

There is no known cure for Huntington's disease, a wasting condition that sufferers acquire from a parent. In this painful account of how their lives were wrecked when his wife started to show the same signs of it as her mother and brothers, the author vents his rage at society, lawmakers, health services and the church for not grasping the need, as he sees it, to legalise compulsory sterilisation and assisted dying.

EB9

# Non-fiction from EnvelopeBooks

www.envelopebooks.co.uk

## My Modern Movement

ROBERT BEST

London's Festival of Britain in 1951 marked the belief that Modern design was visually, morally and commercially superior. Robert Best, the UK's leading lighting manufacturer of the period, thinks the dice were loaded. This is his account of the disputes that raged at the time, based on his diaries.

EB8

## A Road to Extinction

JONATHAN LAWLEY

When Britain colonised the Andamans in 1857, the welfare of its African pygmy inhabitants was of no concern. Nine tribes died out. Dr Lawley now assesses the three remaining tribes' prospects and the legacy of his grandfather, who ran the colony in the early 1900s.

EB2

## From Bedales to the Boche

ROBERT BEST

Bedales, the progressive boarding school founded by J.H. Badley in 1893, instilled values that sustained many of its pupils through the rest of their lives. Robert Best recalls its influence on him as an enthusiastic army recruit in 1914 and, from 1916, in the Royal Flying Corps.

EB3

# Novels from EnvelopeBooks

www.envelopebooks.co.uk

## A Sin of Omission

MARGUERITE POLAND

An emotionally intense novel, set in 1870s South Africa at a time of rising anti-colonial resistance. The book focuses on the tragedy of a promising black preacher, hand-picked for training in England as a missionary, only to be neglected by the Church he loves. Based on a true story. *Winner of the 2021 Sunday Times CNA 'Book of the Year' Award in South Africa.*
EB6

## Mustard Seed Itinerary

ROBERT MULLEN

When Po Cheng falls into a dream, he finds himself on the road to the imperial Chinese capital. Once there he rises to the heights of the civil service before discovering that there are snakes as well as ladders. Carrollian satire at its best.
EB5

## Frances Creighton: Found and Lost

KIRBY PORTER

Love demands trust but trust is a lot to ask for victims of abuse. Having been bullied by two teachers in Belfast as a boy, Michael Roberts suppresses his childhood pains until the death of a girlfriend years later forces him to revisit lost memories.
EB7

# Other titles from EnvelopeBooks

www.envelopebooks.co.uk

## The Train House on Lobengula Street

FATIMA KARA

An anguished but life-affirming novel, set within the Indian community in Bulawayo in Rhodesia of the 1950s and 1960s, about the capacity of women to gain the same advantages as men in the modern world while remaining faithful to traditional Muslim values, and about the cruelty of white oppression. Warm, affectionate and passionate writing.

EB12

## Belle Nash and the Bath Circus

WILLIAM KEELING ESQ.

In Volume Two of *The Gay Street Chronicles*, bachelor Belle Nash returns to Regency Bath from Grenada inspired by a new love that forces him into various pretences that may compromise the ambitions of black circus impresario Pablo Fanque.

BB2

## Spy Artist Prisoner

GEORGE TOMAZIU

Artist George Tomaziu half-expected to be imprisoned and tortured for monitoring Nazi troop movements through Bucharest during the Second World War but thought that his heroism would be recognised when Socialism came to Romania in 1950. He was terribly mistaken.

EB10